AFTER.

F.T. LUKENS

MARGARET K. McELDERRY BOOKS

NEW YORK   LONDON   TORONTO   SYDNEY   NEW DELHI

MARGARET K. McELDERRY BOOKS

An imprint of Simon & Schuster Children's Publishing Division

1230 Avenue of the Americas, New York, New York 10020

Text © 2022 by F.T. Lukens

Jacket illustration © 2022 by Sam Schechter

Jacket design by Rebecca Syracuse © 2022 by Simon & Schuster, Inc.

For information about special discounts for bulk purchases, please contact Simon & Schuster Special Sales at 1-866-506-1949 or business@simonandschuster.com.

The Simon & Schuster Speakers Bureau can bring authors to your live event. For more information or to book an event, contact the Simon & Schuster Speakers Bureau at 1-866-248-3049 or visit our website at www.simonspeakers.com.

Interior design by Rebecca Syracuse

The text for this book was set in Abhaya Libre.

Manufactured in the United States of America

First Edition

2 4 6 8 10 9 7 5 3 1

Library of Congress Cataloging-in-Publication Data

Names: Lukens, F. T., author.

Title: So this is ever after / F.T. Lukens.

Description: First edition. | New York : Margaret K. McElderry Books, [2022] | Audience: Ages 14 up. | Audience: Grades 10–12. | Summary: Arek has managed to fulfill the prophecy and save the Kingdom of Ere from its evil ruler, but the quest is not over because until they free the princess locked in one of the towers he has to asssume the crown himself. When the princess proves to be very dead, Arek is stuck as king; then he discovers that magic requires him to find a bride before his eighteenth birthday or wither away—but none of his female companions are interested, he does not want to marry a stranger, and anyway the only person he is attracted to is Matt, aspiring wizard, best friend, and secret crush.

Identifiers: LCCN 2021031485 (print) | LCCN 2021031486 (ebook) | ISBN 9781534496866 (hardcover) | ISBN 9781534496880 (ebook)

Subjects: LCSH: Magic—Juvenile fiction. | Prophecies—Juvenile fiction. | Kings and rulers—Juvenile fiction. | Wizards—Juvenile fiction. | Gays—Juvenile fiction. | Friendship—Juvenile fiction. | Humorous stories. | CYAC: Magic—Fiction. | Prophecies—Fiction. | Kings, queens, rulers, etc.—Fiction. | Wizards—Fiction. | Gays—Fiction. | Friendship—Fiction. | Fantasy. | Humorous stories. | LCGFT: Humorous fiction. | Fantasy fiction.

Classification: LCC PZ7.1.L843 So 2022 (print) | LCC PZ7.1.L843 (ebook) | DDC 813.6 [Fic]—dc23

LC record available at https://lccn.loc.gov/2021031485

LC ebook record available at https://lccn.loc.gov/2021031486

To anyone looking for their Happy Ever After:

Don't give up!

It may just be in another castle.

CHAPTER 1

I'd been envisioning what it would be like to behead the Vile One since the old wizard had shown up at my door the day after I turned seventeen and told me my destiny—that I would be the person who ended the dark shadow of evil that ruled our realm. Well, okay, not that specific second because who believes a drunken stranger with a crooked hat carrying around a humming staff? No one. That's who. At least, you shouldn't. That's unsafe.

Let me amend. I'd been envisioning this moment since after we'd had tea and he'd explained a few things and told me about *the prophecy*. Though it didn't feel real, as in very likely, and downright probable, until I pulled a magical sword from a bog and a beam of light shot down from the sky, anointing me with supernatural purpose.

After that, I kept a vision in my head about what would happen when I separated the Vile One's head from his shoulders in the final climactic battle. The cut would be clean. There would be artistic arterial spray, and the disembodied head would roll down the steps of the raised dais and come to rest at the feet of my best friend. Everyone would cheer, and I'd finally be the hero I was prophesied to become. I'd *feel* different. Righteous. Awesome. Accomplished. Finally grown-up.

Unfortunately, as things seem to have gone since the start of this whole journey, that did not happen. Not even a little bit.

Fueled by adrenaline and vigor, I swung my blade for the death blow, expecting to cleanly remove the Vile One's head. Instead, the blunted edge buried halfway through his neck and jarred to a stop on his spinal column. Huh. Who knew that prophesied weapons didn't come ready-to-use? Apparently, magic swords that spring from bogs don't rise pre-sharpened.

Stunned at this unexpected turn of events, I froze long enough to draw attention from the party of questors supporting me.

"Arek!" Sionna yelled from somewhere in the chaos. "Finish him off!"

I wrenched the blade from the Vile One's throat, did my level best to ignore the astonished look on his face, the open mouth, the wide eyes, the gush of blood running down the front of his black robes, and struck again. And again. I hacked at the twitching body, which had fallen backward and slumped on the front of the throne, propped up like a grotesque doll, until I was certain he was dead, and no amount of magic could bring him back.

Finally, the neck gave way and the head plopped onto the ground, splattering like an overripe pumpkin. Dead eyes peered up at me from sunken hollows, and thin lips pulled over yellowed teeth in a parody of a scream. A picture that would surely fuel my nightmares for at least the next few months, potentially the rest of my life.

I had also imagined lifting the Vile One's head by his hair and holding it up as a kind of trophy as all the dark magic he'd used to usurp the throne and control the realm would recede like a fierce tide, sucking itself from the world in a flash of light as the populace cheered. Except, the Vile One was bald, and there was no way I was picking the head up by anything else, because *ugh*.

Also, *nothing happened*. No flash of light. No magical reversal. No swell of victorious music. No fanfare. Nothing.

Huh.

Disappointingly, I didn't feel different at all, other than sticky. And weary down to my bones, and nauseated. There were no cheers from onlookers, though the sound of vomiting was clear over my right shoulder.

I dabbed my blood-drenched face with the hem of my tunic, but only succeeded in smearing the crimson more thoroughly. My chest heaved. My arms ached. I turned, swaying on the steps, and surveyed the chaos of the room behind me. The fighting had ceased. My friends were all upright, scattered around like thrown dice, but alive. Followers of the Vile One, distinguishable by their black robes and neck tattoos, were either dead, fleeing, or kneeling in defeat.

I leaned heavily on the sword—barely resisting the urge to sag right there onto the stone steps, next to the jerking corpse, and take a nap. Instead, I stumbled down to the main floor.

"You okay?" Matt asked. He had soot stains on his sleeves, tears in his clothes, and a cut above his eye that leaked sluggishly. His brown hair was matted to his head with sweat. He smelled like ozone and magic. He held his staff in his hand, the bright blue jewel at the tip glowing like a star, but as we stood together in the aftermath, his power faded.

A late addition to the vision of victory I kept in my head included sweeping Matt into my arms and declaring my undying affection. But as I was literally covered in blood, I didn't think Matt would appreciate a hug at this point, or a grand gesture or even a friendly slap to the shoulder. Not when we were both trembling with exhaustion and ebbing adrenaline.

"Yeah. I'm good. You?"

"Yeah." He grinned weakly. "It's done."

"It is." I ran my gloved hand through my hair. "Super gross, though."

"Oh, definitely. That was, for lack of a better word, vile."

"Good one." I held out my fist, and he bumped his knuckles against mine.

Bethany appeared from around a corner, small harp in one hand, wiping clinging bits of vomit from her mouth with her sleeve. She peeled a strand of sweaty auburn hair from her cheek, cast a look at the throne, turned green, then disappeared again. The sounds of her retching echoed in the eerie silence of the previously chaotic throne room.

Sionna rolled her eyes. She wiped her sword on a prone body before sheathing it. Her brown skin was blood-spattered, but far less than mine. She'd no doubt sharpened her sword. Her black hair still swung in her high ponytail, and the wisps that had escaped framed her face, and though her shoulders slumped with relief, her steps were as energetic as ever. Every inch a warrior. Every inch beautiful. Every inch the reason for many of my inconvenient boners while on this quest.

"I'll check on her," she said.

I cleared my throat. "Good idea."

She left the room through the same arch. Matt and I exchanged a glance. Pretty sure we were on the same wavelength about the boners. Even if we weren't, at least he was still by my side. Thankfully, that piece of my vision was fulfilled. We'd been best friends since we were boys and we'd be best friends forever if I had any say, weird wizards, glowing staffs, enigmatic prophecies, and secret crushes notwithstanding.

"You two okay?"

Startled, I spun around.

Lila stood on the ribbon of purple carpet that led up to the throne. Her soft-heeled boots made little noise when she moved normally, but on the plush, she made no sound at all. With her hood pulled up, her features were partially hidden, but I knew the familiar jut of her chin and the bow of her mouth. She had a bulging sack over one shoulder.

"Yes. We're fine. Exhausted and"—Matt gestured toward the headless form—"vaguely traumatized, but . . ." He trailed off; his eyebrows drew together in consternation. "Have you been looting?"

She shrugged. "A little." She dropped the overstuffed bag at her feet with a loud clank.

"Lila!" I placed my hands on my hips, a difficult task when holding a sword. "Put it back."

"No."

"Now."

"No."

"But—but . . ." I sputtered. "What do you even have in there?"

"Oh, you know, loot, spoils, riches. The usual."

Matt pursed his lips. "That's vague."

She smirked. "Exactly."

"Here you are!" The voice came from behind us, and again, I found myself turning quickly, sword raised. Rion leaned on the heavy wooden doors that we'd barged through mere minutes before. Besides his grimy army, he looked almost untouched from battle. He smiled when he saw us, tipping his blood-smeared sword in acknowledgment.

I relaxed and blew out a breath. "Can people please stop sneaking up on me? I've had *a day*."

"Is it over?" Rion asked, not remarking on my outburst. Instead, his gaze drifted around the throne room until it settled on the body by the dais.

"I think so?" Matt said. "I mean"—he gestured helplessly—"this is it. Right?"

Sionna returned from the adjoining room, her arm looped through Bethany's. Bethany wavered on her feet, but she'd stopped actively vomiting. The entirety of our party now stood in the throne room. We looked at one another, no one speaking, merely existing in the moment of sudden calm after the storm.

I surveyed the group, reassuring myself that we'd all made it, that we were all there and safe. Bethany, our bard, rested against the wall, gaze locked on the broken window across the room, and not anywhere near the bloody neck stump that leaned against the foot of the throne. She was charismatic and magic, essential to our success with her ability to talk her way in or out of any situation. Sionna gripped Bethany's arm, lending her strength. Sionna was a fighter, sleek and deadly, as fearless as she was dangerous. Lila, the rogue, stood on the carpet, loot bag at her feet. She was dexterous and conniving, her past shrouded in mystery, as were her motivations. Matt, the mage, my best friend, my confidant, my secret crush, and wielder of arcane spells, held his staff in the gentle curve of his hand. And Rion the knight rounded out the crowd. He was hulking and strong, older than the rest of us, but barely an adult himself, bound to our group by a sacred oath.

Then there was me. Arek. The Chosen One. The fulfiller of the prophecy, awkwardly standing in front of the throne. Somehow, this ragtag mess of personalities, dubious expertise, and questionable hygiene had come together and completed the impossible. We'd saved the realm. Holy shit. *We'd* saved the realm. *This* was the moment. This was victory.

Lila nodded once sharply, then grabbed her sack and threw it over her shoulder. "Great. Well, this has been fun, but I'm out."

"You're out?" Matt hobbled in front of her. I narrowed my eyes. Matt hadn't mentioned an injury. That doofus probably twisted his ankle when we ran up the entryway stairs dodging arrows. "What do you mean by that?"

She shrugged. "The quest is done. It's over. We won. I helped." She hefted the sack. "I took my reward. I'm out."

"Wait." Bethany straightened from her hunch by the wall. "You can't just *leave*."

"Why not?"

"Don't you want to be here for what happens next?" she asked.

Lila raised an eyebrow. "What does happen next?"

Again, we looked around at each other, silent and unsure. The question hung over the room, like the black pennants that swayed limply against the stone in the slight breeze. Bethany shrugged. Sionna blinked. Rion tapped his fingers on his smudged armor. Matt's mouth tipped down in that funny little frown he always got when he was thinking.

Well, at least we all knew the question, but it didn't look like anyone had an answer.

Perfect.

It was Rion who broke the awkward silence. He cleared his throat. "A new ruler needs to be instated. He," Rion said, jerking his chin toward the body, "was the ruler of our kingdom, as ill-gotten as it was. He killed all the royal family save one—"

"Oh," Matt said, straightening from his impressive lean on his staff, "we should find the princess."

I furrowed my brow. "Isn't she locked in a tower?"

"I think we need to wake her from an eternal slumber," Bethany said, "with true love's kiss?"

"I think that's a different quest." Lila dropped her sack, the contents clanging. "Doesn't she have to let down her hair?"

"No," Sionna said. "We have to guess her name."

"You're all wrong." Matt waved his hand. "We just need to let her out."

"Well, that doesn't sound right," Bethany said, hands on her hips. "Are you sure?"

Matt sighed and dug around in the pouch at his side. "The prophecy—"

The entire group groaned. We all knew the prophecy. We'd all read the prophecy. Matt had lectured us extensively on the prophecy. I could recite the prophecy from memory with my hands tied behind my back while being beaten with sticks by angry gnomes. Well, almost all of it, save for a section that was significantly smudged by wine. But I didn't mention that because it was a sore spot, and as fond as I was of Matt's withering glares, I didn't want to be the target of one at the moment.

Undeterred, Matt yanked the scroll from his bag and flapped the parchment in our direction like he was scolding us. "The prophecy doesn't mention true love's kiss or long hair or guessing names."

"You pulled it out just to tell us that?" Lila crossed her arms and quirked an eyebrow.

Matt's lips twisted into a frown. "I'm making a point."

"Is the point that you're pedantic?" Bethany asked, fake smile plastered on her face despite looking a little green around the gills. "Because we're aware."

"You have vomit in your hair," Matt shot back, stuffing the scroll into his pack.

"Okay, okay." I raised my hands and addressed the group. "Let's all take a moment to breathe."

Lila wrinkled her nose in my direction. "Before we embark on any side quests, there need to be baths all around. And food."

"Hey! I just killed the Vile One." I waved at the decapitated corpse behind me for emphasis. "Cut me some slack."

Rion cleared his throat. "Before I was interrupted, I did have a point."

I gestured at him. "Continue, then."

"So commanding," Matt whispered, snickering.

I bit my lip to keep laughter from bubbling out. I was covered in blood, and some of the castle residents had poked their heads out of their hiding places. Hysterically laughing wouldn't be a good look.

"The point is, with no current royal family to assume the

throne, and with you being the individual who hacked off the head of the Vile One, the job to rule the kingdom falls on your shoulders."

Huh. He said hacker of heads. The alliteration was nice, but there could be a better title in my future. Better nip it in the bud.

I crossed my arms. "Let's not go with 'hacked off the head,' please. And there's a princess in a tower who is the lawful ruler. I'm just . . . a prophetic pawn here."

"Yes, but until she is freed, you are the rightful monarch." Rion nodded to the empty throne.

I shook my head. "But I don't want to be the rightful monarch."

"Arek," Sionna said, pinching the bridge of her nose. "We can't leave the throne open while we complete the side quest."

"But—"

"Do you really want to have to do it all again," Bethany whined while flailing her hands emphatically, "if someone even worse sneaks in and sits there while we're gone and takes the throne?" She clutched her harp tighter and absolutely did not look at the headless body slumped nearby. "Or do you want to suck it up and proclaim yourself king for like a few hours?"

I shot a look at Matt. He shrugged, his expression not reassuring at all. Ugh, I really wanted for this all to be over because I wanted to talk to him in *private* and do the whole confessing thing that had been eating away at me for months. Putting on a dead man's crown seemed the opposite of wrapping up the quest, but I couldn't deny that Bethany's point was sound. I *didn't* want to do this all again.

"I . . . um . . . I . . ."

Rion took my stuttering as acceptance. He unsheathed his sword and knelt on the stone floor. "All hail, King Arek!"

"Oh no!" I held up my hands. "No. Stop that. Don't do that."

Bethany strummed her harp, her pale lips curled into a smirk. "All hail, King Arek," she sang, and with the magic of the instrument, the statement amplified into a chorus of voices. *Bitch.*

The proclamation rang out in the small room, and suddenly, everyone knelt. The few servants who had wandered in at the commotion. The remaining followers of the Vile One. And my fellow questors, my friends, those traitorous assholes.

"Get the crown," Matt said, nudging me with his shoulder, positively gleeful. His lips tugged into a smug grin that stuck to his ridiculous face. He sank to his knees. "Put it on."

"No. It's on the head. The *severed* head. That's disgusting."

"You're wearing gloves. It'll be fine."

"And then what? Put it on *my* head? Fuck that. Gore will get in my hair."

"It's already in your hair. It's all over you."

"Don't be a coward," Lila said. She was the last to kneel, but she did, which was surprising. She even pulled back her hood, revealing the long braids of her blond hair, and the pointed tips of her ears. "Do it."

"Do it. Do it. Do it," Matt whispered, cackling.

Lila reached out and pressed a single fingertip to my arm. "Peer pressure."

"Ugh." I marched back to the head, considered it, and nope. Putting on a bloody crown was not part of the vision. Neither was the whole ruling thing. Absolutely not part of the deal. But for appearances, and until the true heir from the tower was freed, I guessed ruling for a few hours wouldn't be so bad. Especially if it shut up the irritating chants.

I yanked the golden crown off the head. It rolled to the edge of the step and teetered for an agonizing second before toppling off and hitting the stone with a gag-inducing splat. I swallowed down bile, desperately trying not to pull a Bethany in front of my soon-to-be subjects. Knocking the lifeless figure off the dais, I ascended the remaining stairs and stood in front of the throne.

It was ornate, in a menacing way, with terrifying monsters etched into the decoration, and intimidating all on its own. It shouldn't have been—it was only a chair—but I did pause at the idea of plopping down where the guy I just killed used to sit.

I took a breath. "Well, all right then." Despite my misgivings, I placed the crown on my head, turned quickly, and dropped onto the throne. It was not at all comfortable.

I don't really know what happened in that moment, but something in the room swelled, and crackled, then broke over me in a wave of warmth and potential. The hair on my arms stood on end and a shiver traced down my spine. It was like standing in a field during an oncoming storm as the pressure and expectation of something much bigger than myself bared down on me, a reminder of the wonder inherent in magic and in the world, and my place in it. In an instant, I was suffused with the song of everyone who'd come before, and how all roads had led me there, to that place, to that moment, to that role.

It lasted the length of a breath, then evaporated.

The chanting ceased. I squirmed, trying to find a position that didn't twinge my back. All eyes stared at me. Yeah, this was a bad idea. Almost as bad as leaving my house in the middle of the night nine months ago, clutching the prophetic scroll that landed me here with Matt trailing behind me.

"Say something," Sionna hissed.

"Oh." I leaned forward, shaking myself out of a stupor. "Uh. The Vile One is dead. I killed him. So, I hereby assume the throne of Ere in the realm of Chickpea and declare myself King Arek." I licked my chapped lips. "But only until we free the princess from the tower. My rule will be for a few hours. Tops. An interim king, if you will. Yay. Huzzah. And all that."

Sionna snorted.

"Spoken like a true statesman," Matt said with a grin.

Lila rolled her eyes. Bethany, still pale, picked a few strings on her harp, and my words echoed outward, throughout the castle and the grounds.

A round of polite applause followed.

"Can . . . uh . . ." I swallowed. "Can we have the room please? And maybe a cleanup crew?"

The few interlopers scattered, including the last remaining living followers of the Vile One, and soon the room was clear save for us and the dead.

"Did you lot feel that?"

They blinked at me.

"Feel what?" Bethany asked. She clutched her stomach with one hand. "Sick? Because yes."

"No. The magic? Matt, did you do something?"

He furrowed his brow. "Not that I'm aware of."

"Huh." It could have been the release of stress, the receding of adrenaline, leaving me chilled and shaking. But I knew better. After nine months of prophetic fuckery, I recognized the presence of magic. The way warmth and power washed over me on the throne mirrored the prickling shock when Matt used his staff, or the sweep of mystical promise when I touched the sword for the first time in the bog. There was more brewing in the throne room than I wanted to be part of, and the sooner we found the princess and installed her as queen, the sooner I could be done with being destiny's pawn.

I slapped my hands on the arms of the throne and stood. "Well, let's find this princess, then."

"Now?" Bethany asked.

"Now," I said with a sharp nod.

Lila frowned. "But baths and food."

"And rest," Sionna said.

"Now." I pointed to the crown. "Consider it my first act as king."

"Your first act as king is to not want to be king," Matt said, smile lurking around the curve of his mouth. "Sounds about right."

Bethany snickered.

"Come on," I said, descending the dais and striding quickly out of the room. "The sooner we find this princess, the sooner we can put this whole quest behind us."

CHAPTER 2

"Rion, I swear to all the spirits in this realm and the next that if the princess *isn't* in this tower, I'm going to charm you to walk off a turret," Bethany threatened as we climbed to the top of the tower. She huffed and puffed loudly. Bethany consisted of soft curves, an ample bosom, and a round face. She was not above using all her assets, including her magic, to get what she wanted. In this case, it was a faster way up the never-ending spiral staircase.

I did not blame her as this was the third tower we'd climbed, and I was exhausted. And still quite sticky and anxious to have a conversation with a certain someone.

Matt continued to hobble. I continued to eye him. He didn't complain. I wanted him to complain. It would be better than seeing his little grimace and the tight lines around his mouth every time he stepped too aggressively.

"This will be the one," Rion said. "I'm sure of it."

"Good, because I regret not changing my clothes and taking a bath before we chose to embark on this journey."

"We *all* regret it," Sionna muttered.

I placed a hand on my tacky crimson tunic, right over my heart. "You wound me."

"Don't tempt me."

"Oh, stop it." Matt's pain finally emerged as irritation. "It's not like any of us smell like roses right now. We all stink. But if we can convince this princess that we're the good guys and that we're here to free her, she might let us stay, at least for the night."

"Oh! I see the door!" Rion ran ahead, his armor clinking, his enthusiasm not exactly contagious. "And it's locked! This is a good sign."

"Shouldn't there be guards?" Lila squinted in the gloom.

I scuffed a heel through the layer of dust on the stone steps. "Not if there are locks. Right?"

She squeezed past me on the stairs and peered ahead. She pulled her ring of tools from her belt, intent on picking the lock at the door, the same way she'd gotten us around the portcullis a few hours before, but Matt beat her to it. He leveled the jewel of his staff at the lock, said a jumble of magic words, and the door blasted open.

"No need for subtlety," he said, tapping the end of his staff on the floor. A swirl of motes puffed into the air. "It's not like we're sneaking in this time."

She tilted her head, considering. She slipped her tools into her hip bag and slid silently back into a position by the wall.

Wait. There was an awfully thick layer of grime on the floor. No one had been up here in a long time. But that door was definitely padlocked from the outside. A sinking feeling took hold in my gut, and despite Rion's zeal, unease prickled through the rest of the group as well.

I picked my way to the front, my steps leaving distinct footprints in the dust, and pushed on the opened door. It swung inward a few inches on creaking hinges. Cobwebs dislodged and fell in graceful wafts to collect on my borrowed crown. An uncannily cool breeze barreled past my right shoulder, followed by a stale smell that made me lift my sleeve to my nose.

A lump formed in my throat. Somehow this was scarier than bursting into the throne room, blood pumping, magic sword in my hand, to finally face my destiny. Because if my gut was right about what I thought lay deeper in this room, then my life was fucked. My hands shook. Sweat beaded along the back of my neck. I pushed the door harder, and it scraped along the stone.

On the other side sat a skeleton. An honest-to-spirits skeleton propped on a low bed near a sliver of a window. She wore a brocaded dress that sported moth-eaten holes, had glittering rings on her fingers, and an open journal sat at her right hand. The last princess of the former royal family had died a long time ago, locked in a tower, and all that was left was her bones.

Bethany craned her neck to look. "Well, your princess isn't in another tower. She's dead."

Matt stood next to my shoulder. "Huh. I guess you are the rightful ruler."

Panic seized my heart. I froze. *Shit!*

The group shuffled past me, poking around and rifling through the small room's contents, seemingly unbothered by the big reveal that the princess was dead, and I was king.

"Well, what do we do now?" The question erupted from me in a shout, echoing in the enclosed space, bouncing off the stone. My pulse thudded at the thought of being *responsible* for a whole kingdom. I clutched the hilt of the sword at my side with a death grip.

"We should probably do something with this body." Lila tugged on a piece of finery, and the skeleton slumped over. She inspected a bony hand, then slid a jeweled ring off a finger.

"Have some respect for the dead, Lila." Rion crossed his arms, his tone stern.

"I'm sure she doesn't mind."

"Lila."

She sighed. *"Fine."*

Rion's posture eased.

"We shouldn't leave her up here, though." Lila poked the skeleton's shoulder. "Funeral rites are important."

"Okay, noted. But what about our other problem?" I pointed to the bloodied crown, which kept sliding into an incongruously jaunty angle on my head.

Ignoring me and my existential crisis, Matt pushed aside a pair of fluttery curtains and peered out of a tiny window, more of an arrow slit than anything else. He stilled, and the tip of his staff pulsed with a warm glow.

"Matt?" Sionna asked, wary. "What's wrong?"

He gestured to the window with a frantic flap of his hand. "Him."

"Him?" I asked, voice cracking as my thoughts immediately went to the Vile One. I pushed forward, stepping around Rion's bulk, trying to ignore the uptick in my pulse as I squeezed close to Matt. I'd beheaded him, so he couldn't possibly be back. Unless his corpse was somehow shambling around outside. Hopefully not, because ew. "Him who?"

"Him! The wizard!"

Sure enough, the old man who'd declared me as the chosen one now tottered around the gardens inside the castle walls.

I'd recognize the pointy-hatted bastard anywhere. If there was anyone who could fix my current predicament, it would be him.

"That's the guy who gave you the scroll?" Bethany asked, voice pitching high in incredulity.

"Yes," I said with a sharp nod.

"And you followed it? What the hell? I knew you two had extraordinarily little self-preservation skills, but honestly."

"It seemed like a good idea at the time. And hey, it worked out in the end, kind of. Anyway, Matt, did you call him?" I asked, eyeing the glowing tip of Matt's staff.

"Ha! If I knew how to call him, I would've asked for his help ages ago."

I didn't know how to take that, so I decided to move on. "Look, you lot take care of the princess. Matt and I will talk to the wizard. He had to have popped up here to offer advice or another prophecy or something. Matt and I will figure it out. Okay? Okay."

I slapped my hand on Matt's shoulder and dragged him out of the room before anyone could object.

It took us a few minutes to find the door that led out of the castle into the correct garden, but once we finally did, we tumbled outside in a hurry. Craning my neck, I searched for the tower where our friends remained and spied Lila's pale hand waving from an arrow slit up above us. Well, at least we had witnesses to whatever would happen.

"Hey! Hey, you!" I shouted, striding across the lawn.

The old wizard turned, his worn robes swishing around his ankles. His long, gray-streaked hair fluttered in a non-existent breeze. He was so old and gnarled that his wrinkles had wrinkles, and his shoulders hunched. Despite his feeble appearance, he radiated power. The air shimmered with magic, and it prickled along my skin.

"Me?" he asked innocently. Then he squinted. "Oh! Hello."

"Hello. Hi. How are you?"

He made a humming noise, then turned his attention to Matt. He stared at the slow flashing light emanating from the staff in Matt's hand. "Ah, I see," he said with a nod. "You've done it, then?"

Matt blinked. "Done what?"

"Succeeded. Congratulations!"

"You're . . . not here to take back the staff, are you?" Matt pulled it closer to his chest. I didn't want to break it to him, but I was fairly certain that if the wizard wanted it back, proximity wasn't going to be an issue.

"Hm? No. No, that's not why I'm here."

"Great," I said, clapping my hands, drawing the attention back to me. "Why are you here? Because we would love some help. We just found the rightful ruler dead in a tower, and somehow I've been named king, and I don't think I want to be king, much less know how to rule a kingdom. So, do you have another scroll you could give us? Wise words? Direction?"

He peered at me under bushy eyebrows, looking confused. "Ah, no."

Matt and I exchanged a glance. "No?" I asked.

The wizard shook his head. "Correct."

"Wait, what?" Matt asked.

"Exactly."

I clenched my hands so tight my fists trembled. "Okay, so why are you here?"

He blinked his ancient eyes, and then his gaze traveled the length of my body, from the scuffs of my boots to the golden monstrosity of the crown on my head. He laughed. Not a tinkling sound or a chuckle but an outright deep belly laugh. He bent over, grasping his knees as he guffawed loudly and enthusiastically and totally at my expense.

"You know," I said, arms crossed, annoyed down to my bones, "you were much more talkative when you persuaded me to run away from home nine months ago to fulfill my destiny, which, I might add, included almost dying multiple times."

The wizard continued to giggle.

"You do remember, right? Appearing the day after my birthday? Telling my best friend he could wield magic? Handing me a prophetic scroll?" I flapped my hand in Matt's direction, and he yanked the offending parchment from his pouch. "Does this look vaguely familiar?"

The wizard finally regained his composure, clearing his throat. He regarded the scroll with an arched eyebrow. "Yes. Of course it does."

"Well?" I prompted.

"That is the prophecy detailing the end of the tyrant known as the Vile One."

Okay. Not wrong, but not information I didn't already have. I leaned in. "And?"

The wizard shrugged.

I waited, thinking there might be more information forthcoming, but a solid minute passed in silence. I threw up my hands in disgust. "Can you at least tell me what to do about being the king? Am I even supposed to be king?"

He rubbed his chin. "No."

"No, you can't tell me, or no, I'm not supposed to be king?" *Please let it be the second option. Please let it be the second option.* I hoped for an answer, but as another long pause stretched between us, I realized there wouldn't be one. My frustration and fatigue reached a breaking point. "This is useless!" I yelled. "Absolutely useless! Come on, Matt. I bet the others are dying of laughter up there."

The wizard snorted. With a wave of his hand, he unrolled his own scroll from midair and plucked a quill from nothing. Pinching the feather between his fingers, he made a single tally mark on the parchment.

"What's that?" Matt asked, craning his neck. "What are you doing?"

Sighing, the wizard snapped his fingers, and the parchment and quill disappeared in a spark. He folded his hands in the wide sleeves of his robes. "There are thousands of prophecies in the world," he said. "Not all of them are true. This one happened to be. I'm marking it down in my records."

"Wait, *what*?" Matt asked again, his voice a screech. "You keep data?"

Though I echoed Matt's outrage, I felt like he missed the bigger issue. "Do you mean to tell us there was a chance we could've *failed*?" I'd never felt more betrayed in my life. The one bedrock of this whole journey was the prophecy, and it could've been *wrong*? My entire world tilted. "We could have *died*? What the fuck?"

"You didn't," the wizard offered helpfully. "This prophetess has a ninety-five percent accuracy rating. It's quite astonishing."

Matt made a very complicated face at that information.

I felt like my soul left my body. We had relied on that prophecy like it was truth, and now I found out that *it might not have been.* I went light-headed and staggered over to lean against the castle wall to keep from face-planting.

The wizard was unfazed. "This has been nice, but I have a few more of these visits to complete today, so I better be off."

"Wait." Matt stepped toward the wizard, hand outstretched. He had already squirreled the prophecy back away in his bag. "Do you have another prophecy about Arek? Or about someone in our group? Did the prophetess write anything else?"

Good thinking, Matt. Always the one to ask the right questions. One of the many reasons I liked him so much. I currently couldn't be trusted to do so. I was in the midst of a mental breakdown, because the wizard clearly said he had a few more visits. A few more visits? How many prophetic schemes was this guy running? How many teenagers did he send out on quite-possibly-fake adventures?

The wizard's eyebrows angled oddly. "No."

Matt deflated.

Ignoring him, the wizard pinned me with another intense look. "Enjoy your reign, King Arek." Then he smirked.

Oh, that was uncalled for. I pushed away from the wall, grabbed the hilt of my sword, intent on doing something brash and kingly, but the wizard merely waved his hands and popped out of existence.

Matt shook his fist at the sparkles hanging in the air in the wake of the wizard's departure. "Well, screw you!" he yelled.

"Wow. Such language," I said. "Who's the mature one here?"

Matt swung his head and, oh yes, *there* was the withering glare I was so fond of. He took a steadying breath, one hand pressed to the center of his chest, the other curled around his staff in a death grip. "Let's go find the others," he said. "And give them the wonderful news that we have no plan, no help, and that you are indeed the king of Ere in the realm of Chickpea."

"Yay. Long live me, I guess." I gave him the best smile I could muster.

Matt narrowed his eyes, then shook his head as his expression softened. He even huffed a laugh as he stomped to the door. I followed, because the only solid thing in my world was Matt, and I was certain that, together, we'd figure something out.

CHAPTER 3

"He reigned for forty years." The firelight played across Bethany's features, and her eyes reflected the funeral pyres. "I don't know why we anticipated finding anything different."

"Anything different than a pile of bones? Really?" I adjusted the crown. It was so heavy it gave me a headache and pinched my ears when it slid down too far. I considered tossing it into the fire as well, but Lila would probably snatch it out of the air and squirrel it away before I could blink. And throwing it away wouldn't relieve the burden of ruling the kingdom. I'd declared myself king. Bethany broadcasted it throughout the castle, the grounds, and the surrounding village with her magic harp. I was royally screwed.

"I mean, I guess you hear the term 'princess' and automatically assume, you know, a typical princess." Matt gestured helplessly.

"You know what they say about assuming things. It makes an ass out of you and me." They all glared at me. Matt even groaned. "What? I make jokes in uncomfortable situations. You should know that about me by now. It's not like you haven't spent the last several months of your lives trying to keep me from becoming a corpse."

Sionna rubbed her thumb between her eyes. "Yes, we have, despite your jokes."

The fire crackled. Sweat rolled down my spine. The heat pouring from the flames was unrelenting, even with the cool evening. It had been a solid four or five hours since we'd raided the throne room and I'd unwittingly become king. The day was waning and so was my patience and energy. And I still hadn't found a bath.

"And the wizard had nothing to offer?" Rion asked. "At all?"

Matt and I had already provided the painful details of our conversation with the wizard, but I could see how it would seem unbelievable. I had actually talked to the guy and I could scarcely believe it.

"Nothing," Matt said on a sigh. "We completed the quest and now we're a tally mark in his records." He tossed a twig into the fire. "And Arek is king."

The group stood in silence, the only sound the popping and crackling of the fire. Embers floated in a soft breeze. The sky inched toward twilight. We needed a plan, at least for the night, but everyone was exhausted and, for the moment, content to merely exist in the same spot for a while.

"You know," Lila said, breaking the silence, "for a dead lady, she's very poetic." She held up the journal from the tower. "Listen to this: 'If I ever get out of here, I'm going to tell her I love her.'" She pressed the book to her chest. "That's so sweet. Sad as all the hells, but sweet."

Matt shifted next to me, staff grasped in his hand, looking pained. His ankle must be hurting again. He refused to sit down when I offered to pull a chair from one of the many castle rooms into the garden.

I huffed in Lila's direction. "Did you steal the journal?"

"What? Not like she needs it." She tilted her chin toward the dual pyres.

Bethany grabbed it from her hand. She flipped through it. "This might have information we need to figure out how to rule this blasted kingdom."

Cocking my head to the side, I considered the group. "We? Rule?"

She blinked. "You're the king."

"Yeah. So?"

"So. That means you are in charge."

"I realize that, kind of." I was trying hard not to think about it. "But what does that have to do with you?"

Scoffing, Bethany leveled a thoroughly unimpressed look in my direction. "I'm not leaving. This is a castle. There are beds here. And food."

"And the rest of you?"

"This is just getting interesting," Lila said with a grin. "I'm staying, at least for a bit."

Sionna rolled her eyes at Lila but nodded. "Same."

"I swore an oath to you," Rion said. He shrugged. "The God of Vows heard my words and would not look kindly upon my breaking them."

"But the quest is over. You don't have to protect me anymore."

Rion's brow furrowed. "You're king of this land. You need protecting now more than ever."

I opened my mouth to retort, but snapped it shut. I hadn't

thought of it that way. I'd barely thought of anything beyond fulfilling the prophecy since I'd found out about it, and since our victory, I hadn't thought beyond the next few minutes at a time.

"I don't want to be king."

"You don't?" Sionna asked.

Lila crossed her arms. "You literally put on the crown."

"Under duress!"

Matt nudged me with his shoulder. "You'll be fine. We'll all be fine. Those of us who choose to stay will help you. Like we've *been* helping. We're ... we're a—" Matt cleared his throat. "Well, we're a group. We've congealed into something that works. We wouldn't have made it this far if we didn't."

"Matt is right," Sionna said, standing from where she had sat cross-legged on the paving stones in the courtyard. "We work well as a party."

It had been her idea to burn both the Vile One and the last princess as our first task after finding the bones. Lila and Sionna were adamant about adhering to the funeral rites according to the princess's beliefs. I wanted to ensure the Vile One couldn't be resurrected via his own dark magic. Even headless, we couldn't risk him returning. Because that would be terrifying and gruesome, and I was certain his first order of business would be to exact revenge on the individual who made him headless in the first place.

"We'll continue on this journey, together." Rion crossed his arms over his chest, the greaves of his grimy armor clanking together. With his feet shoulder-width apart, his posture ram-rod straight, he moved into what I had dubbed his righteous stance. He used it often when addressing us because, though we were all roughly the same age, he was the one with the strongest moral compass while the rest of us ran around like feral barn cats.

I couldn't stop the swell of affection that I had for this group, surprised but grateful that their friendship extended beyond the confines of a written prophecy. I rubbed my hands together. "Okay. That's great. It's settled." In an attempt at leadership, I tried to infuse my voice with the confidence of someone who was comfortable with the idea of governing a kingdom. "We'll look into this ruling thing. Tomorrow, though. Right now, I'm exhausted and gross."

"Food too," Bethany said. Matt agreed, nodding like his head was on a spring.

"Okay, food too. We should find places to rest for the night. Or one place. We'll room together for safety, just in case. And baths. And dinner. We should do that. Eat. Sleep. Be merry because, hey, we won. We fucking won!" My voice cracked on the last word, but my false cheer lifted the heavy mood. Because, despite the odds, our months of toil hadn't been for naught. The Vile One was dead because of us. The land was free.

I breathed a deep, cleansing breath, then gagged on the smell of burning flesh and ash. Huh. Not a good idea. I coughed into my hands, and Matt pounded a fist between my shoulder blades until I regained my composure.

"Yes. We did win," Rion said. "We deserve rest. Our situation will look different in the light of a new day."

"Sure, it will," I said with as much enthusiasm as I could

muster, which wasn't much as my energy flagged. "It'll be great."

Lila slapped my shoulder. "Nice speech, your majesty."

Sionna's lips quirked into a smile. Bethany winked.

"For the record, I hate you all," I said, turning on my heel. "Come on, this is a castle. There have to be amenities around here somewhere."

I walked back toward the entrance, careful to stay slightly ahead of the group so my face would be obstructed from their view and they couldn't catch my expression. As grateful as I was to know they were sticking by my side, at least for the time being, an uncomfortable feeling rose up through my exhaustion. My chance of telling Matt how I felt about him—free and clear of any obligations to quests and prophecies—was slipping further away.

Chapter 4

"What the fuck is happening?" I yelled as I careened out of sleep to the sound of someone pounding on the door. I scrambled out of bed, tripping as my feet tangled in the sheets. It would be comical if I were the only one flailing, but my friends were just as harried.

"Oh shit, they're after us!"

"Who?"

"I don't know!"

"Where's my harp?"

"Where's my *sword*?"

The evening prior, after we all bathed in a fountain in the garden and ate what we could find, we'd retired to a grand bedroom in the castle. We'd locked the door and dragged a heavy wardrobe in front of it, and Matt set a magic ward. Even with all our precautions, months of constantly living on edge—of sleeping with our boots on and bags packed in case we had to run in the middle of the night—meant all six of us were on our feet with weapons in hand before we even realized what was happening.

Well, almost all of us. I disentangled myself from the blankets, grabbed my sword, and had it halfway out of the scabbard before the voice on the other side said, "Good morning, sire. I'm here to serve you breakfast!"

I paused, brought up short. "What?"

"Breakfast, sire! Sent up from the kitchens."

Frowning, I exchanged a glance with my disheveled compatriots.

"Isn't it a bit early for breakfast?"

"The sun has been up for two hours."

I jutted my chin toward the window, and Lila leapt like a fox from the floor to the edge of the bed to another table, not making a sound as she did so, and creaked open the shutters. Indeed, the sun was up and bright and shining. Huh. The world hadn't ended overnight. That was a bonus.

"Yes, um, well, give me a moment." I pitched my voice low. "What do we do?"

"Opening the door seems like an appropriate action," Rion said, completely seriously. "It is time for breakfast."

It took every ounce of my limited restraint not to roll my eyes. Rion's earnestness didn't deserve my ire.

"Yes. But what if he's here to kill us?"

"You," Bethany said brightly. She had her harp clutched in one hand, the other on her hip cocked jauntily to the side. "If he's here to kill anyone, it's you. Not us."

I did roll my eyes at that. "Thanks, oh so helpful."

Sionna gripped her sword. "We'll protect you if that's why he's here."

I wanted to believe her. After all, they had protected me for several months now. But the prophecy was completed. Their bonds to me were no longer mandated by a higher power. And Lila had one leg out the window.

Matt nudged me with his elbow. He tapped his staff against the floor, and the jewel in the tip glowed blue.

I cleared my throat. "Quick question," I called. "How did you know I was here? How did you learn that I am the king?"

"I heard the proclamation yesterday, sire. You declared yourself King Arek. The whole castle heard it, as did the grounds, and the village. I must admit, it did take a bit of time to find the room you'd taken for your quarters, which is why your breakfast is here an hour late."

"Right. The proclamation." I glared at Bethany. She flashed a flirty grin. "Fine. Um . . . seriously, only a minute longer."

I nodded toward the others. Sionna and Rion crept closer, weapons at the ready. Matt raised his staff and, with a whisper, levitated the heavy wardrobe and moved it softly out of the way.

With shaking hands, I slid the bolt, grabbed the large ring, and took a breath. I pulled the door open a crack and peeked around the worn edge.

The sight that greeted me was the exact embodiment of everything I would've expected in someone who would deliver breakfast to a king. He was tiny. Okay, not *tiny* tiny. Not like the pixie we'd encountered in the forest that made us answer questions before she'd allow us to pass through her meadow. But short for a human. Pint-sized. The top of his head brushed my shoulder. And he was slim, like a willow branch. He had steel-gray hair and wrinkles around his eyes and mouth. He wore a fine shirt with a brocaded vest over his chest and a pair of slim-cut trousers. He held a silver tray of food.

"Um . . . hello."

"Hello, sire." He lifted the tray. "Your breakfast."

I opened the door farther and leaned toward the food. I sniffed. It smelled like fresh biscuits and cheese and sausage. And was that gravy? My stomach growled. I resisted the urge to fling the door open and dive face-first into the covered dish because, though he looked the part of a servant, he could be there to kill me. I'd hate to die over a biscuit.

"May I come in and set it down?"

I glanced over my shoulder. Sionna gave me a sharp nod, but her knuckles were white where she gripped her sword.

"One thing," I said through the crack. "Who are you?"

He blinked his large blue eyes. "My name is Harlow, and I'm the steward of this castle."

Matt elbowed me in the back. "The steward runs the castle," he whispered.

"Was he loyal to the last guy?" I whispered back.

Matt shrugged. "I think he's loyal to whoever is lord of the castle."

"That's you," Rion said helpfully.

"Right." This was the guy who could tell us how to navigate the castle without starving to death or committing a faux pas that would result in our ousting, maiming, or assassinations. "Come on in."

I stepped out of the way, and he walked smartly into the room, stopping short at the group crowded along my back.

"Oh," he said, a short sound of surprise, though his tone remained even. "I don't believe I've brought enough to feed everyone." His eyebrows quirked. "But there is more in the kitchens."

"Great. Um . . . so, Harlow." I put my hands in my worn trousers' pockets and rocked back on my heels. "Are you . . ." I searched for the right words. "Going to poison me?"

He looked positively affronted, and his already pale face went translucent.

"I mean," I added quickly, "are you Team Vile One or Team Arek? Are you upset that I beheaded your previous king? I literally hacked off his head. It was gross. You may be mad about that. I just need to know because, if you are, I'd rather not eat the food you've brought and die."

Harlow's mouth pursed so violently he looked like he'd sucked on a lemon.

Bethany's eyebrows were in her hairline. "We really need to work on your charm, King Arek. And your mouth and the sewage that spills out of it."

"What?" My shoulders lifted to my ears, and I spread my palms. "I'm being honest."

Harlow's gaze wandered over Matt's staff, Rion's sword, and Lila, who clenched her dagger in her teeth even as she was mostly out the window.

"Well," Rion prodded, gently resting the tip of his sword on the fabric of Harlow's starched jacket, "where does your loyalty lie, Harlow?"

He blinked. "With King Arek, of course. My loyalty is to the castle. King Arek defeated King Barthly and became our rightful ruler."

"Barthly?" Matt asked, his tone mirroring my own incredulity. "The evil wizard who used dark magic, usurped the throne, and kept our realm in shadow for forty years was named *Barthly*?" He flailed his hands. "Barthly!"

Harlow squinted. "He did not prefer to use his name."

"Well, would you? If your name was Barthly?"

I stepped on Matt's uninjured foot because he seriously needed to chill.

"Anyway, so you run the castle, correct?"

"Yes, as I have for the last twenty years."

"And during that whole time, you didn't think to, oh I don't know, try to stop what was happening?"

Harlow finally brushed past all of us and set the tray down on the table, then turned smartly to face our group. "No."

"Why not?"

"It wasn't my place."

Huh. "But you continued to work here. Why didn't you find another job? Somewhere else? Like in the village we stormed through?"

Harlow wrinkled his nose. "Find another job? That pays well? In this economy?"

Fair point.

Harlow continued. "Myself and my fellow servants had no place else to go, though we knew it was unsafe here. When you six charged the gates, when you crossed the moat, and entered the keep, when you ran up the stairs to the throne room, my fellow servants and I did not hinder your progress. In fact, we cheered, as quietly as possible in the event you failed, but we did." His mouth twitched into a small smile. "I hid and prayed to my gods and hoped you would succeed. And you have."

I cleared my throat. "Well, then I'm glad we could be of assistance."

Harlow gave the group a curt bow. "If the rest of your party would like, they can follow me to the kitchens for their breakfast."

I pinched the sleeve of Matt's tunic between my thumb and forefinger but nodded for the others to dress and follow Harlow.

"Then, if his majesty desires, we could reconvene after," Harlow said, "in the council room adjacent to the great hall."

"Sure!" I chirped. Harlow appeared disconcerted, so I amended. "I mean, his majesty does desire. That sounds like a fine idea. We'll meet in the council room. Thank you, Harlow."

Amid a few grumblings, the group, save Matt, prepared themselves for the day. I sat on the bed, cross-legged, and didn't stare as Matt made himself comfortable against the headboard, lounging in the sheets. I also didn't stare as Sionna braided her long dark hair and donned her leather armor, her muscles flexing beneath her dark skin, and as Bethany primped and applied her makeup in the large mirror affixed to the wall. I really didn't stare at Lila, because she'd stab me, and I wouldn't realize it until she had already fled and was leagues away. And I didn't stare at Rion because, despite the muscles . . . Okay, well, I did stare at the muscles. Who am I kidding? His forearms were chiseled, and his abs were works of art. Of course I peeked. Who wouldn't?

Did I mention I was seventeen and had been living in close quarters with five beautiful people the last nine months?

Anyway, the group met Harlow in the hall, and he raised his eyebrows as Matt didn't move from his place on the bed.

"Oh, he's injured," I said. "His foot was wounded in battle. He shouldn't walk on it."

"Then he should see our court physician."

"We have one of those?"

Harlow clasped his hands in front of him, and I could only imagine the thoughts running through his head. They were probably along the lines of *How the hells did this ignorant peasant-child defeat the most powerful being in ages?* "Yes," he said, clipped. "Perhaps your majesty would like to meet the castle's staff after his meeting with his advisors."

"That would be great."

Once they were gone and the door was firmly closed, Matt burst into laughter. "Did you see his face? When you asked about the court physician?" He clutched his sides. "That man is going to have a conniption when he realizes how unprepared you are to rule a kingdom."

"Thanks. Real helpful, Matt." I flopped theatrically backward onto the bed.

"Dramatic, much?" Matt grinned at me and poked me in the side.

"Yes. Very."

He sighed through his nose. "So, are you going to eat that?"

I waved my hand toward the table, and Matt hobbled over and pulled off the cover. "There's enough food here for you and me and half our village."

A pang hit my gut at the mention of our village. We'd hadn't been back since we left. It didn't really hold anything for me anymore, since my parents and Matt's mom had both passed, but it was the only home I'd known. I couldn't believe we'd been away for so long.

Matt sank onto the bench seat and lifted a biscuit from the basket as gently as one would hold a priceless artifact. He held it in his palm and inhaled. "Magic, save me," he said. "It smells like butter."

The corner of my mouth lifted. "Is there gravy in that?" I asked, nodding toward a small pitcher set on the side of the tray.

Matt lifted the lid, the ceramic plinking as he did. "Sausage gravy at that."

"Shove over," I said, hopping off the bed and sitting next to him. "I haven't eaten since yesterday."

"I can definitely get behind these spoils of war."

I knocked my elbow into his while we each reached for the decadent food. "Almost makes all that running and fear worth it."

"Almost," he agreed.

A glint of light caught my eye, and my gaze landed on the crown, which sat abandoned on the table. It was a gold circlet with five vertical ornaments. Each one was shaped differently, though I didn't know their symbolism, and centered within each was a different jewel. It was beautiful, once I was able to get past the fact that it used to sit on the head of evil. I still wished it wasn't mine, though.

What if Sionna had beheaded him? Would she be declared queen? I'd trust her more than myself. What if it had been Matt? I reached out and ran the tip of my finger over one of the gold ornaments. My fingernail caught on a jewel.

"Hey," Matt said. "I've been thinking."

"Dangerous," I quipped.

He ignored me. "If you really don't want to be king, we could leave. You could place the crown on the throne and walk out.

Leave it for the next adventurer who fancies themselves king."

"I can't," I said, fingertip dropping from the gold. "Who's to say that they'd be any better than who we defeated?"

"We could let the people decide," Matt said around a mouthful of sausage. "Or let a council of lords choose."

"I don't think it works like that, Matt." I remembered the wave of magic that swelled over me when I sat on the throne and declared myself king. It had felt weighty, significant, like I'd been tied there.

"Why couldn't it? You're the king. You could choose a successor and pass the crown on. Right? Then we leave and head back to the village before the snows start. Or anywhere really. Where do you think the others would want to go?"

That sounded perfect and exactly what I had hoped would happen after we completed the quest. I wished we could walk off into the world together, with endless possibilities stretching in front of us, including a chance at a relationship. It seemed within reach yesterday, but now it felt further away than ever.

I pinched the bridge of my nose. "I just . . . It won't work."

"Why not?"

"Because I think I'm stuck?" It came out as more of a question than a statement. I picked up the crown, my thumbprint smearing the glossy metal and my reflection distorting in the gentle curves of the circlet. "You didn't feel it when I put this on my head and sat on the throne. I don't know how you missed it. It was a burst of magic, like my very soul was tied to that moment, to the earth beneath that spot. Whatever kind of magic was in this . . ." I turned to him and held it up. "It bound me to the throne."

"What?" His voice was a breath of disbelief. "Why—why didn't you say anything?"

"I did. Remember? I asked if you felt it."

Matt swallowed down his bite of biscuit and rubbed a hand on his chest. "I didn't feel it." He studied the tray of food. "Are you certain?"

"No. But I think if we do some research, we'll probably find something about it. Maybe Harlow knows and can tell us."

"You might not be able to leave." He fisted his hands on his thighs. "I should've realized it. I should've known."

"Hey, no, don't do that. We couldn't have known. I don't even know if what I felt was *real*. Maybe it was just the adrenaline drop. Maybe I could leave if I wanted."

He raised an eyebrow. "The prophecy—"

I bit back a groan.

"—was explicit that you had to kill Barthly. Not defeat him. Not usurp him. Not imprison him and ask him nicely to hand over the crown. Kill him, Arek. I thought it was because he was evil, but maybe that's how succession works. The throne has to change hands through death."

Yikes. That wasn't good. But Matt wasn't wrong. The prophecy had been clear that Barthly had to die, and it even gave me a sword to do it with, if not a sharpened one. "Are you suggesting that if I decide to not be king . . ."

"You may have to go the way of Barthly."

A chill shot down my spine. Well, that was bad. Wow. Really should've read the fine print before shoving the crown on my head and declaring myself interim king. "Huh. That is a horrible system for transitions of power."

Matt sighed in frustration. He dropped the shard of biscuit

back to the plate and ran a hand through his dark brown hair, tugging on the ends. "Look, don't take this the wrong way, but after we found the princess's corpse and everything spiraled out of control, I was betting on your abdication."

"Hey!" I said, vaguely offended, even though I had the exact same notion.

"You didn't want to be king. You didn't even want to put on the crown!"

"Because it was covered in decapitated evil guy!" I protested. Matt wasn't wrong. I didn't want to be king, but the disrespect in his tone was a little too sharp. "And may I remind you that you dared me to do it!"

Matt ignored me.

"Last night, I thought, hey, this is fun, my best friend is king, right? Because we'd wake up this morning and realize that it is utterly impossible that you're meant to be a ruler."

I made a high-pitched noise of affront, but he plowed on.

"None of us are suited for this. Lila stole a dead woman's diary."

"To be fair, Lila steals everything. And the princess really didn't need it."

"Bethany vomits at the sight of gore."

"You can't blame her. It was *really* gross."

"Rion is not the sharpest sword in the armory."

"Well, now you're just being mean."

"And I was convinced we'd play rulers for a day, a week at most, and that when this got weird or too tough or we got tired, we'd leave. That we had *options*. That we might just be waiting on someone else to fulfill *their* prophecy to become king and relieve us, relieve *you*, of this burden. That you were a stand-in for, well, someone better prepared for this enormous responsibility."

"Wow." He was not wrong, but a little tact would go a long way. "Weren't you the one who said last night that we'd congealed into a group? That we worked?"

Matt glared at the opposite wall. "That was a vote to stay together, not necessarily to rule a kingdom. We aren't equipped."

"Thanks for the vote of confidence there, Matt."

"Shut up. *None* of us know what we're doing. We both thought the princess was alive and she'd step in."

"Well, she's dead, so not much we can do about that. I'm not disagreeing with you that this is a bad idea. I was fully prepared to hand this stupid crown over to someone who was born to do it. But there are currently no other options. There's just us."

"This isn't fair. We followed through on the quest. We fulfilled the prophecy. This"—he waved his hand around the bedroom—"is beyond our obligations. The prophecy *ends*. We're supposed to be done. I thought we'd find a person who was . . . a responsible adult."

Matt was clearly freaking out, and if he saw me upset, then he'd lose it even more, and then we'd both spiral. There was only room for one of us to stress, so I had to muster the ability to stay at least outwardly calm. It was surprisingly easy when I thought about how all I wanted was for Matt to be happy. "I hate to break it to you, Matt, but the closest thing we have to a responsible adult is Rion."

"Spirits, save us."

"Right?"

"But you can't leave." He rubbed his eyes. "You can't leave. *You can't leave.*"

Okay. Wow. That reaction was a little strong. Did . . . did that mean that Matt wanted to leave? The thought shook me to my core, and my heart threatened to break. The idea of being stuck here without him was too much to bear. I had to do something, even if it was a bad idea. I cleared my throat.

"Matt—"

He held up his hand, cutting me off. "Okay. Give me a minute. I have to think."

"Matt—"

"Shh."

"Are you shushing your king?" The wilting glare he shot me was totally worth the comment. "What I was trying to say is that we could test it. I could undeclare myself king and see what happens."

Matt's mouth dropped open. "Test it? Test magic we know nothing about? Magic strong enough to determine the fate of an entire kingdom? You want to roll those dice?"

"Yes?"

"Oh, okay. Sure, King Arek. Let's tempt fate and possibly trigger an earthquake or destroy the realm or kill everyone in the castle! Or even worse, possibly kill you!"

I raised my hands in surrender. "Fine. Okay. I won't play with magic."

He sighed and dropped his head into his hands. "If only the princess was alive," he muttered.

"Wait," I said, snapping my fingers. "Barthly didn't kill the princess. She would've been heir after he killed all her family, and the magic would've recognized her as the rightful ruler.

But she was at least alive in the tower for a few years while he sat on the throne. Which means that maybe death isn't necessarily involved with succession."

Matt nodded slowly. "Huh. Good point. She was the rightful heir." He hummed. "We're missing something important. We need more information."

"Right. Yes. Of course." More knowledge would be helpful. It would be beneficial to know if I was well and truly stuck, in case we didn't get the hang of this ruling gig. Last night everyone seemed on board to help, but that was when we were all giddy with victory and exhaustion. Who knew what would happen today? Or tomorrow? They could all decide to leave, and then what? I couldn't rule a kingdom by myself. All alone. Without them. Without *Matt*. I couldn't bear it. "Okay, so plan. You look into all this, and I try to . . . rule."

He snorted.

This time I ignored him. "And we should look at the prophecy again. Together."

Matt's mouth tipped down. "You literally groan when I bring it out because we've been over it so many times. I've studied it backward and forward."

"I know," I said quickly. "I know, but maybe it's changed? We've encountered so much magic we never thought existed, so maybe it's magic too."

A line appeared between Matt's eyebrows, and I resisted the urge to smooth it away.

"Maybe," he agreed, rather reluctantly. He smiled, and my stomach flipped. I'd known Matt for so long, I could differentiate between his cheerful smiles and the ones he forced to appease others. This was one of the latter. He nudged a hard-boiled egg toward my side of the tray. "Eat up. Wouldn't want Harlow to think you didn't like your breakfast. I think it would crush him."

My appetite had fled, but I took the egg anyway and choked it down my dry throat.

CHAPTER 5

Sitting around a large table in the council room, my group of fellow questors stared at me. Harlow hovered behind my right shoulder with a pitcher of wine, waiting to refill the goblet that had magically appeared before me. Matt sat next to me on the left while the others slumped, reclined, and perched around the table.

Matt and I had decided to keep the fact that I may be trapped by magic to ourselves until we had more information. But it wouldn't hurt to gauge everyone's feelings about our initial plan.

I awkwardly cleared my throat. "In the light of a new day, one in which we're all fed and rested and living our best lives, Matt and I thought about revisiting the proposal from last night."

"About ruling?" Sionna asked.

"That would be the one."

The group exchanged glances. Lila shrugged. "It's certainly not your worst idea. Not like when you decided to run toward the people trying to kill us instead of running away from them."

"I wanted to see if a different strategy would work. No harm done."

"You were stabbed," Sionna said.

"I healed."

"Oh, what about the time when—"

"Okay," I said, cutting Lila off before she could recount another of my best mistakes. "Thanks for that."

Bethany laughed obnoxiously as she and Lila fist-bumped.

"Anyway," I said, clapping my hands. "Ruling. Thoughts? Suggestions?"

Matt sighed in that long-suffering way of his. "We figured the best place to start is with the prophecy," he said as he rolled the parchment out to its full length. The flowing script started at the upmost left corner and spilled down the page, stopping in the middle of the scroll about an inch shy of two feet. The edges were tattered from our journey, and there was one section about a third of the way down that had been smudged out when Matt spilled wine across it very shortly after the wizard had given it to us.

I touched the beginning where the prophetess's beautiful lettering documented Barthly's usurpation of the throne and reign of tyranny in two succinct lines. The rest of the scroll detailed the journey I would take to defeat him.

Bethany tapped her fingernail on a line of script that mentioned the "Bard with the Harp." "This is when you met me," she said with a soft smile. She had changed into a beautiful dress with a low-cut neckline and a sweeping hem. I have no idea where she found it, but it hugged her every voluptuous curve. "I saved you from being thrown into a pillory."

"You did," Sionna said. She patted Bethany's shoulder. "And you did it wonderfully."

A light blush filled Bethany's cheeks, and she ducked her head. I was certain it was an act.

We'd found Bethany in a pub where she played her harp and sang for coins. She didn't realize she was influencing her customers then, only that she made amazing tips, especially when she used her harp. She'd always had a talent for persuasion, and since she'd joined us, her powers had only grown. It didn't work on other magical beings, though, or on nonmagical people when it came to matters that originated in someone's heart. We learned that in the face of a large troll and in the case of the innkeeper's son who inconveniently fell in love with Matt.

The parchment didn't provide the names of my fellow questors, only their roles, otherwise when Matt and I found the first village outside of our own, we would've yelled Sionna's name instead of trying to subtly distinguish which warrior would help us from the warriors who would rather kill us than look at us.

Not to be outdone, Lila slapped her hand on the paragraph that pertained to her. "And this is when you met me."

"Trying to steal from us," Matt said. "This very scroll."

Lila laughed. She tipped back in her chair and propped her boots on the table. "Ah, those were the days."

"That was literally less than a year ago," I said.

She winked. "That it was."

Sionna leaned in and ran her hand over the wine stain. "I wish we knew what was under these words."

Matt stiffened. "I don't remember. It happened when we first had the scroll."

"I know," Sionna said, frowning. "But it might be helpful. Maybe your magic—"

"I've tried," Matt snapped.

I winced. The stain was a sore spot for Matt. He'd tried to fix it when it happened, but he couldn't. The missing words weren't important anyway, since they didn't hinder our ability to complete the prophecy. Just in case, though, I moved my full goblet of wine as far away as possible.

"What would be helpful," I said, switching the subject, "is if it didn't just end."

Rion craned his neck to read. "And he shall be defeated by the chosen's hand with the sword from the Bog of the Undead, and his reign will end. Then the realm shall be freed from his dark magic, and the kingdom of Ere will enter a period of peace lasting a thousand years."

"Like, what the fuck?" I said, flailing. "Not helpful at all."

"We're off the map," Matt said, lower lip sucked between his teeth in thought. "Here there be monsters."

"The only monster here is the one in the moat," I said. "We're fine. We just need some clarification on who exactly is supposed to usher in this period of peace."

The group exchanged a glance.

Rion coughed politely, drawing everyone's attention. Shoulders back and spine straight, he leveled his serious gaze at me. "It's our obligation to try."

Lila quirked an eyebrow in Rion's direction, then looked away. "Yeah, why couldn't it be us?" she asked, tone defensive. "We're just as good as the next lot. And I don't see anyone else lining up for the job."

"You were literally hanging out of a window this morning, trying to escape," I said.

She shrugged. "The situation has changed."

"How?"

"We had breakfast."

I resisted banging my head on the table, but just barely. This was not how I was expecting this conversation to unfold. Not that I wanted them to leave, not until I figured out if I even could, but Matt was right: this was beyond the prophecy, beyond the quest, beyond their original commitment.

"I agree with Rion and Lila." Sionna crossed her arms. "Why not us? We're capable. We merely need guidance."

Matt pursed his lips. "Lila, do you still have the journal?"

Lila rummaged in her bag. She found the leather-bound book and tossed it toward us on the table.

Harlow cleared his throat. "May I make a suggestion?"

I startled. I'd forgotten Harlow was there. Oops. I craned my neck and found him closer than he'd been before.

"Sure."

"The first step any good king should take is to appoint a council to act as your inner circle and guide your decision-making. Each council member typically leads a certain aspect of the kingdom. For example, you should have an individual who manages your treaties and relations with other kingdoms."

"Bethany," I said without hesitation.

She perked up from where she had been leaning on the table, her head in her hand. "What?"

"It makes perfect sense," Matt said. He twirled his staff

absently in his hand, the tip of it spinning on the stone floor, making a soft susurration. "You're the most well-spoken, and even without the magic, you're great at persuasion."

"Oh," she said, batting her eyelashes. "Are you coming on to me, Matt?"

"No," I answered for him, trying to tamp down the prickle of jealousy her words elicited. "He's not, but he's not wrong, either. Bethany, you're the head of whatever that department is called." Well, in for a penny, may as well go in for a pound. For now, anyway. "Okay, what's next?"

I could tell that Harlow was refraining from slapping his hand against his face, but just barely. His nose twitched.

We established the council of King Arek within a few minutes. Lila would head the treasury, since she had an uncanny ability to know the value of everything, and her fae heritage would be beneficial when figuring out planting seasons and grain stores and all the technical stuff that would keep the kingdom from starving. Sionna was the head of the military because of course. Rion would lead the knights and castle guards, since he had experience dealing with the sons of lords. And Matt, well, Matt was my court mage.

"And advisor," I said.

"Are you sure?" Matt said nervously. "I'm as clueless as you are about all this."

"Pfft. You're the smartest person I know. And you can read all the books in the library for research," I said with a pointed glance. "There is a library, isn't there?"

Harlow sighed. "Yes."

"See?" I slapped Matt on the shoulder. "No problem."

"Right." He said it like he didn't believe me, but I knew

better. Matt would be the perfect advisor. He's always been much more levelheaded than me. Besides, I wouldn't mind keeping him close for a lot of reasons, but especially his hideous beautiful face.

"Anyway, now that's settled. Harlow? Can you show my council to their quarters and get them started on their duties?"

"Of course." Harlow clapped his hands and several servants slipped through the door. They ushered the group to follow them.

Lila squinted at the girl at her shoulder. "I need quarters with a large window located near a garden."

"Of course, my lady."

Sputtering, Lila shook her head. "I'm not a lady. I'm a rogue."

The girl's gaze flickered from Lila to Harlow. He waved his hand. "Yes, Miss Rogue?"

"Uh . . . sure. We'll go with that."

"Oh, we get to pick our rooms?" Bethany asked, harp in hand. "I'd love one with a big bed. And a fully stocked wardrobe."

"And I would like one with a direct path to the training grounds." Rion pulled back his shoulders. "As I will be training the castle knights."

Sionna rolled her eyes. "How quickly they adapt." She patted my hand. "Don't look concerned," she said, a small smile teasing at her lips. "We'll be fine. You'll be fine."

"I'm not concerned," I said, though my heart thumped at her touch. I couldn't tell if it was from the anxiety that our group was separating again, or because she touched me. Like I said, inappropriate boners. I shifted in my seat. "Have fun."

"Of course."

She left with the others.

Matt poked me in the side. "Now what?"

I looked back to Harlow. "Yeah, now what? Do you want me to meet the castle staff?" I lifted my goblet and took a sip of the strong-smelling wine.

Harlow sniffed. "Now that you've chosen a council, you must choose a spouse."

I spat out my wine. *"What?"*

Chapter 6

I paced the room. I tugged at the collar of my tunic as sweat rolled down my spine. My heart raced. "I'm seventeen years old!" I spun on my heel. "I can't choose a spouse. I can barely choose my clothes in the morning."

"We're aware," Matt said dryly. He hadn't moved from his chair by the table. He wore the same expression as when we'd scared that skunk in the tall wildflowers on the outskirts of the village when we were boys. We'd been sprayed and spent several nights sleeping outside because neither of our parents would allow us back into our respective homes.

"Not helpful," I snapped. "Why do I need a spouse? *Barthly* didn't have a spouse."

"Technically." Harlow raised a finger. "He did."

"Huh?"

"He what?"

Clearing his throat, Harlow picked up the journal and hefted it in his hand. "Before he imprisoned her, he forcibly bonded with her in spite of her protests. Their spirits were tied in the sacred words."

I sent Matt a wide-eyed look, the conversation from the

morning fresh in my mind. That was the piece we were missing. "What kind of backward misogynistic assault-y realm do we live in? I mean, honestly!" I threw up my hands.

Matt took the journal from Harlow. He didn't quite snatch it away, but it wasn't gentle, either. Matt must have trusted him about as much as I did.

"As much as it pains me to say it, Arek is right. He's too young." His lips pressed into a tight line. "And Barthly did it to secure his claim to the throne. There is no one left of that line, and Arek is the rightful ruler. He doesn't need a spouse."

"Exactly!" I dramatically pointed a finger in Harlow's direction.

"It is the law."

"I'm the king. I'll change the law."

"It's a *magic* law."

I stopped short, sliding as the worn soles of my boots failed to find purchase on the stone. Magic. Fucking magic. Always the problem and the solution rolled into one.

Matt scowled.

"Explain."

Harlow eyed me like I imagined he'd eye a fellow servant who spilled a bowl of soup—with a veneer of patience thinly stretched over disdain and exasperation. I'm fairly certain it would be his permanent state for the next several years of my reign. If I got that far.

I nodded toward him, urging him silently to talk before my feet followed my heart and I bolted from the room.

"How is it you know so little of the history of your own land?" He raised an eyebrow.

"We were unwashed peasants up until yesterday late afternoon," Matt said, voice flat.

Sighing, Harlow creaked toward a seat and sank into it. "In the beginning—"

"Nope." I sat down across from him. "We're not starting from the beginning. We're starting in the middle, or wherever we are right this minute. You can lecture us on history later. Now, start talking about why I need to choose a spouse."

Matt opened his mouth to speak but cut his gaze over to me and snapped it shut. He crossed his arms and slouched in his chair. I didn't know why he was being so moody. It wasn't like *he* was the person who had to rule a kingdom and apparently *get bonded*. Unless he was pissed at the reveal of another barrier that would make it difficult for us to leave. I clenched my jaw and bit down on the worries and confessions that dared to spill out just thinking about the future and my foiled plans.

"Fine," Harlow said, voice clipped. "There must be a co-ruler. Someone to offer balance. It's a fail-safe to protect the kingdom and the people."

"From someone who would do unspeakable evil," Matt said slowly. He sighed and rubbed a hand over his face. "Like Barthly."

"Okay, did we miss the fact that Barthly did unspeakable evil? This magic law didn't seem to have worked that well."

Harlow scowled. "Believe what you must, but it did temper him. Without the influence of her soul, he would've been much worse."

"Much worse?" My voice went high. "How could he have been any worse?"

Matt shook his head. "It still doesn't make sense. She died. Presumably, her soul left. You said you only came to the castle twenty years ago and she was already dead. He reigned for forty. Why didn't the magic force him to bond again?"

"That is the part I don't understand." Harlow shrugged. "I only know the law. The magic is beyond me."

But I knew. I knew the second I opened that tower door and stepped over the threshold. I knew when that gust of wind blew past my arm. She hadn't just been physically trapped in that tower.

"She was here," I said. I gulped. "Her soul was here until we opened the tower door."

Matt's eyes widened. "You felt her?"

"Didn't you?"

He blinked. "Yes, I did. I didn't realize it was her soul, but I felt the magic." He cleared his throat. "Lila's lockpicks wouldn't have worked. It's why I blasted the door with my staff. It was warded with strong spells, but I thought it was just to keep her physically trapped. I didn't realize. . . . Well . . . Now I know."

Matt's brow furrowed. "What are the consequences?" he asked. "If Arek doesn't bond with someone."

Good question, Matt. Excellent question. "Yeah. What if I don't? Is the castle going to kick me out? Famine? Plague? A good drought, maybe?"

Harlow's lemon face reappeared. "Possibly. I also assume you'll die."

My stomach dropped. "Well, that's unfortunate, isn't it?" I snapped.

Matt was decidedly paler than he was seconds ago. "Are you sure?"

"It's the law."

"Perfect. Absolutely perfect." I crossed my arms. "Amazing. Wonderful. Being king just gets better and better, if I do say so myself."

None of this was *fair*. The idea of being king was terrifying, but I could accept it. Because honestly, I didn't have much of a life to return to in our little village on the edge of the kingdom. But bonding? That was a whole other matter. That involved another person's *life*. What if magic had a say in that, too? What if I wasn't allowed to choose? I glanced over at Matt. What if the person I chose didn't want to choose me back?

He gave me a suffering look. "You're being difficult."

"I'm being difficult?" I pointed emphatically to my chest. "You're the one throwing my life under the metaphorical cart because of a magical law we know nothing about."

Matt jerked as I threw his words from the morning back at him. Arms crossed, he looked away. "I'm being realistic," he said to the wall.

"I don't—" I started, my voice catching. I took a breath to steady myself. "I don't want to bond with someone just to save my life." I looked back at him, and we locked eyes. I felt exposed in that moment, like every feeling I had was scrawled across my face for Matt to read. He held my gaze, and I swear I saw something like an inkling of understanding flicker across his expression, and for a desperate second, I thought he might reach out toward me, might say that I didn't have to worry, he wanted me as more than a friend, and we didn't need to go looking for my soul mate because he was standing right here. Matt opened his mouth to speak, then hesitated, breaking our gaze and looking down at his lap. My heart pounded heavily in my ears as he looked back up at me. *Say it*, I pleaded silently.

He took a deep breath and said, "We should tell the others."

"No!" I stood, the chair clattering across the stones. I don't know why I'd expected anything different, but his words had hit me like a punch to the gut. I turned on my heel and paced the length of the table, then back again, trying to push down the sudden irrational surge of hurt that rushed through me. I thrust my finger at them. "No fucking way. You are not telling anyone. In fact, this information doesn't leave this room. This is for the three of us to know."

"Arek," Matt said, voice tired. "It's magic."

"It's a mistake."

"It's the *law*."

"It's asinine!"

"Arek." He pulled on his hair, brown locks tangled in his fingers, a lethal amount of irritation packed into the two syllables of my name.

"Matt." My counter didn't quite have the same effect. In fact, it came out more a whine than the clipped word I wanted it to be. He didn't really deserve my anger—it's not like I'd actually confessed my affections to him and he'd shot me down. But somehow, it had felt like that in the moment, and I wasn't above being petty.

Matt stood, fingers spread on the table. He stared at the glossy wood grain, refusing to look at me, his head sagging between his tense shoulders. "I'll—I'll . . . search the library. It'll take time. I'll see what I can find out about magic and the law, but Arek . . ." He trailed off. "I'm worried about taking too long to follow through, especially now that we freed the princess."

I exhaled. "Okay." Shaking my head, I grasped the back of a chair. "Okay." I unclenched my jaw and willed the stress to ease from my body. "But we don't tell the others a word of this until we have more information. Or a plan. That's . . ." I swallowed. "That's a command from your king."

Matt made a face like he'd smelled that skunk from our childhood again.

Harlow bowed. "Of course, sire." He snapped to attention. "And now if you allow me, I'll prepare the servants to meet you in the throne room." He strode to the door. "My lord?" he addressed Matt. "Would you like for me to have someone show you the library?"

"That would be lovely." He licked his lips, gaze never leaving mine. "But first, please give me a moment with the king."

Harlow bowed again and slipped out.

Once the door was closed, Matt stalked forward, all pretense of politeness gone. All that was left was barely controlled anger and a slight, pained limp.

"Matt?"

"Don't." He bit out. "Don't *ever* command me again." His face flushed red. His body shook. His eyes were glassy. "I'm your *friend*, and you may be a king, but I'm not your subject."

I raised my hands. "I'm sorry. Matt, I'm sorry. That was more for Harlow than for you. I swear."

He blew out a breath through his nose like a bull, and he looked away. He knuckled the weariness from his eyes. "You're my best friend," he said, voice low. "Don't forget it. Please."

Friends. Right. "Never."

He nodded, then strode out. He left me standing in the center of the empty council room, wondering how I was suddenly all alone.

CHAPTER 7

"After an afternoon sitting on the throne and meeting with every single one of the castle staff—from cooks to stable boys to tailors to maidservants and manservants and everything in between—I was starting to think that running away from home to follow a vague prophecy hadn't been a good idea. The duties were suffocating. Not to mention the threat of nebulous bad things happening, including but not limited to my own death, if I didn't choose a spouse. If nothing else, it was enough to put some distance between me and the tense moment I'd had with Matt earlier.

At least the servants had been fairly nice, if a bit skittish.

I'd be skittish too, especially if I had to meet the new ruler who had beheaded my previous boss.

I didn't realize how many staff it took to run a castle, or the amount of income the castle needed to generate to be able to pay all their wages. It wasn't something I'd ever thought of before. Liquid money, as in coin, was rare in my village. We had a few pieces, but mainly we bartered or raised what we needed. And it wasn't until I met Lila that I realized there were levels of nuance that came with coin as well. There was so much about the world I didn't know. How was I going to bring peace to our realm for a thousand years if I couldn't calculate the cost of paying three cooks?

Castle income and expenses swam through my head as I legged it out of the throne room and into the grounds under the guise of perusing the vegetable gardens. The head cook, Matilda, was a middle-aged woman who had three daughters all working in the kitchen. She'd given a soliloquy about the gardens that I only half listened to while my thoughts swirled around the words "*soulbond*" and "*partner*" and "*magic*," which then inevitably circled around to Matt. When she asked my preferences, I almost blurted out "brunettes," then realized she meant food. To cover, I rambled about soups and stews because those were Matt's favorites.

I needed time with my thoughts. I needed fresh air and sunshine, and where better than a garden to get those things? Better yet, I had actual working knowledge about gardens, how to plant and water and weed. I was in my depth in a garden, and I wouldn't mind sinking my fingers into tilled earth; inhaling the sharp, fresh scent of growing vegetables; and spying the spring green of new growth.

Following a well-worn path of packed earth, which wound through overgrown bushes teeming with late-blooming flowers, I found the large flourishing garden laid out in neat rows next to the kitchen area. It was beautiful and reminded me of home so fiercely that my stomach ached with a sharp pang of homesickness. Swallowing hard, I walked along the edge, bending to run my fingers over the veiny leaves of a head of cabbage.

"Sire?"

I jerked to standing, startled. "What?"

A girl knelt in the middle of a row, watching me with a raised eyebrow, a pile of carrots in a basket in front of her. She looked vaguely familiar.

I wagged my finger at her. "Have we met?"

"Just now in the throne room. I'm one of Matilda's daughters."

"Melody?"

"Meredith," she corrected with a soft smile. "Melody is my sister."

"Ah, okay. Sorry. I didn't mean to interrupt your work."

"It's fine, sire." She tilted her head, her pretty lips pursed. "Are you all right?"

Now, *that* was a question. The answer was a solid *no*, but I couldn't tell her that. Instead, I shrugged, something flippant on the tip of my tongue that died and turned into a choked shout as an arrow sank into the ground at my feet. The metal head nicked the toe of my boot before forcefully embedding upright in the ground, the shaft quivering from the force. I jumped back. Wow. Okay. Odd and a little alarming.

Craning my neck, I looked to the outer wall to find another lone arrow sailing over in a high arc. It speared through a head of cabbage upon landing.

Meredith gasped.

The telltale twang of bow strings sounded, and within seconds more arrows followed, thunk-ing into the soil all around us—*thunk*—and oh shit, someone was shooting at me! I looked to Meredith, meeting her wide eyes. At *us*! Someone was shooting at *us*!

Heart pounding, I ran and grabbed her arm, hauling her to her feet.

"Come on!"

"But the carrots!"

"Leave the carrots!" I yelled, just as an arrow plunged through the basket. She made a high-pitched noise of panic that I wholeheartedly agreed with as another whizzed through the small space between our faces. An inch to the right and my nose would have acquired a new nostril.

I tugged her behind me as we tripped into a run. She kept a grip on the basket, carrots scattering behind us as we dodged the rain of projectiles, while her other hand clasped mine. What the hell? I couldn't be so unpopular as a king already. Could I? An arrow thudded right in front of us, and I skidded to a halt, yanking Meredith hard to the side to prevent us from stumbling over it. Another sank next to her boot, catching the hem of her skirt. She squeaked, and I echoed the sound.

Luckily, as far as I could tell as I hurriedly glanced over my shoulder, the shots all emanated from the same outer wall, which meant we could scurry out of range. Or if not, at least take shelter.

If I'd had that thought at the first arrow, we'd have made for the kitchen buildings, but as I was fueled by panic, we'd already sprinted past. And I was not going to double back, not when the arrows continued to dot the landscape. Another pierced the air next to my ear, the fletching catching the tip, stinging like an angry wasp.

"Toward the path," I shouted, though it came out more of a wheeze. "I think we'll be okay once we're on the other side of those bushes."

Meredith didn't answer. Our grasp had loosened with sweat, our fingers slipping until just the tips of mine hooked against hers. I risked a look behind me just in time to see a bolt hit its apex and tilt downward, headed right at her cheek. Adrenaline coursing through me, I did the one thing I could think of in the moment. I dropped to the ground and kicked her feet out from under her while she was mid-stride. We fell in a tangle, momentum pushing us into a roll. We toppled over each other, the arrow embedding nearby, the *thunk* of it too close for comfort. As we tumbled, I caught her knee in my stomach and her chin in my throat, hard enough for an oomph of discomfort to escape. I also lost my crown somewhere.

When we finally slid to a stop, I was on my back on top of the remaining carrots and under the bushes with her sprawled half across my heaving chest. Breathing hard, I made sure to grip the leaves and roots beneath me instead of anywhere on Meredith's body.

She peered at me through the mess of her hair. "You saved me."

I held up a finger. "We might not be safe yet. So, hold that thought, yeah?"

She nodded as she leveraged herself into a sitting position, her elbow digging into my ribs. Gracelessly, I followed, scrabbling in the undergrowth to sit hunched over beneath the thick growth of the bushes. Leaning forward, I peered cautiously out of our hiding place. The ground was littered with arrows and . . . scrolls? Pieces of parchment flapped in the soft breeze like little flags.

Squirming, I found the crushed woven basket and the arrow that had pierced it. I yanked it free and removed the small scroll wrapped around the shaft.

"What's that?" Meredith asked.

"I have no idea," I said, unrolling the note. I read it and blinked.

Return our golden peacock, or we will challenge your reign. Signed, the Su Family.

Meredith squeezed closer and looked over my shoulder. "What does that mean?"

Shaking my head, I turned the parchment over and inspected all sides. Finding nothing else, I allowed it to fall into my lap. "I think the Su Family wants their golden peacock back."

She wrinkled her nose. "Is that a euphemism?"

"I don't think so?"

Meredith crawled partway out of the hiding spot and snatched another arrow. She handed it to me. I unrolled the missive.

Two cows, five chickens for our allegiance, or expect retaliation. Signed, the River Hooks Estate.

"Two whole cows," I said, rubbing a hand over my chin. "That . . . uh . . . I don't know what to think of that. Is their allegiance worth two cows?"

"And five chickens," Meredith pointed out helpfully.

I held up the notes between my fingers. "This is weird, right?"

"I don't know. There hasn't been a regime change in—"

"Forty years. Right. Right." I sighed, clenching my eyes shut. A headache bloomed in my right temple. This ruling thing just kept getting better and better.

"Sire?" Meredith said, voice a whisper. "I think someone is—"

"Here," an all-too-familiar voice said.

I opened my eyes to spy a pair of boots and skinny legs. I wiped a hand over my face, smearing dirt, as Lila ducked down and peered under the bush. She had my crown in one hand and an arrow in the other.

"There you are," she said with a smirk. She looked to Meredith, then back at me. "Interesting."

I frowned. "I guess the shooting has stopped."

"Yeah, I think it's safe."

With all the grace of a wounded sheep, I scrambled out of the bushes and bramble to stand on the path with Lila and Meredith, the two notes clutched in my hands. Meredith fished the destroyed basket with the two remaining carrots from beneath and clutched them to her.

"Carrots," Lila said, snickering. "Nice."

"This isn't funny."

"Oh, it's kind of funny."

I huffed in annoyance. "Give me that," I said, reaching for the crown.

She snatched it away, clucking her tongue. "I don't know, Arek. Finders keepers. It might look better on me any—" She suddenly hissed through her teeth and dropped the crown in the dirt. "Ow!"

She clutched her wrist, her palm up, a slash of red across her pale skin.

"What was that?" I asked.

Lila shook out her hand, scowling down at the gold circlet. "Magic theft deterrent, I think." She didn't sound entirely convinced.

I picked the crown up and gave her a dark look. "Well, you

shouldn't be stealing my things anyway. Especially after I had to run for my life." I stepped around her to see the garden and the surrounding field. Hundreds of arrows littered the ground. I was amazed that Meredith and I made it out relatively unscathed.

"Sire," Meredith interrupted softly, "you're bleeding."

Well, mostly unscathed. I touched the sting of my ear. My fingertips came away bloody. "Huh. So I am."

Lila's mouth tipped down. She tilted her head to the side, her eyes narrowed, her lips flattened, and then she moved, quick as a flash of lightning, pushing me to the side and thrusting her hand out. She caught an arrow, snatching it out of the air, like a cat with a bird. Her fingers clutched the shaft near the fletching. Blood welled from between the creases.

The original trajectory of the arrow without Lila's intervention was through my eye and out the back of my head.

I gulped. "Maybe not so safe after all."

"Maybe not," she said, expression pinched. "Let's get inside."

Chapter 8

"You know what these are, right?" Bethany asked as she plucked a strip of parchment from the substantial pile.

I would have shrugged, but the court physician hovered around my ear, and I didn't dare distract him from whatever the hell he was doing to it. I sat still as stone on the stool next to the overstuffed bookshelf, my crown on my lap, with a smear of blood marring the gleaming gold. I picked a leaf from the folds of my shirt and flicked it away. "Petitions?" I guessed.

"Demands." Sionna crossed her arms. "Outright challenges to your reign."

Lila and I had escorted Meredith to the kitchens before finding Bethany, Rion, and Sionna in a room filled with parchments and books. My guess was that it was Barthly's office. It had a desk and an inkwell and blank parchments. Oh, and *a human skull*, which stared judgmentally at me from a shelf with its sightless gaze. This room would need to be redecorated before I would even consider using it myself.

A large window had been flung open to let in light and to air out the musty smell. Four of my five advisors stood around the large, heavy desk—examining the scraps of parchment fluttering in the soft breeze. The mound was . . . not small.

"Awesome. What do we do with them?"

"What do you want to do with them?" Rion asked. "You're the king."

"Yeah, quit reminding me." I flinched as the physician did something to my ear. "I don't know. Burn them? Ow! What the—"

"Here." Meredith had returned with wine, bless her, and she shoved a full goblet into my hand. Before I could thank her, she retreated into a corner, holding the pitcher and trembling like a leaf. Sionna eyed her with a look I couldn't decipher, which more than likely scared Meredith even more.

Bethany huffed, and Sionna's gaze slid away. Tossing a parchment aside, Bethany picked up another one. "Have you read any of these?"

The wine was strong, and after a few sips, heat prickled along my cheeks. "Yes, apparently, the Su family wants their golden peacock returned."

Lila snorted. She had a bandage wrapped around her palm, which she kept tucked in the crook of her elbow. "Like I'm returning the peacock," she said under her breath.

I narrowed my eyes at her. "What?"

"Huh?"

Bethany rubbed her forehead, then blew out a breath. "You realize we're fucked, right?"

From the angle, I couldn't tell if the physician's hand slipped or if he meant to jab a needle into my ear. "Ow! Ow!"

"Apologies, sire," he said, his tone dry. "You required a stitch."

"It's fine. We're fine." I was not fine. Based on everyone's expressions, *we* were not fine. I held my tongue as the physician completed his care, then packed his things and left.

"Okay, now that he's gone—care to explain, Bethany?"

"Oh no." She tossed her auburn hair over her shoulder. "I'm not explaining this twice. We need Matt."

"He's in the library, I think." Trying to solve my other problems and probably still mad. Because Matt could hold a grudge like nobody else. I downed the rest of the goblet.

Meredith shot from her spot in the corner and plunked the pitcher of wine on the edge of the table. "I'll fetch him, sire."

She spun on her heel and opened the door to the hallway just as Matt pushed from the other side. Both caught by surprise, Matt stumbled forward. Meredith fell back. I jumped from my seat to catch her and keep her from braining herself against the desk, but Sionna beat me to it and steadied her before she fell to the stone. Matt on the other hand, with his injured foot, and unwieldy staff, tripped his way into the room, careening around Sionna and Meredith. He crashed into my chest, knocking the wind out of me.

I staggered back, catching him under his arms instinctively. My hip knocked into the edge of the table, hard enough to send a jolt of pain down my leg and causing the wine pitcher on the edge to teeter, then fall. Red wine erupted everywhere.

"Matt!" I said, pulling him up as he winced. Our faces were inches from each other, his forehead level with my chin. I clutched his body against mine, surprised, flushed, and not nearly as steady as I wanted. My heart pounded and fingertips tingled where they pressed into his back.

He pushed me away, righting himself, a deep blush in his cheeks that crept down his neck to disappear beneath his tunic. I hid my wince at Matt's obvious aversion to being physically close to me. Another little stab of rejection right into my heart. It certainly hurt worse than my ear.

"Oh no! The wine!" Meredith wailed, then dropped to her knees, her dress soaking up the red liquid, as she grabbed the overturned pitcher. "I'm so sorry, sire. I'll go right away and retrieve more."

"It's okay," I said, internally lamenting its loss. I waved my hands. "It's fine. It was an accident. There's no reason to be upset."

She stood, clutching the pitcher to her chest, wine wicking through the fabric of her skirt. Her face was sheet white, and tears spilled out of the corners of her eyes. I thought she would pass out, even with Sionna's hand on her arm. "What?"

"We're good." I gestured to the rest of the group, who stared at the scene that had gone from slapstick to serious in an instant. "Right, council?"

They erupted in reassurances. Even Lila, who wasn't one to offer comfort, told the terrified girl that everything was a-okay.

"Hey," I said when Meredith still looked like a rabbit in a snare. "We're really not mad."

She swallowed. "You're not going to put me in the stocks?"

"No! Why would I do that? That sounds awful."

She blinked.

"I literally saved you from arrows this afternoon. Why would I order you to the stocks?"

Matt stiffened and paled. "Arrows?"

I waved my hand. "We were shot at. It's fine now."

"Your ear is bandaged."

"Mostly fine. Anyway, I don't punish people for honest

mistakes. Seriously. Please don't be frightened of me. Of us." I nodded toward my merry band of doofuses.

Rion waved.

She licked her lips. "I'll . . . I will get something to clean this up."

"Wait," Matt said, raising his hand. "It was partly my fault. I'll get it." He tipped the head of his staff toward the mess on the floor and table. The large puddle lifted from the stone, as did the splashes from our clothes, congealing into a large floating sphere of wine that poured itself into the pitcher she clutched to her body. "There," he said once the stream finished. "All cleaned up. I wouldn't drink it, though. I'm uncertain about the cleanliness of the floors."

Her mouth dropped open, then snapped shut, then opened again. Her eyes were saucers. "That was . . . amazing."

I didn't like the way she gazed in open wonder at Matt, like she was half in love with him from his magic trick.

Matt didn't notice. Or if he did, he didn't comment.

"You're dismissed." It came out far harsher than I meant it, and she fled from the room.

Sionna frowned at me in disapproval.

I sat back on my stool and crossed my arms. "Now that Matt is here, we can actually talk."

Matt glanced at me and shook his head. "I was in the library at your command, sire."

Ouch. Yeah, definitely still annoyed.

Bethany snapped her fingers. "Can we focus, please? Because we're in trouble."

I groaned. "Okay. Feel free to explain."

She grabbed a scrap of parchment and waved it in my

general direction. "These are demands. Tests of strength. The shooting today was just to get a point across. They weren't trying to kill you."

"Well, that's a plus." I gave them a weak smile. "People don't want me dead."

"Yet," Sionna said, ever the optimist.

Bethany pinched her nose. "Yeah, no. We have to sort through each of these demands and decide which allegiances we can afford to buy. If we don't, we will lose the support of our own kingdom and you'll probably be usurped."

"Okay. And if that happens?"

"They'll kill us," Sionna said, voice flat.

Damn, Sionna, read a room. I looked to Rion, who reluctantly nodded in agreement.

"Wait," Bethany said, holding up her hand. "It gets worse." Of course it does.

She held up several pieces from a different pile of parchment and fanned them out. I couldn't see the details from across the table, but I could see the wax seals of other kingdoms on the bottom, along with flourished signatures.

"I researched every treaty our realm has had with other kingdoms since the last royal family before Barthly. He broke all of them. Every other kingdom hates us, and now that he's gone, they'll likely try to invade or absorb us."

"Wait," I said, standing and crossing the room. "That doesn't sound so horrible. Another kingdom who has infrastructure and the ability to rule could come in and fix this, and we wouldn't have to." Depending on what Matt had found in the library, that option could get me out of this mess. That could relieve me of the absurd magic-bonding law.

"They'd kill us and all of our people," Bethany said.

I deflated again. "Well, then never mind that idea."

"Yeah. We need to fix things fast, or there is going to be definite bloodshed. Probably ours."

"Great," I sighed. "Okay. To recap, we are being tested by our supposed allies. And other kingdoms hate us. Do we have any defenses?"

Sionna leaned against the wall and crossed her arms. "We don't have a military. The members of his followers we didn't kill have fled. And since Barthly used fear to keep his soldiers in line, there was no loyalty, save the loyalty their heads had to their bodies, so those who didn't exactly agree with him ran off as well."

"This is helpful. So helpful. And as awesome as we are, I doubt we'd be able to hold off an entire kingdom's army on our own." I rubbed my temple, careful of my damaged ear. Death began to appear more like a viable option. "Dare I ask for your update, Rion?"

He fidgeted. Rion never fidgeted. "There are no knights. The vassals refused to send their sons to . . . Barthly, but he didn't quite need them anyway, did he? Not when he had his followers. And all the dark magic."

"Ugh. So we have no allies, no military, no knights, and no clue. Great. Just great."

"Good thing we're loaded." Lila perched on the windowsill; a cheeky grin spread across her features.

I raised my head from where I studied the rug, which depicted flames and a mound of skeletons. Yeah, redecorating jumped several slots up on my to-do list, right under surviving and figuring out how to rule a kingdom. "What?"

"We're literally the richest kingdom, basically ever." She shrugged. "The amount of gold I found made me bug-eyed, and I don't say that lightly."

I perked up. Enough gold to impress Lila was a lot of gold.

She continued, "Not to mention the grain stores. The staggering amounts of jewels and finery. The full stable. And the livestock."

"We're rich?"

She twirled a piece of her pale blond hair around her finger. "We're not rich. We're swimming in it. I could do laps in the mountains of coin that's stowed in the dungeon alone."

"The dungeon? He kept his gold in the dungeon?"

Lila shrugged again. "It's not like he kept prisoners there."

True. He seemed to just kill anyone he didn't like. And the one prisoner we know he kept was locked in a tower, not a dungeon.

"Wealth doesn't solve everything." Matt leaned over the parchments and ran his fingers over several of them. He hunched as he scanned the missives, the weight of our predicament seeming to bear down on his shoulders.

"No, it doesn't," I agreed. "But it helps a lot. First thing, we give all the servants in this castle a raise."

Lila raised an eyebrow.

Sionna furrowed her brow. "Money won't buy their loyalty."

"No, but if we have happy staff, then our lives are going to be much easier. I don't know about you, but if we don't have to focus on our next meal or who is going to clean our linens, then we can focus on the broader problems."

"Makes sense," Sionna said.

"Now, we're going to organize these, and start working on the reasonable ones. Cows and peacocks and gold are doable. Anything weird, place in a separate stack."

"This person wants their daughter to marry you, Arek," Lila said with a smirk, flapping the parchment in my face.

I absolutely did not glance at Matt. "That one obviously goes into the weird stack. Thanks. Lila, we need an inventory of everything. Have Harlow assist."

She straightened from her sprawl. "Okay. I can do that. Sure."

"Great. Bethany, find out which of the kingdoms are struggling and what they need. If it's grain, we can spare it. If it's debt relief, we can help with that, too. Let's start there, and extend a hand of friendship and assistance where we can. That may ease tension and buy us allies. But most importantly, it will give us time."

"That's not a bad idea." She smirked. "I'll throw in a little charm, too, and see where that gets us."

"Good idea." I drummed my fingers on the table. "What should we do about the knights, Rion?"

Rion perked up. "We should . . ." He sucked his teeth. "We should invite the sons of kingdoms' lords to squire here."

"Uh . . . just ask? Politely, I assume?"

"Before B-Barthly," he said, stumbling over the name, "it was a great honor to be invited to the castle to become a knight. It's a good option for second sons, who don't stand to inherit any land from their fathers."

"Well, that sounds unfair."

Rion made as close to a "those are the rules" gesture as I'd ever seen him make. It was a slight raise of the shoulders and a tilt of his mouth. Huh. Rules of nobility were so weird.

"Then send messages, but invite all their children that are of age. We have plenty of evidence sitting around this table that other genders can fight just as well as men."

"Who will train them? We have no senior knights."

I blinked. "You will, Rion."

"I was only a squire when—"

"When we met you. That was ages ago." I shrugged, dismissing his concern.

"Seven months."

"You've more than proved that you're a knight. At least to me." I looked to the others for confirmation, afraid I'd missed something about knightly duties other than fighting, keeping people alive, and being loyal to a fault. "Right?"

"None of us would be alive without Rion," Lila said, the faintest blush pooling in her cheeks. "Including me."

"Arek," Matt said softly, "you have the power to knight him."

"I do, don't I?" I smiled for the first time since we'd gathered. I could do this for Rion. I could give him something he'd always wanted, something he was denied because of Barthly. It thrilled me to the core, my first act as king that I could be proud of. "Okay, from this point forward, you are Sir Rion. Done." Matt kicked my shin. I jerked my knee and slammed it into the lip of the desk. "What the hells, Matt?"

"There's a whole ceremony—"

"No," Rion said. His eyes were wide and wet. His hands clutched the edge of the table. It looked like he was about to cry and was restraining himself from running around the table and giving me a hug. "I don't need a ceremony. This is fine. This is perfect."

"Great. Bethany, you have a pile of parchments there; please document that Sir Rion will train the knights."

Bethany grabbed one of the blank squares, dipped her quill in the inkwell, and scribbled.

Rion beamed. "Thank you, sire."

"Oh no, don't do that. I'm Arek. Just Arek."

Rion nodded. He ran a hand over his face, then grabbed his goblet.

Sionna cleared her throat. "We should do the same for our military. Offer the common people of the kingdom a wage to be a soldier. They can be a part of the forces for a few years, and then return home if they choose."

"Lila?" I asked. "Do we have enough for that?"

She snorted. "We have enough for anything. And if we run out of coin, which we won't, we can liquidate our other assets."

"Bethany, please add that General Sionna will develop the procedures to fatten our military. No, wait, don't use 'fatten.' That's not a good word. How would a king say that?"

"'Strengthen,'" Sionna said. "Strengthen the military."

"Yes. Is 'General' okay? Or would you rather be—"

"'General.' I like it."

"Perfect. Record that please, Bethany."

"What about *his* followers?" Sionna asked, tenting her fingers. "They're still out there. They may try to attack us. Especially as our defenses right now are limited to the individuals at this table."

"Arek cut off Barthly's head," Matt said, blunt to a fault. "Do you think they'd risk it? He was the most fearsome ruler in centuries, and this"—he jerked his thumb in my direction—"is the person who defeated him."

I didn't know how to take that. But it did give me an idea.

"We should offer them a pardon." I expected the chorus of grumbling from around the table. After all, his followers had pursued us day and night for months, but I spoke over the objections. "We offer them a pardon in exchange for pledging loyalty to their new king, joining our military, and accepting a reduced wage. It beats tracking them down and executing them."

"That's . . . not a horrible idea." Sionna said it slowly, as if she spoke while still processing and only accepted the idea after she'd voiced her approval.

"I do have good ideas sometimes."

"We could debate that." Lila stretched her long arms over her head. "But this one isn't the worst. And we have the money."

"Rion?"

"The proposal is sound. I agree."

"Matt?"

Matt sighed. "I have no objection as long as we have someone keeping an eye on them."

"Great. Lady Bethany, did you get all that?"

"I did." She paused. "Are you giving everyone titles now? Not that I'm complaining." She batted her eyelashes. "I always did consider myself a lady."

"Sure. How about you, Lila? Fancy a title?"

Lila made a face, then waved my question away. "I'm fine, thanks."

I nodded. I took a moment to mull over all the information from our conversation, then exhaled. "Okay," I said. "Okay. We have a plan." I scanned the table around me, taking in everyone's energy. Lila looked inordinately pleased with herself, her lips tipped up into a smile as she balanced on the window-sill as only a fae could manage. Bethany's energetic scratching on the parchment filled the room. Rion looked over Bethany's shoulder, nodding along as she wrote. Sionna picked through the pile of parchment scraps, reading and sorting. And finally, finally, I felt a bit better about this mess.

"What about you, Matt?" Sionna asked as she leaned back and dabbed her cheek with a napkin. "How was your day?"

"Oh yeah." Lila tipped forward, propping her elbow on her knees, with her chin in her hand. "What did you find out, Matt?"

Matt ignored my intense glare of *Don't even* and idly spun his staff. "I researched in the library." He glanced at me. I resisted the urge to kick him. He made a face that conveyed he thought I should just tell them about the soul mate law. I narrowed my eyes.

"And?" Bethany asked, interrupting our silent conversation.

"I found a book of spells and a book of laws."

"Anything relevant?"

"I'll have to study further."

Which meant he had found something. Matt didn't outwardly lie. For one, he was horrible at it, and his mother saw right through him whenever he tried—spirits guide her soul. For two, Matt had always said he didn't like having to keep up with different stories and found telling the truth was easier. But Matt could evade and skirt like a fish swimming upstream dodging rocks and bears.

Bethany held up her quill. "Are you Lord Matt now?"

"Yes. Of course he is."

"I'm not a noble."

"Like I am?" I asked, tone still slightly annoyed. But I couldn't stay mad at Matt for long. I never could, and already I could feel my irritation melting away. I held up my blemished crown. "I'm the son of farmers, but I'm now King Arek. You can be Lord Matt."

He sighed. "Fine."

"Good." I stood. "I'm happy with our plans. I'm happy that we're all here. I'm happy that we have food and beds and a roof over our heads." I raised my goblet. "Cheers!"

The others didn't have glasses but cheered nonetheless. "Hear, hear!"

I took a gulp and slammed the goblet on the table. "Okay, I have a headache. And I'm exhausted. I'm going to rest."

"Feel better, Arek," Sionna said, touching my hand. "Rest well."

A flush worked its way into my cheeks. "Thanks, General Sionna."

I left the room and walked the quiet hallway to my quarters, only getting lost once in the process. I went in, closed the door behind me, and leaned on the wood, the back of my head thudding. I took a breath. My room had been cleaned. My sheets had been changed, and my wardrobe filled with clothes far finer than anything I'd ever worn in my life. There was firewood stacked by the hearth. A bowl of fruit sat on the table. A pair of slippers peeked out from beneath the large bed, and a basin of water steamed on the night table.

I tossed my crown on the table, washed, changed, and slid into the bed. It was late afternoon, but I felt like I could sleep the night through. Instead, I stared at the ceiling. Over the last nine months I had grown accustomed to not being alone at bedtime, so now it was strange not to have another warm body next to me.

I wished for Matt to come slide in next to me, like he did often when we were on the road, following a vague prophecy toward our waiting destiny. I waited for him for a long time, counting sheep, thinking about the problems that lay in wait for us, remembering how Barthly's head had splattered on the stone floor, and how the princess's spirit escaped the tower, caressing my arm as she left. I waited until my eyes were too heavy and my mind finally slowed.

He didn't come.

Chapter 9

"You were always a heavy sleeper. At least, before all of this happened."

I opened my eyes to slits. The sun streamed through the cracks in the shutters.

"What?"

"You missed dinner last night. Harlow just brought your breakfast."

I blinked. I was warm and my pillow was soft, and Matt sat stretched out on the bed next to me. He leaned against the headboard, fully dressed, his new, shiny boots crossed at the ankles. He wore a blue tunic, and a pair of brown trousers, and his hair was as long and as messy as it had ever been. It curled around his ears in brown tendrils and fell across his forehead in an adorable sweep that made me forget I was upset with him for a whole moment as my brain moved from sleeping to waking. But then I remembered how lonely I had felt the night before. My gut churned in equal parts embarrassment and anger, and I rolled away from him and curled on my side.

"I waited for you last night." My voice was tight, but hopefully muffled enough by the pillow that Matt wouldn't hear it.

He huffed. "I knew you probably would."

"You didn't come."

"No. I was mad."

"Well, now I'm mad."

Matt poked me in the side. I squirmed away from him. "You can be mad at me all you want, but we do need to talk."

Snuggling down in the blankets, I ignored him. "No."

"You're the worst."

"I'm the king."

He prodded me again, a little harder that time. "Then act like it. I'm here as your advisor."

"Not as my friend?"

Matt paused. The moment turned tense. Then he let out a breathy chuckle. "Of course as your friend, doofus. I'll always be your friend."

I cringed internally.

He grabbed my feather pillow and wrenched it from under my head. Then he smacked me with it.

"Ugh." Snatching it away, I tucked it under my body and rolled to face him. I propped my head on my elbow and half-heartedly glared. He smirked at me with his annoyingly perfect face. "Do I need to remind you that I was shot yesterday with an arrow? In my ear?" I waved my hand at the bandage where the wound throbbed beneath.

"You're fine."

"I needed stitches!"

"One. A single stitch, Arek. You've had worse."

I frowned. "Hey, you try running away from a barrage of arrows! It was terrifying! Probably took years off my life!"

Matt's expression softened. "Are you okay? Really?"

"Yeah," I grumbled. "I'm fine."

"Good, because I found something."

"Other than new clothes?"

He picked at the fabric of his shirt. "They were the only thing in my wardrobe besides robes." He pursed his lips. "I'm not wearing robes. I know both the wizard and Barthly did, but I refuse."

"Noted." I said it in my flattest, driest tone.

"Wow, you're tetchy."

"You did wake me up."

"You should be awake. It's almost midmorning."

"If you're a chicken."

That earned a chuckle. His smirk tipped into a full smile—not the forced one either—the one that came so easy when we were home but had become rare in the months since. A bloom of happy warmth spread from my middle at having made Matt laugh.

"Look, your lordship, do you want to know what I found now, or should I wait until we're all seated in the council chamber later today?" Matt rubbed his knuckles on his new shirt, trying to act nonchalant but failing miserably. "I'm sure they'd want to know all about your impending nuptials."

I flopped back on the mattress. Acid climbed my gullet. "Fuck you, but fine. Tell me."

"I have good news and bad news."

"The bad news," I said before he could ask which I wanted first. Better to face the problem head-on, my father would say, spirits guide his soul, instead of running away. A hilarious sentiment, if I thought about it too long, since I had done just that—run away. But I had been running toward my destiny, not from it, barreling like a hothead toward adulthood. Now that I'd made it, I just wanted to go back to how everything was before.

"Fine. The bad news is that, yes, there is a magic law that says you must be bonded to be king of this realm. Your soul must be tied to someone, and as long as that other person's soul is with yours, you'll be king."

"Wait." I shot upright and crossed my legs, facing him. "What does that mean?"

"I'm not sure. The spell itself is quite vague. I don't know if that means if your spouse dies, you're no longer king, or that you die with them, or if you can just remarry. Barthly obviously trapped the princess's soul in the tower to reign even after she died, so there must be some element about the soul staying in this realm for Barthly to have remained king."

"But why?"

"It's a fail-safe. Just as Harlow said. Your entwined souls are meant to complement each other, bring out the best and temper the worst."

I snorted. "Yeah, like that worked."

"Right? Can you imagine? If he had been on his own, how horrible it would've been? I kind of wonder if her soul was the reason the prophecy was able to be written and come true."

That was a lot to process. A lot. The implications were massive. Did that mean if I died, my poor soulbonded person would die as well? If someone wanted to assassinate me, could they just target my soulbonded spouse? If I hated my soulbonded person, would I be stuck with them not only in this life but the next? I shook my head. "Okay. This is the bad news, right? That I am stuck with a magic law and will have to bind my soul with someone."

He worried his bottom lip between his teeth. "The spell is clear that if you don't, you're in trouble."

"What kind of trouble?"

Matt wrinkled his nose. "You'll wither, if I translated it right."

"Wither?" I patted my chest. "Like fade away?"

Matt bit his lip. "Like die, I think."

Rubbing my hands over my face, I slumped, with my elbows on my knees. "Please tell me the good news. I need the good news."

"The good news is that you have until you turn eighteen to find your spouse."

"That's not good news! I turn eighteen in three months. Three months!"

"Better than three days!"

"So if I don't find a soul mate in three months, then I'm going to . . . die?"

Matt raised his hands. "All signs point to yes. But I don't know for certain. I'll see what else I can find."

Any appetite I'd gained over the night disappeared. I slid from the bed to the floor in a perfect imitation of slime.

Matt leaned over the edge of the bed. His face contorted into concern, his lips pressed together, his forehead drawn. "Are you okay?"

"No." I sighed. The stone was cold against my skin, even with my trousers as a barrier. A carpet would not go amiss on the floor of my room. "Did you happen to find anything about the magic succession laws when you flipped through those books?"

"Not really. According to a servant, Barthly destroyed most

of the history scrolls, so I couldn't find anything about the previous king other than his name. Nothing about how he inherited the throne."

I pinched the bridge of my nose, face scrunched. "Based on what we know, the princess was bonded to Barthly and trapped in a tower that locked her soul inside when she died. So Barthly was king both by bloody usurpation and by being tied to the last remaining heir."

"Yeah, he didn't leave anything to chance."

"If I'm king, then I have to tie myself to someone or I'm going to wither."

"Correct."

Well, this was the exact opposite of what I had hoped. My plans for what would happen after the prophecy was fulfilled were all but unraveled now, the threads of them cut and falling limply to the stone. A lump sat in my throat as I tipped my head back and glanced at Matt. He stared off at the wall, brow furrowed in contemplation. I couldn't decide which would be worse—confessing to Matt and him bonding with me out of some sense of obligation to keep me from withering, or living a life bonded to someone else and with Matt so near but beyond reach. I don't think I would survive either, not to mention how unfair it would be to everyone involved. No. I couldn't. I wouldn't.

"Okay, that settles that. I'm going to test the magic."

Matt's eyebrows disappeared into his hair. "What?"

Using the bed for leverage, I stood. "I'll take off the crown and declare my abdication and see what happens." At Matt's horrified expression, I plowed forward before he could object. "Look, destiny and prophecy and magic have pulled me around by the nose for the last year. I'm kind of done with it. Being king, okay, sure, fine, at least there are meals and shelter here, and there is no way I can be worse than the last guy. Even if I'm terrified of sucking at ruling. But bonding with someone? That's a step too far." I wanted a choice. I wanted Matt, but that was a conversation for another time, not when I was under duress and not when he could interpret it any other way than genuine feelings.

Matt frowned; his eyebrows pinched in concern. "You'd rather risk the consequences of taking off the crown than soulbond with someone?"

I threw up my hands. "We don't know the consequences! I'm just saying I'd like to know if there's a chance that my future could hold something beyond finding someone to bond with me to save my life. If I can abdicate, we could leave here. We could have *options*."

Matt didn't respond. He chewed the inside of his cheek, his ridiculous beautiful face scrunched in thought, probably thinking of ways to talk me out of this course of action.

I didn't give him the chance. I crossed the room to where the crown sat on the table. I grabbed it and shoved it on.

"Come on," I said, tugging Matt's sleeve as I headed for the door. "We're going to the throne room."

"Are you sure you want to do this?" Matt asked as he stepped down from the dais, then turned and faced me.

"No." I sat on the throne, crown on my head, Matt and Harlow looking up at me. Harlow happened to be in the throne room when Matt and I burst in on our mission, and well, it might be good to have another witness. "But I should at least try. Right?"

The uncertainty on Matt's face was a sight to behold. He scratched the back of his head, his cowlick standing on end, and didn't dare to meet my gaze.

"Well, don't both of you agree at once."

"It's just seems . . . drastic."

"This isn't drastic."

"Testing magical laws is drastic, Arek."

I made a rude noise with my lips. "It's not."

"I think we may have lost perspective on what's considered drastic over the last year of our lives. But trying to abdicate a throne with potentially deadly consequences to keep from bonding with someone meets the criteria." Matt stated in a way only Matt could, completely deadpan yet with a hint of long suffering.

"It's not just marrying. It's a soulbond. We're stuck. Together. *Forever.*"

Matt ducked his head. "Would that be so bad?" For a second, I thought about telling him how I felt right then and there, that it wouldn't be so bad to be stuck forever with someone, not if that someone was Matt. But then I realized there probably had never been a less romantic time in the history of the world to profess your love to someone.

So instead, I said, "I'd just like the chance to have more than three months to figure that out. And to not die if I don't."

Matt winced. "I don't want to see you hurt."

"I appreciate the concern. But I'd rather know I'm no-kidding really awfully stuck with this situation before I conscript someone into spending the rest of their existence with me."

"Sire." Harlow spoke for the first time. "It was an honor serving you for the past days."

"Thanks, Harlow. That wasn't ominous at all."

"Being prepared, sire, for any result."

Oh my spirits. Harlow for real was betting on my death. Great. Wonderful. Awesome. I clenched the arms of my throne and steadied myself. My heart beat so hard, I thought it would break my ribs. I broke out in a sweat.

"Here goes nothing," I muttered. I stood and took off the crown, placing it on the seat of the throne, then stepped to the side. "I, King Arek, sovereign ruler of Ere in the realm of Chickpea, hereby do abdicate—" That's as far as I made it before overwhelming pain punched through me. It felt like I was being crushed from the inside out. My whole body spasmed. I gritted my teeth against the sudden and tremendous torment, but it did little to stop the waves of agony.

I fell to my knees, then pitched forward onto my elbows. The taste of copper filled my mouth, and with a shaking hand, I touched my face to find my fingers covered in thick, red blood.

Shouting filled the room, but I was too far gone to recognize one word from another. My hearing fizzed out, and the room darkened on all sides until all I saw was the pattern of the carpet.

Hands pulled at my body, and someone jerked me upward, clasped their arm over my chest. I swayed on my knees. My head flopped forward, blood dripping in a stream from my nose. An image of Matt wavered in front of me. He jammed the crown onto my head, then gripped my shoulders.

"Arek! Take it back! Do something! *Say* something!"

He grabbed my chin and tilted my head up. My tongue was thick in my mouth. I gagged on blood.

"Arek!" Matt yelled again. He shook me. "Take it back. Come on. You have to do something. I can't combat this magic."

"I'm," I tried. "I'm—I'm . . ." Everything *hurt*. Oh spirits, this was a bad idea. At least I would see my parents again. And Matt's mother. Maybe. What if I became a ghost and haunted the castle? What if I was truly stuck here like the princess? Bound even when trying to leave? I couldn't do that. I couldn't do that to Matt.

"Arek!" Matt cupped my cheek. "Take it back. Say you're the king. You can do it. Say you're the king."

Frantic Matt was terrifying. Tears ran down his pale face. His body glowed with impotent power. I'd never seen him so afraid. I didn't want to be the cause of it.

I took a wet, shuddering breath and gathered every bit of my ebbing strength. "I'm . . . the king of Ere."

The relief was instantaneous. I sucked in a ragged breath. Tears streamed from the corners of my eyes. As I sagged backward, the arms around my body lowered me to the floor.

"Fuck," Matt said. He bent down low and met my gaze as he pushed my hair out of my eyes. "That was a bad idea. A horrible idea."

"No shit."

Matt laughed and it was deranged and hysterical, and he carded his hand through my hair while he cried and smiled. He was the most beautiful person I'd ever seen.

I tried to match his smile, but I couldn't. My lips wouldn't twitch. But my heart still pumped. And I was alive.

Matt's relieved chuckles and calming touch were a bonus.

My eyes fluttered shut, and I didn't try to stop them.

To say our experiment was an epic fail was an understatement.

I was well and truly stuck as the king of Ere in the realm of Chickpea.

"Hey," I croaked when I woke up. Matt sat next to me on the bed, his fingers twisted into knots, his face pale and drawn.

He startled. "Oh, thank fuck. You're awake."

My sentiments exactly. "How long have I been out?"

"A while." He poured a vial into a goblet of water and held it to my lips. "Here, drink this."

"What is it?"

"A fortifying potion the physician left for you. He said you're lucky that your organs are still intact."

"Lucky," I agreed derisively. I sipped it carefully, unsure if I had the strength to hold it myself. It tasted terrible, but I drank it down anyway, because Matt looked as awful as I felt, and I had an inkling that it was my fault. "Ugh. That was foul," I said, when he pulled the cup away. I could already feel the potion working, warming me from the inside as the liquid worked its way down my gullet.

"Serves you right," Matt said primly. "I've had to cover for you all day, and you know how I feel about lying."

"You're horrible at it." I stretched my legs and grimaced. Oh no, that was a bad idea. Moving in general was unpleasant. Pain lanced through me, traveling from my head to my toes like a lightning strike.

"How do you feel?"

"Like I almost died."

Matt's bloodless lips pinched together. "Don't ever do that again. Understand? That was terrifying, and I thought . . . I thought . . ." He took a deep breath. In an attempt to reassure him, I reached over and patted his hand where it lay next to me on the bed. Damn. Even that hurt. But even with as much pain as I was in, I couldn't help but feel happy to have Matt next to me in bed, just like old times.

"Anyway," he said, composing himself, body shuddering as if shaking off his fear. "Abdication is out."

"Right out," I agreed. Which was less than ideal. My stunt confirmed I was king until death, which apparently could be in three short months if I didn't find a soul mate.

Matt clapped his hands and startled me out of my own thoughts. "New plan." He stood and gingerly crossed the room to his satchel. He rummaged through the bag and tossed a book onto the mattress, next to my shoulder. I craned my neck and raised my eyebrow when I recognized the cover.

"The princess's diary?"

"Start there."

"Huh?"

"Think about it. You've been locked in a tower. You don't know when you're getting out, if ever. You'd write the important stuff down, wouldn't you?"

I struggled to sitting, my muscles the consistency of noodles. Leaning heavily on the headboard, I picked up the journal and ran my fingertip along the cracked leather spine. This journal held the last thoughts of the last royal of the last dynasty. It was an heirloom, an important piece of history that probably belonged in the library under glass. I bounced it in my hands. It had heft, and I didn't just mean in the physical sense. "I guess."

"You study that and recover, and I'll head to the library."

"Matt."

He held up a finger. "Don't 'Matt' me. I'm in it now. I'm going to research magic laws and counter spells and maybe find a way to undo all this. Or at the very least, a way to mitigate the damage."

I flipped through the pages with my thumb. "Thank you."

"You should thank me, especially after what you pulled today. Harlow and I had to lug your dead weight around. Luckily, we didn't run into any of the others. I wouldn't have been able to keep your ridiculous secret then."

The corner of my mouth ticked up. It seemed that my brush with death had more or less wiped out the awkwardness between us from the other day. "You're such a jerk."

"You won't be calling me that when you're out of this mess." He yanked open the door. "You better throw a feast in my honor."

"You better go see the court physician before your foot falls off."

Matt made a rude gesture with his hand.

"Hey! At least send for him while you're in the library. That's a—"

Matt whipped his head around, eyes narrowed.

Smiling cheekily, I winked. "A strong suggestion from your friend."

Shaking his head, he left the room, satchel over his shoulder, staff in his hand. "I'll tell the others you're taking dinner in your room," he said, glancing over his shoulder. "I'll come back later." Concern softened his tone. "If you're up for it."

My body ached. I felt like death. I probably looked like it too, but I forced a grin. I waved away his concern and stifled a groan behind my clenched teeth. "I'm fine. I'll see you in a bit."

He nodded, lower lip bitten red, and closed the door behind him.

I sighed and looked down at the book. "All right, princess," I said, smoothing my palms over the cover, "let's get to know each other."

Chapter 10

In the days since my attempt to abdicate, I'd thought a lot about my options. If I was considering only my own feelings, there was an obvious solution to my current predicament: bonding with Matt. Unfortunately, I cared enough about Matt's happiness not to force him into lifelong bondage if he didn't feel the same way. The issue was gauging his interest without putting him in a position where he felt like he had to bond with me to save my life. Because Matt was nothing if not loyal and willing to do anything for his friends. Spirits, he'd followed me on my quest to kill the Vile One without hesitation. I couldn't ask him to put his life on the line like that for me again. Besides, the only thing worse than having to find someone willing to bond with me was the idea of bonding with someone who wasn't. I didn't want my reign, as inauspicious as it had started, to echo anything of Barthly, and forcing someone was definitely a Vile One move. So despite my contemplation thus far, I'd come up with zero solutions to this predicament. Nothing. Zip. Zilch. Luckily, the princess's diary was a compelling distraction. I reclined against a plush pillow, stretching comfortably in a beam of sunlight and picking up reading where I'd left off the night before.

She had the audacity to call me arrogant. But she was the one who forgot to prop the door to the tack room next to the stable. After our ride, in which she refused to speak to me and only talked with the maids who accompanied us, she followed me into the room and the door swung shut behind her, locking us both inside. I was so mad at her. We were stuck for hours, waiting until our families realized we weren't at dinner. But in those hours, she deigned to talk to me. And I learned more about her than I ever thought I would know, and that was the first time my heart softened toward her.

"There you are!"

I slapped the book closed and straightened. Bethany flounced through the open door of the sunroom, all rich fabric and curled hair. Sionna followed at an even pace, her hair in loose waves down her back and her sword attached to her hip. Lila was the last of the trio, her long pale blond hair pulled away from her face in intricate braids that accentuated her high cheekbones and pointed ears.

"To what do I owe the visit of my top three councilors?"

Bethany rolled her eyes. "We all know Matt is the top, so don't try to ply us with compliments."

I rested my forearms on my bent knees and acted as if the three of them standing around me wasn't intimidating at all. "Fine. What do you want?"

Bethany smirked. "That's better." She folded her hands. "We wanted to inform his majesty that all of the missives to the realm's vassals and neighboring kingdoms have been sent."

I perked up. "That's great. Any responses?"

"Not yet. We literally just sent them. It took us a while to figure out how to word everything ... diplomatically."

"Especially the 'noes,'" Sionna said, her right hand tight

around the hilt of her sword. "But we did our best to ease the sting when we couldn't grant their demands."

"We also didn't want to rub it in that we had a lot of stolen riches," Lila added.

"Did you give back the peacock?" I asked, giving her a knowing look.

She sighed and crossed her arms. "Yes," she grumbled. "I sent back the peacock."

"Good to know you're capable of growth, Lila."

Bethany cleared her throat. "Anyway, we used a combination of messenger birds and paid envoys on horseback. It will take at least a few days for all of them to reach their destinations, some as long as a week. You may want to stick to staying inside until we get a sense for whether our efforts are received well."

"Noted." I scrambled to my feet, the book dangling from my fingers. "Sionna, any word about the military?"

She stood with her feet shoulder-width apart. "Per your request, we have sent heralds to all the towns and villages with the invitation."

"Wonderful. Hopefully, with the promise of wages, we'll get a few farm kids and apprentices for you to train."

"I've increased the wages to all the castle staff." Lila pursed her lips. "They're calling you 'King Arek the Kind.'"

"What?"

"And I found a few more caches of riches stashed throughout the castle. I've moved a few and consolidated others but have decided to leave deposits in a few different places. Just in case we have to leave in a hurry and can't empty the vault."

"I'm sorry, I'm still stuck on 'King Arek the Kind.' What is that about?"

"You literally saved Meredith." Sionna tilted her head to the side. "And you've given the staff a raise and pardoned the followers of Barthly if they abide by the laws you've set."

"And you've offered aid to kingdoms who've suffered because of our previous ruler," Bethany added. She cocked her hip. "I may have used harp magic to spread the rumor faster than it would have otherwise, but the staff and the townspeople know about your plans and have been talking."

I was at a loss for words, which was rare for me. I made a noise through my nose, which sounded like a cross between a dying songbird and a chittering squirrel.

"Are you okay?" Sionna nudged me with her elbow.

"Arek the Kind?" I asked, incredulous. "Not the Fearsome? The Chosen One? The Killer of Evil? The Hacker of Heads?"

Lila laughed so hard she snorted. It was a little mean.

Bethany pinched my cheek. "Oh, how cute."

I squirmed away. "I hate you," I said, but it had no heat, and she wasn't offended if the pat to my head was any indication. I shouldn't be upset, really. There were worse things to be than kind, but it felt like weakness. Is that how the populace would perceive me? Kind? Naive? Gullible? Soft?

Distracted by Bethany and her pinching fingers, I loosened my grip on the diary enough for Lila to nab it from my hand. She flipped through. "You're reading the diary?"

"Yeah, it's full of information, and it's interesting."

She nodded, then gave me a knowing glance. "Have you gotten to the part where they kiss yet?"

I snatched it back. "Don't spoil it for me! And no, they were just locked in the tack room together."

"You're just at the start!"

Bethany squinted. "What are you two talking about?"

"The love story between the princess and the lady."

Bethany and Sionna both made a motion for the book, but I danced away. "Nope, it's mine right now. I get to read it first; then you two can squabble for who gets it next."

Sionna raised an eyebrow. "Being locked in a room together doesn't sound like a particularly promising start to a love story."

"No," I agreed. "But the encounter turns out sweet, according to the princess. They learn about each other."

"I never took you for a sap." Lila punched me in the arm.

"Oh, Arek, are you a secret romantic?" Bethany clasped her hands together and held them next to her cheek. "Do you want to swoon into someone's arms? Or have someone swoon into yours?"

Lila snickered.

"Huh?" I asked, decidedly not thinking about Matt or the fact that romance of some sort would have to happen within the next three months if I wanted to remain whole, solid, and of this world. "What? No."

"If I were to fall in love," Sionna said thoughtfully, "it would be with someone I know well. Someone who understands me."

"I get that," Bethany said. "But for me, I'd like the excitement of a dashing hero, a person who would swoop in and rescue me, and then my bosom would heave, and I'd swoon into their strong arms." She fanned herself. "Someone hot and daring and strong and beautiful."

I rolled my eyes. "Not a tall order at all."

She stuck out her tongue at me, her cheeks pinked.

"What about you, Lila?" Sionna asked.

Lila snorted. "No thank you. None of the above. I don't need to be rescued, and I don't need anyone to know me. Everyone knows love is pheromones and proximity. For it to be real for me, I'd have to be struck by lightning." She snapped her fingers. "Instant attraction."

"Immediate lust, then?" Bethany tapped her fingers along her mouth. "I could see that for you."

"Okay, okay." I dusted my trousers in an attempt to hide my discomfort. "This is all getting a bit too personal."

Bethany huffed. I could see that she was about to bring up the fact that we had lived in each other's pockets for several months and that we'd all pretty much seen each other naked enough times to get a little personal.

"What I mean is don't you all have things to do? A kingdom to run, perhaps?" My attempt to change the subject didn't work.

"It's not like there is anyone here to woo us anyway." Bethany pouted. She flipped a lock of her long auburn hair. "Not unless anyone takes us up on our messages."

Hold up. I hadn't thought of that. There *wasn't* anyone here to woo, really. The castle was fairly vacant for it being a castle. Other than the staff and our quest party, there wasn't anyone. No lords or courtiers or squires or knights. There wouldn't be many options for me to find a spouse until the messengers returned. But that didn't mean I couldn't gauge interest.

I suddenly had an idea, something that would allow me to reveal my affection to Matt in a *Hey, I've liked you since forever* kind of way and not in a *Hey, I'm going to die if you don't soulbond with me* kind of way. It would require tact, which might be difficult, but I had to try. And that's where the three people in front of me came in, as well as Rion.

"Is there something wrong?" Lila said, nose scrunching. "You look like you're in pain."

Sionna placed a hand on my shoulder. Her touch burned through my tunic. "You're making a face, Arek."

"Huh? No. I'm fine. I've—I've remembered something. I have to talk to Matt."

As exits go, the one I made from the sunroom was less than graceful, as I all but ran away from three of my closest friends. But I had an idea. An epiphany. A plan that had potential. I had a book that detailed a successful real-life romance. And I had three months to make it work.

Chapter 11

"I have an idea!" I said, slamming the journal onto the table in front of Matt.

He peered at me over the edge of a book, eyebrow raised, mouth pressed into a wry expression. "What?"

"What's my idea? Or a general 'what'?"

Matt narrowed his eyes and uncurled from his position on the low sofa. He wasn't wearing his boots, and his foot was wrapped with a bandage, though the swelling had all but disappeared. His toes looked like toes again instead of sausages. Not that I was usually one to notice toes, only Matt's toes.

He closed his book. "A general 'what.' Or how about, what are you doing in here?"

"Good question." We'd been living in the castle for just over a week, and I hadn't yet disturbed Matt in the library. This was my first time stepping into it, and that said more about me than I wanted it to. The room was spacious with floor-length windows that led onto a veranda. The abundant natural light had faded the edges of the lush carpets and the cushions of the sofa Matt relaxed upon, which sat directly in the path of the afternoon sun.

There were books everywhere. They bowed shelves beneath their weight, lined every inch of the walls, and were stacked in unruly piles on the floor that stretched toward the ceiling. Knowledge and light permeated the entire space, a perfect reflection of Matt, who looked like he innately belonged among the fluttery parchments and the beams of sunlight.

He swung his feet over the edge of the couch and sat up from his repose. I joined him, perched on the edge of the cushion. "I figured out a potential solution to my soul mate problem."

Matt raised an eyebrow. Okay, here went something.

"I'm going to woo one of my friends."

"Again. What?"

"The journal." I picked it up and pushed it into his face. He batted it away. "The princess details how she falls in love with a lady she despises in the beginning. It's a love story. A story I can replicate."

"I still have no idea what you're talking about. You think you're making sense, but all I hear is babble about wooing and love stories."

"You're being difficult." I studied him, looking for any nuances in his expression other than outright confusion, but I found nothing. Huh. I might have to be more direct.

Matt pointed at himself. "I'm being difficult? You're the one who started a conversation in the middle."

Sighing through my nose, I gave him my best kingly glare. "I have to marry someone and join our souls before three months pass."

"Yes." Matt picked through the pile of books at the base of the couch's armrest. He grabbed one and held it up.

"According to this, that is true." The golden lettering flashed in the sunlight—*Enchantments, Curses, and the Binding Magical Laws of Ere in the Realm of Chickpea.*

Well, fuck that book and whoever wrote it.

"I don't want to marry someone I don't know."

"Makes sense."

"I have decided to woo one of my friends."

"And that's where you lose me."

I punched Matt in the shoulder while my insides twisted. "Doofus. It makes sense. My friends know me. I know them. I won't have any other options until people start visiting us in the castle, which won't be for a while. Until then, I should at least try."

Matt looked so skeptical, it hurt. "And how are you going to do that? We've known them for nine months, and not one of them has been remotely romantically inclined toward you."

Ouch. Okay. Straightforward. No mincing of words, and I couldn't help but note he'd left himself out as a possible participant. "That you know of," I snapped.

"Trust me, I know." Okay. So, this wasn't going great. Maybe I needed to hint a little more heavily.

"So . . . no one at all? Not one person from the entire group of people who participated in the quest has any feelings for me at all?" There. That should do it.

He crossed his arms and raised an eyebrow. "That's a no."

I huffed. My breath swirled the dancing motes. He certainly wasn't making this easy. Also, rude. "We've been basically running for our lives, trying to fulfill a prophecy, not knowing when we'd have food or a bed or if we'd need to flee in the middle of the night. It wasn't the time for romance." I gave him a sly smile to cover up my inner turmoil. "At least, not for some of—"

"If you bring up the innkeeper's son one more time, Arek, I swear I will turn you into a toad." He pointed his finger at me with all the threat of a hissing, puffed-up kitten.

"You can do that?"

"That's not the point."

"Kind of is the point."

"I haven't learned it yet, but I bet the spell is in here somewhere!" He flailed his arms to encompass the room.

"Okay, whatever, I'll never bring it up again. Anyway, the princess basically lays out a template for wooing in her journal. All I have to do is follow it."

Matt eyed the book. He took it from me and flipped through the pages, forehead wrinkled in thought. "Don't you think they should have a choice?"

"They will have a choice. They can always say no, even after the wooing. But there's . . . a group of us. It only takes one person to like me back." I tried to catch his gaze, hoping that looking me in the eye might help him see the true meaning behind my words.

"What about you?"

"What about me?"

"Do you even like any of our friends romantically?"

This was it. The moment. I took a breath to steel myself and began, "Well, there is someone I've been wanting to—"

"And if they're not interested?" Matt cut me off so quickly, so pointedly, as he glared at the pile of books on the floor with his brows furrowed. He wouldn't look at me with his big brown eyes, even as I stared at his ridiculous, beautiful profile. His shoulders scrunched near his ears, his body tense as a bowstring. Oh, he knew. He *definitely* knew, and he was obviously uncomfortable. He couldn't even stand to hear me say it. My heart sank to my toes. "What then? Move on to the next one? A string of second places?" he asked, voice tinged with something sharp.

I shrugged, desperately trying to appear as nonchalant as possible while I pretended Matt's words didn't pierce as deep and painful as an assassin's dagger. "Friendship is a good start," I said quietly, touching the edge of the journal. "Don't you think? I mean, the princess despised the lady when they first met, but they ended up falling for each other. I feel like I'm in a better starting position than she was." As I said this, a small spark of hope kindled in my middle for me and Matt in all this. That maybe, as he saw my efforts with the others, it might awaken something in him. I couldn't forget the way he sounded when he thought I was dying on the floor of the throne room, the relief in his voice when I finally woke up. Those moments made me believe there might be something there.

Matt rubbed his brow. "I'll concede it's not a horrid idea. I just..." He sighed, shoulders slumping, his face drawn in pain. I wondered if he'd moved his ankle the wrong way when he made room for me on the couch. I glanced down but didn't see anything amiss. "It's not ideal."

"'Ideal' would be me not having to woo anyone at all. 'Ideal' would be me not being bound to a throne, either. But 'ideal' walked out the minute the wizard showed up on my doorstep with a prophetic scroll detailing my destiny."

Matt winced. "I guess your life wasn't ever going to be normal, was it?"

"I guess not."

"All right then. Well, good luck with your plan."

My body froze. "You're not going to help me?"

He scoffed. "No thanks. Leave me out of it."

"Seriously?"

"Yes." He held up a book. "This is me helping you. Trying to find a way to undo it all. Keep me out of your romantic schemes." This plan could not go any more wrong if I tried. I needed a way to keep him invested on some level.

"But . . . I need your help."

Matt rolled his eyes. "Really? You need help with flirting?"

"Of course!" I said, doing my best to appear lighthearted. "Yes! That's it! I need an inside man. Someone to help give me advice."

"Someone you're not pursuing," he said, mouth pressed into a firm line.

Okay, Matt, no need to *rub it in*. I got it the first time. Loud and clear.

"Yes, someone I'm not pursuing," I said, forcing my face into a casual smile. "So you'll help me? I can't do this without my best friend."

"Right," he said softly. He shook his head, gave a half-hearted smile, and slapped my shoulder with the book. "Right. Of course I'll help you. I want you to keep living, even if I turn you into a toad."

Relief flooded through me. Okay. We could get past our really awkward conversation about my feelings and move forward. I still held out hope that the princess could help me change his mind, and in the meantime, I could start on my backup plan. I'd actually have to woo the others. But Matt would help me. Matt would always help me because he was loyal to a fault and really the best person I knew. I didn't realize how important Matt's approval was until I was scared I wouldn't have it. But now that I did, I could allow the apprehension to ease, and the tension in my body fled. I slumped against the cushions and tipped sideways until my cheek smashed into a throw pillow.

"Perfect."

"What just happened? Did you faint or fall asleep?"

Groaning, I poked his side. "Neither. I'm tired, and I'm thinking."

"Ah, that's why I smelled smoke."

"Funny."

"I'm hilarious. I thought you knew."

I snorted. "Okay, so, my plan." My first instinct was to wiggle close to Matt's side, but I was wounded and embarrassed from our conversation, so I sprawled on the cushion opposite him on the sofa, half turned to face him. I hadn't thought this far into the plan before barging into the library, my hopes pinned on Matt, so I had to come up with the next steps on the fly. Luckily, I was kind of good at improvising. I just needed to start at the beginning. "The first bit where the princess says her heart softened toward the lady was after they were trapped together in the tack room and started to understand each other better."

"And?"

"And . . . that's what Sionna said she wanted in a potential partner." Ha! Good thing I paid attention during that conversation.

"I thought it might be Sionna," Matt muttered.

"What?"

"Nothing." Matt shook his head. "So," he said, drawing out the vowel sound, "you want to become trapped in a room with Sionna."

"Yes."

"So you two can talk and get to know each other."

"Exactly."

"Here's a thought: Why don't you just ask her on a picnic or on a walk with you in the garden?"

"Reason one: arrows. And reason two: because then she'll know that I'm trying to woo her."

"And that's bad?"

"Yes."

"So you're stealth wooing."

"Exactly."

"Why again?"

"Because it needs to feel natural, like destiny brought us together. That's what happened with the princess."

"And destiny is going to be . . ."

"You. You're my destiny." I tried not to blush too hard at those words. "I mean, you're going to trap us together."

Matt went rigid.

"Arek." He fiddled with a loose thread on his blue tunic. His dark hair fell in his eyes. "I don't know. I said I would help, but I'm not going to deceive our friends."

"It's not deception. You're just going to lock us in and then let us out after a few hours. No lying involved on your part. No big deal."

"And then what? You'll be in love? You'll marry Sionna right then?"

The thought made my throat tighten with anxiety. "Don't be foolish." I choked the words out past my dry mouth. "Of course we won't fall in love right away. It will take time. The trapped-together part is only the beginning. To test chemistry and see if either of our hearts soften."

"That sounds like a medical problem."

"What? That's how the princess described it. But don't worry, I don't see Sionna as someone who is going to jump into my arms and beg to be bonded." Then to shift the focus, I added, "She's not an innkeeper's son."

Matt lunged for his pile of books, his face a brilliant red. "Toad! I'm turning you into a toad right now!"

Laughing maniacally, I dove after him, my hands clutching his waist. It was instinctive, to reach out for him, to tease him. We'd been physically close since we were boys, but now it held a weird connotation, a split second of awkwardness that I decided to push past. This was Matt, and if I felt a tinge of excitement mixed with heartache, that was my own problem. I jerked him backward away from the book of spells while he pulled forward. We overbalanced and fell off the couch, and I ended up tackling Matt to the floor. We bumped into the table and rolled around like puppies, playfighting and generally being destructive while knocking over a pile of books. Matt laughed as we wrestled, just like old times, when we played in the fields or in the hay loft.

"Get off me," Matt said, pushing his hands against my face,

his own flushed, as he wheezed with giggle-filled breaths. "You oaf."

"How dare you call your king an oaf."

He kneed me in the ribs, and I tumbled to the side, squished between Matt and the sofa, our bodies flush from our shoulders to our knees, squeezed into the small space between the ornate couch legs and the table.

Matt huffed. His chest rose and fell quickly as he panted from the short minutes of exertion. "You're horrible," he said, but he smiled, all teeth and eye crinkles. "Truly horrible. I don't know where they came up with 'King Arek the Kind.'"

I groaned. "You heard about that?"

"Who hasn't?"

"I don't suppose you found anything in here that will make me not 'King Arek the Kind.'"

The atmosphere between us changed in an instant. "No. I have not. I found a book of spells to study. I found a book of laws. I found a book of magical laws. But nothing to undo what happened when you sat on the throne with the crown on your head."

"Other than death?"

"Other than death."

"Well, then I better get to wooing."

Matt released a long-suffering sigh. I was used to them, especially when I was trying to talk him into some foolish, fun adventure back in the village. And I'd heard them quite often on our journey to fulfill the prophecy. Despite its negative connotation, it was a comfort to hear, because it meant Matt was there by my side, listening to my harebrained schemes, and about to get in trouble right alongside me.

"Fine," he said. "I'll suggest you and Sionna search the princess's tower together, and I will lock you in. Happy?"

I grinned at the ceiling. "Very."

"Good. Now leave me in peace. I have studying to do."

"Yes, Lord Matt. I will leave you to your scholarly pursuits."

"You're an ass."

"And yet, you're my best friend, so what does that make you?"

"Best friends with an ass."

I laughed, loud and inelegant, like a donkey's bray. As I stood, he threw the princess's journal at me, and it thudded squarely against my chest.

"Fine, fine. I'll leave, but first thing tomorrow, I want myself and Sionna locked in that tower. Understood?"

As Matt sat up, his smile fled once again, and he shook his head. "Don't push your luck, sire. Especially around a grumpy mage." The way he said 'sire' sounded more like an insult than a title. I wasn't sure how I felt about that, besides impressed at his execution.

"Noted." I placed my hand on the door and paused, deciding to throw out one last olive branch. "Thanks, Matt. You really are my best friend."

"I know," he said so quietly, so small, that I was sure he was in pain again. I almost turned back, but then he added, "Oh look, there *is* a spell to turn someone into a toad."

I changed my mind and fled.

Chapter 12

"Shouldn't Lila be accompanying you on this mission?" Sionna asked as we climbed the stairs to the tower. "She's the best at looting."

"She does have the stickiest fingers," I agreed with a nod. The entirety of my body was damp with anxious sweat, because as great as an idea as this was yesterday, it didn't seem so great now that it was in action. Sionna was as shrewd and knowledgeable as she was beautiful, and other than Matt, she had known me the longest in our little band. We'd barely started, and she was already poking holes in my plan. *Deflect, Arek. Deflect!* "But I would actually like to have a chance to look at the items we find—and not have to fight her for them before she squirrels them away in her stash, never to be seen again."

Sionna nodded sagely, her loose black hair falling around her shoulders. She wore an embroidered tunic and a pair of loose trousers, her leather boots, and her sword. My face flushed when I glanced at her, and I hoped that she wouldn't notice in the gloom of the stairwell.

"She's grown, Arek. She might let you hold them before she hides them."

"Was that a joke?" I held the torch higher over my head and squinted in the firelight. A small smile played around Sionna's lips. "It was a joke! Oh my spirits, ring the warning bells. Sionna told a joke!"

"I've told jokes before."

"When?"

"I have."

"I don't remember any."

"Well, I have. Maybe you didn't hear them over the sound of your own voice."

"Ouch." I covered my heart with my hand. "Your words strike true, General. I'm wounded."

She shook her head. Her deep brown eyes caught the light. "What's that word you and Matt use to insult each other?"

"'Doofus'?"

"Yes." She snapped her finger. "That's it! You're a doofus."

"Sire."

"What?"

"If you're going to insult me, at least use my new title." I gave her my best smarmy grin. "Say, 'You're a doofus, *sire.*'"

She chuckled, a low and throaty sound that shivered through me. "You're something else, Arek. I don't understand you at all."

My heart flipped, then promptly sank into my belly.

"What do you mean?" I held out my arms, the torch flickering against the stone in the small hallway that circled up toward the tower. "I'm an open book."

"In a different language."

"That's not true. I'm an easy read."

She hummed.

Okay. This wasn't funny anymore. Yes, the whole purpose of my ruse was to get to know Sionna better, and I'd figured that she'd need to get to know me better as well for us to feel a spark toward each other. But it stung that she thought she didn't know me *at all*.

"Seriously, Sionna. You've known me for months."

She raised her shoulders. "I've known a version of you, yes."

"A version?" My pitch went high. Clearing my throat, I tried again. "A version?" Nope. Did not come out better. Still sounded hurt.

She nodded. "And you've known a version of me."

I stopped short on the stairs and teetered. My heel slipped off the step, and I almost fell, but Sionna caught my elbow and steadied me.

"You're upset."

Sionna had this annoying, and by annoying I meant accurate, ability to make statements of things that should be questions. She possessed an emotional perception years ahead of anyone else in our group, which also made her appear far more mature than the rest of us, save maybe Rion, even though she was only a few months older than me. In fact, her birthday would be soon. I think.

"I'm not upset."

Her face pinched. "You are."

"Fine. I am." I pulled my arm from her grasp. "Can we get this over with, please?" I was the most mature king in all the land. There would be songs written about my wisdom and aplomb.

Stomping in the dust, I brushed past Sionna on the stairwell and headed for the tower landing. Feeling like this mission was doomed before it even started, I wondered at the prudence of continuing with searching the tower, but it would look strange if I suddenly turned and headed back. She'd think I was madder than I really was if I did that, and I honestly wasn't that mad, just caught off guard that after traveling together for several months, Sionna felt like we didn't really know each other at all.

"Arek." She easily caught up to me, her long legs eating up the small distance between us. "Arek, wait. I want to explain."

The landing was much the same as we'd left it from the last time we were here, though the dust was marked with a new set of footprints. The lock and chain hung off the door, blasted by Matt's magic. Propped open slightly, the door swung freely on the hinges when I pushed it open.

"Oh, look, there's nothing. Great. Let's go."

She caught the door with her hand before I could close it.

"Arek, you're being childish."

Ugh.

"And?"

"I didn't say that we weren't friends or that I don't care about you. I do. I stayed because of you."

Crossing my arms over my chest, I leaned on the stone wall, just on the outside of the tower door. "What?"

"I can't speak for the others," she said, measured, brow furrowed, as if tasting her words before saying them, "but I couldn't go back to the life I had before you and Matt fell into that tavern."

"We didn't fall. We gracefully entered."

"You were lost and soaked to the bone, and you would've been eaten alive if I hadn't stepped in to save your hides."

I stuck out my chin. "I remember it differently, but fine." She was one hundred percent correct; we would've died.

"I've been trained to fight my whole life. That's all I've ever done. That's all my father taught me. Do you know what I was supposed to be doing in that tavern when we met?"

That took me by surprise. We'd never talked about it before. Or rather, I'd never asked.

"No, I don't know. What were you doing in that tavern?"

"Waiting for you."

"Bullshit."

She laughed again, and I realized belatedly it was another joke. She continued, "I was waiting to meet a man about a job."

"What kind of job?"

"The mercenary kind."

I blinked. "You were a mercenary?"

"No." She raised a finger. "I was almost a mercenary. My father had fallen ill. He hadn't taught me how to run his blade-smith forge, only how to fight with the weapons he made. I sold everything he had completed to anyone who would buy it, for whatever price, which as you know—"

"Probably wasn't much because the Vile One was stealing everyone's wealth."

"Exactly." She dropped her gaze and picked at her nails. "I found a guild who would take me, and they set me up with my first chance at a job. I was seventeen and petrified."

"But Matt and I bumbled in."

"And the rest is prophecy." She spread her hands, palms up. That small smile lingered around her mouth, peaceful and placating my dimming hurt.

Rubbing my hands over my face, I wilted against the wall. "What happened with your father?" The question chased the smile away, and Sionna tipped her face down, stared at her fingers. A bead of blood welled at her cuticle. Wow. I was awesome at wooing.

"He died, several weeks before I met you. My mother and my younger sister moved to live with my uncles in another village, but I had already contacted the guild, and I thought I'd try life on my own. Maybe even make a bit of coin to send to them." Her shoulders sagged from her perfect posture. "I couldn't go back now, even if I wanted to. I can't imagine the guild would be happy with how I left. And the village life isn't for me."

"I didn't know."

"How could you have? I didn't tell you. I didn't tell any of the group."

"Yeah, but—"

"That's what I meant about you knowing a version of me. The version in your head is of a capable warrior who saved you and fought by your side and helped you defeat the Vile One."

"Because that's true."

She shook her head, her brown hair splayed over her bare shoulders. "But in reality, I hadn't killed anyone until that night in the tavern—I hadn't even been in a real fight before. I was just a terrified teenager sitting at a table, drinking watered-down mead, and waiting for someone to show up and tell me who I had to hurt and when, so I could earn coin for my mother and sister."

"That mead *was* watered down," I said. She made a face. "Sorry. Sorry. I'm an ass."

"That, I do know."

"I'm sorry. I'm sorry that happened to you. I'm sorry I didn't know."

"It's fine, Arek. But that's my point. Your perception of me is not the real me."

Frowning, I squeezed my crossed arms closer to my body. "Okay, I get what you're saying. But Sionna, that was a destiny ago. You're the most capable person I know. You're amazing. Whatever version of you that I met in that tavern, the version who is standing in front of me is the version that is my friend. I put the Sionna I know in charge of our whole military. It's the version I trust."

"That's very kind of you, Arek."

I rolled my eyes. "Please don't start about King Arek the Kind."

"I'm not, but it is very kind of you to say so."

"I'm sorry, Sionna. I'm sorry I didn't take the time to know you better before this moment."

She shrugged and looked away. "We didn't have the time."

"I know, but I wish we had."

She nudged my arm. "We have it now. Thanks to our group. We have plenty of time."

How little she knew. I should tell her about the soul mate situation. But that wasn't a tower conversation. We should be seated, and there should be cake. Lots of cake.

She jerked her chin toward the door. "Shall we complete our task? Then we can have lunch with the others."

Stomach roiling, I peered into the room, knowing that if we entered, we'd be trapped for an indeterminate amount of time based on Matt's whim. Matt's words about asking Sionna on a picnic felt wiser now than they had yesterday. "Actually, Sionna—"

"Shh," she said, turning on her heel. A dagger appeared in her hand from *somewhere*, and she crouched into a fighting stance. "Someone is coming."

Matt.

Panicked, I grabbed her arm, marveling as her muscles flexed beneath my fingers, and tugged. "Wait! It's—"

She elbowed me hard in the sternum and I stumbled backward, straight through the door and into the tower.

CHAPTER 13

I caught my heel on the edge of a throw carpet and fell on my ass, knocking my head against the princess's small but sturdy table. Stars flashed behind my eyes, and pain shot up the length of my spine. For the first time, I wished I was wearing the crown. Maybe it would've taken the brunt of the blow.

The door remained open, but it quivered as if in anticipation. I squinted at it through my blurry vision but was unable to see into the darkened hallway beyond where Sionna stood. The torch, at least, fell away from anything that could catch.

"Who's there?" Sionna demanded, crouched into a fighter's stance on the other side of the threshold.

"It's me."

"Matt!" Sionna yelled. She placed a hand on her chest in apparent relief. "You startled me!"

"Sionna!" he yelled back. He sounded winded, like he'd run up the stairs, and there was a hint of fear there as well, probably at the sight of Sionna's outstretched dagger. "Where's Arek?"

I opened my mouth to respond, but clamped it shut when bile rose in my throat. *Oof.* I'd hit my head hard enough to rattle my stomach. I groaned.

"Arek!"

Matt brushed past Sionna, knocking her aside and skidding into the room along the dusty stone from where the rug had curled away during my stumble. Once he crossed the threshold, the door creaked and slammed behind him, right in Sionna's face. A thud resonated and a quiet *ow* followed.

"Oh shit!" Matt stalled, head whipping between the closed door and my sprawled self.

Sionna pounded on the other side. "Matt! Arek!" The door rattled in the frame.

I waved off Matt's concern and hoisted myself upright, then promptly pitched to the side and ended up curled on the floor. The back of my head pounded in time with the beats of Sionna's fists against the door.

"Sionna," Matt called. His gaze was trained on me, but he kept his voice calm. "It's okay. Just find Lila and see if she can pick the lock." He grimaced as he said it, like he tasted bad milk.

"Is Arek okay?" The handle twitched. "He surprised me. I didn't mean to knock him so hard."

"He's fine," Matt said quickly. "He's hit his head, but I don't see any blood."

Reaching back, I touched the quickly growing knot. My fingertips came away red, and again, Matt made a face. Good thing Sionna couldn't see him. He really was the worst liar.

The lock rattled again. "Why can't I open it?"

"It's locked."

"You broke the lock, remember? When we first came to the tower."

"Magic, then," Matt said, lips twisting into a wry smile.

"There's probably a spell. Hopefully Lila will be able to finesse what's left of the lock, or maybe Bethany can charm it open."

I tilted my head and mouthed, "Really?"

Matt shook his head. He raised both hands in the quintessential *oops* gesture, and that's when I realized he didn't have his staff.

Awesome. We really were stuck.

There was another loud thud on the other side, and Matt looked toward the ceiling, hands on his hips, shaking his head.

"Sionna," he said in his best Matt voice, flat and patient yet tinged with annoyance, "you'll only hurt your shoulder if you continue."

There was a short pause followed by a pained grunt. "Can you open it from in there?"

"Nope." Matt popped the *p*. "Dropped my staff. Can you take care of it? I don't want it falling into the wrong hands."

"Can I use—"

"No!"

"*Fine.*"

"Find Lila. I think I last saw her in the dungeon." Again, he squished his features. Horrible liar. The worst. No wonder we'd almost been killed in that tavern. Between my mouth and his inability to bluff, we were doomed from the beginning. "And Bethany was walking around the grounds. At the very least, maybe you and Rion together can break the door open."

"I'll be back soon. We'll get you out."

"We'll be fine."

Matt waited by the door until the sound of Sionna's footsteps disappeared.

Once I was sure she was gone, I wet my lips, my mouth dry.

"I take it that Lila won't be able to pick that lock."

Snorting, Matt crossed the room and sank down by my side. "No. I spelled the door to close once two people crossed the threshold and only to open after several hours."

"And she's not in the dungeon."

"Yeah. I have no clue where she is. I thought sending Sionna on a wild goose chase for the others would be better than trying to explain this whole situation when Lila fails to pick the lock."

"Good call."

"Are you okay?"

With his help, I managed to sit up. My head spun, but focusing on Matt's face seemed to help center me.

"I'm fine."

"Okay. Good. We can't have a concussed king."

Raising my eyebrow, I took in Matt's expression. Despite his calm countenance when speaking with Sionna through the door, he appeared unsettled.

"Are you okay?" I waved my hand. "You look distressed."

"Huh? Oh well." He ran a hand through his dark hair, over the part in the back that stuck up from a cowlick. "I just watched my friend be vaulted through a door and heard a crash. Sionna is strong. I thought she'd really hurt you."

"Oh, Matt." I placed my hands over my heart, only half joking. "You do care."

He shoved me in the arm. "Yeah, whatever. It would have been a shame to keep you alive for nine months just for you to meet your demise at the hands of your newly appointed general."

Truth. That would've sucked.

"Thanks."

"Anyway, I only came up here because my trap hadn't been triggered, and I wanted to make sure being stuck with someone was still part of your brilliant plan."

Slumping forward, I propped my elbows on my knees. "Yeah, about that. As much as it pains me to say this, I should've just asked her on a picnic."

"Wait, what?" He cupped his hand behind his ear. "Did I hear that correctly? Did you say that I was right?"

"Yes. Don't gloat. I have a horrible headache."

"Whose fault is that?"

"Yours!" Matt ducked, narrowly dodging my flailing arms. "And on top of that, you were almost on the receiving end of Sionna's dagger. Things may have been relatively calm here in the past week, but we're all still on high alert."

Matt drew his knees to his chest and crossed his arms atop them, mirroring my pose. "Yeah. Sometimes I flinch at sounds in the library, especially when I'm alone. And I hate it when the servants sneak up behind me. I'm terrified I'm going to accidentally blast one with my staff!"

"That would be unfortunate. That Melody makes a very nice tea."

Nudging me with the toe of his boot, Matt gave me his disapproving face. "Can't you ever be serious?"

"I can't sleep," I confessed, quickly, quietly, as honest as I ever was. "I just stare at the canopy over the bed until I'm so exhausted, I pass out."

Matt's expression softened; then he nodded. "I think we're all dealing with a posttraumatic stress response. We did spend nine months on the run. We should probably check in with the others and see how they're coping."

"That's a good idea."

He looked away, stared at the stone. "So what happened?"

"I fell and hit my head."

"No." His exasperation was a familiar, reassuring sound. "With Sionna." He cleared his throat. "You didn't enter the tower."

"Yeah. Sionna ended up opening up to me without much prompting. I think the trapped-together scenario is more for people who aren't willing to share their feelings readily and may need proximity and long silences to encourage conversation."

Matt shifted on the ground. He stood suddenly and picked up the dying torch from the corner where the flame licked at the stone walls. He held it up, and the flickering flames cast weird shadows along the walls.

"We should look around and see if there really is anything in this tower."

"There's not."

Matt flipped back the ratty blanket that was on the small bed tucked into the corner. "Are you sure?"

"Lila has already removed everything of value. I asked her to do it the day after I became king." Sitting on the bare stone was startingly uncomfortable. I crawled to the carpet that had tripped me and sprawled across the thick plush. My head pounded, and I tucked my arm beneath it as a pillow, careful not to press on the wound.

"No offense to our friend, but she doesn't consider things to be valuable unless they're shiny."

"That's not entirely true. She was spot-on about the journal."

"Yeah?" Matt said, tugging on the wooden bed frame to peek behind the bed. "How's that working out for you?"

"Don't be a dick to me right now. I'm in pain."

"Silence it is, then."

Eyes narrowed, I craned my neck to stare at him and pouted. Matt ignored me and hummed as he continued his search. He went through the wardrobe in the corner, then moved to the heavy curtains. I closed my eyes to the sounds of opening drawers and furniture being moved. After several minutes, I heard a heavy sigh from Matt and a series of creaks as he presumably flopped onto the ancient mattress. A puff of dust escaped into the air, and I sneezed.

"Spirits bless you," Matt mumbled.

I wiped my sleeve under my nose. "Thanks."

Lapsing back into silence, I kept my eyes closed and let my thoughts wander. My relationship with Matt was typically full of easy banter that could fill spaces and didn't leave much room for silence. I'd always thought it comfortable and familiar, a habit to slip into each time I saw him, but sitting in the quiet, I wondered if it was just that, a habit, a way to avoid tougher subjects. Of course we'd had serious conversations, the weighty ones you can have with friends about life and existential dread, and when we were on the road with the others, we kept close in the beginning when our trust in the newcomers was thin at best. But as the journey went on, there'd been less and less time for drawn-out discussions. And even though my attempt yesterday to delve into something deeper hadn't gone quite the way I'd hoped, maybe I could still use this tower scenario to my advantage.

"Why did you not want to help me with this?"

Matt sucked in a quick, surprised breath. "What?"

"The wooing. You help me with everything, all the time. Even when we were kids. You've been by my side since the start." My forehead wrinkled as I tugged at the blood-sticky hair at the back of my head. "Why not this piece?"

It might be unreasonable to hope that maybe I'd misinterpreted something, that he might be holding back for some reason. But if there ever was a time to push the envelope, it was now. Matt didn't respond right away. I kept my mouth shut and gave him time. The longer he waited to speak, the more I wished I'd swallowed the question.

"Nevermi—"

"I didn't want to be involved."

The words came in a rush, slurring together so that it took me a beat to comprehend them. I pushed myself to sitting, then faced him.

The pink of his mouth turned down at the corners, and I could have sworn I saw a glisten in his dark eyes.

"You what?"

Matt puffed up, straightened his posture, as if bracing himself to face down an enemy instead of a friend. It hurt, in a strange way, that Matt needed to bolster his resolve to talk to me. Me! The person who stayed beside him when his mother died. The person who defended him from the other village children. He was the reason I'd thrown my first-ever punch when an older boy had pushed him. I'd hurt my hand and then endured a lecture from my father; not about the punching—he'd agreed with that bit—but how to throw a punch that would inflict damage and not damage me.

"I don't want to talk about it."

"Tough luck. We're stuck. There's nothing else for us to do. We're talking about it."

"I'm not Sionna." His face went red, the flush working up his cheeks and down the column of his throat. "I don't want to be a tick mark on your to-woo list."

Ouch. Well, those words sealed it that Matt was not interested in being my soul mate. A little tact would've been nice. Tears pricked at my eyes that weren't a result of the head wound. I felt the hurt flare up again, and suddenly I was mad. Mad at the Vile One for being such a jerk that someone had to usurp him, mad at the wizard for sending me here in the first place, and mad at myself for thinking Matt would ever want to be with me.

"No, you're not Sionna. You're Matt. My best friend. And for some reason, you didn't want to help me not die."

He refused to look me in the eye. He stared at a point above my head and across the room. "It doesn't matter. I'm helping you now." And now I was *pissed*. I was sick of the evasiveness. If he really didn't want me, I wanted to hear him say it. I *needed* to hear him say it.

"It does matter. It matters to me. Now, answer the question."

"Is that a command?"

I flinched. "What? No."

"Then screw you, *sire*."

"Wow. Fine. Whatever. Be a prick."

His gaze shot to mine as quick as a flash of lightning. "Fine. You want an argument? Is that what you want?"

Despite my headache, I sat up straighter. I didn't like that

Matt loomed above me on the bed. But I didn't trust my legs with making it over to the chair, and spirits be damned I'd ask him for help.

"Your plan is absurd." He crossed his arms in response and glared. Damn, was he stubborn. If I wasn't so mad, I would have teased him about it.

"Yeah, my plan might be absurd, but it's all I have right now. Unless you want me to die. Which I guess you do, since you initially refused to help me."

He rolled his eyes. "Why are you stuck on it? I'm helping! I set up this stupid trap for you like you asked."

"Because I want to know."

"Because I don't understand the magic!" Matt exploded with sound and movement, throwing his arms out to the side. "Okay? I don't know a thing about magic succession laws or soulbonds. And I don't have any experience with *romance*!" He spat out the last word like it tasted bad. "Is that what you want to hear? I'm not skilled enough in either realm to help you. I want to, but I . . ." He clenched his hands into fists. "I *can't*. I don't know how to help you with this, Arek."

That brought me up short. "What?"

Matt shot me one of his classic annoyed glares. "I've never . . . You know this. I don't know why I have to explain. You grew up with me, and you know the other villagers weren't knocking down my door to be my friend, much less a significant other. I was the weird kid who was run out of their previous village because of a rumor of magic. I didn't have any friends other than you. I don't know how to help you with relationships or with *flirting*." Matt flopped dramatically backward on the mattress, and another wave of motes erupted from the bedding, twirling in the weak sunlight.

And just like that, my anger dissipated and was replaced again by that stubborn little flame of hope. "That's it?"

"That's it? That's *it*? Oh right, I forgot who I was talking to, the King of Flippancy. It shouldn't be King Arek the Kind—"

"On that we agree."

"It should be King Arek the Asshole!"

"Hey!"

"You have no idea what it's like not being able to help with the one thing I'm supposed to be good at."

"Matt. You do a million amazing things a day with magic. You can clean up spilled wine and blast open doors." He gave me an exasperated look. "Okay, so maybe those aren't the grandest examples of your magic. But you're the only person I would trust to help with this." I paused. "Wait, can you do those things without the staff?"

"Of course I can. The staff focuses my power and makes me stronger, but I've always been able to . . . do things with magic."

"Huh. I just realized . . . I always wondered how you were able to complete your chores so quickly."

Matt's mouth twitched into a smirk.

"And you never helped with mine? All those years and we could've had so much free time!"

He raised a finger. "Exhibit one as to why I didn't tell you when we were kids. I did not want to be subjected to your whims. I was an impressionable youth, and you would've coerced me into playing pranks on the farmers."

I flailed my hands. "Of course I would have!"

Matt shook his head, smiling, then sobered, leveling me

with a hard look when he remembered he was supposed to be mad at me.

"And come on," I continued. "You had plenty of chances at relationships. You were the one who was aloof." I did not allow one hint of bitterness to seep into my tone. "It's not my fault you didn't branch out beyond me."

Matt shot to his feet and pointed his finger into my face. "You don't get it! Barthly had already reigned for over twenty years when you and I were born. He'd destroyed our realm. He'd destroyed our neighboring kingdoms. He had waged war. He'd killed thousands of people. And he'd done it with *magic*."

Oh, I was not for this lecture or for the height difference. Planting my hand on the edge of the table, I hauled myself to my feet. My world spun, and my vision darkened at the edges, but at least this way I was taller. At least I could handle Matt's righteous anger from this angle.

"I'm aware, thank you. I may be *flippant*, but I'm not ignorant. What does that have to do with anything?"

Matt laughed, a cruel, biting sound. He took a shaky breath, and his hand trembled when he pushed it into my chest. His touch burned through my tunic.

"For an entire generation, Barthly was all the villagers knew of magic. Not the hedge witches who brewed healing potions that he had rounded up and killed in the first years of his reign. Not the pixies and other magical creatures of the forest who hid from his wrath. Not even the storytellers like Bethany who disappeared because they wove magic into their songs. No. Our people only knew of the Vile One and everything he'd done and everything he planned to do. And no matter how good I was or how innocent or kind, my magic would be associated with *him*. It didn't matter if I used it for the benefit of the village. They'd only see the same power flowing through my veins as it did his. I'd be lucky to only be run out of town."

My temples pounded, but physical pain was inconsequential to the anger and hurt that throbbed in my middle. "Oh."

"It's not that I didn't want relationships. It was that I couldn't have them. I couldn't allow anyone to get close." Matt shrugged. "Except you. You didn't give me a chance to push you away."

A lump formed in my throat. "Well, I wanted to be friends with the weird kid even if he didn't trust me with his biggest secret."

"I couldn't trust you. Not when we first met. And not later when I didn't know if you could keep it to yourself and not blab it to any pretty person who batted their eyelashes at you."

"That's not fair." It was totally fair.

Matt scrunched his face and shook his head. "Even now, it's all about you. And not about me and what I was feeling."

"Well, maybe I'm a little concerned that my closest advisor might not trust me." The more I raised my voice, the more my head hurt. I gripped the table; my knuckles turned white. "Do you trust me now, Matt? Huh?"

Matt pressed his mouth into a flat line, his lips thinned. He didn't answer.

"Well?"

"Of course I do, Arek!" he yelled. "But do you understand? I had one friend." He pushed me again. I took an unsteady step back, my sweaty fingers sliding across the lacquered wood until I could grab the edge. "One! One person who even pretended to like me, and I couldn't risk that. For anything."

I froze at his words. Was it possible . . . Could he be talking about our present? Was he afraid that my affection toward him would ruin our friendship? Especially since he'd made it clear that he didn't return those feelings? I understood. I'd harbored the same fear, which was one of the reasons I'd kept it to myself while on our quest, but I didn't like it. I didn't like it at all. That he was so afraid of losing my friendship. He took a breath and continued before I could answer.

"You were well-liked by everyone, as was your father. Everyone wanted to be your friend, and I was lucky enough to be allowed in your orbit. After my mother died, I was the village orphan. The village *burden*. Your acceptance meant everything. It opened opportunities you didn't even realize, people who would allow me to do their odd jobs, just because they saw me walking with you around the square. I couldn't imagine what my life might have been without you. It would've been even worse if the rumors about magic were proven true."

My cheeks colored in shame. Matt was right. Here I was fixated on my own feelings when he was standing in front of me pouring out his heart about all his struggles that I was oblivious to back at home. "I didn't know."

Matt's mouth lifted into a half smile. "No. You didn't."

"I'm sorry."

Shrugging, Matt put his hands in his pockets and rocked back on his heels. He stepped away, and only then did I realize how close we'd been, how we'd been yelling into each other's faces.

"It's in the past. You can't change anything now."

"No. Well, yes, I could. I'm the king. I could do a lot, maybe, technically." I shook my head, which was a bad idea. I locked my knees to keep from crumpling. This was an important conversation, and I couldn't leave it by passing out. "But I'm sorry I didn't know. I'm sorry you went through that. I'm sorry I wasn't observant enough to realize it and do something to make it easier for you."

"You did enough, just by being my friend."

"That's a low bar, Matt."

Matt shrugged again. "You gave Bodin a bloody lip when he pushed me in with the pigs. That was a solid friendship move."

"He deserved it. Pigs are dangerous, and we were what, ten? You were small and could've gotten really hurt."

Matt smiled, his real one, and my world righted. Well, not literally. Everything was still fuzzy, and I was in danger of losing my battle with consciousness, but Matt was still my best friend, and I understood things about him I hadn't before. Huh. Maybe proximity and long silences worked for friends, too, not just enemies.

"I'm sorry I can't help you more," he said, voice low. He knotted his fingers. "I don't want you to wither. But I don't think this plan to woo our friends should be the only one you have."

"Okay. That's fair. We'll come up with a contingency plan. Just in case."

Matt nodded. "Okay. I'll do what I can to help. With magic and with . . ." He scrunched his nose. "Flirting."

"Thank you." I blew out a breath. "Besides, you can't be all that bad. I mean, the innkeeper's son—"

"Arek!" Matt said, exasperated and beautiful, his mouth ticking up into an incredulous smile.

I grinned. "We should've talked about all that a long time ago."

"Agreed."

"Oh," Matt said, voice breathy. "The door."

I turned, and the door was popped open. "It's not been several hours, has it?"

"No." Matt's cheeks colored. "I ... uh ... put in an extra condition on the spell. We must have met it."

"What was it? And no lying," I added when Matt's expression pinched.

"The door would open when true understanding passed between the people inside. Happy?"

Well, huh. Look at that. My plan wasn't horrid after all. "Of course. It's open."

"Right. Let's get you to the court physician. I think you may have hurt yourself more than you let on."

"I'm not going to argue."

"That's a first."

Matt threw my arm over his shoulder, and we left the tower, leaning on each other as we climbed down the steps. I felt lighter than I had in a long time—emotionally, not physically, if Matt's remarks about rich food and addled kings were any indication—but at least I still had him, and we were closer than before. I also had confirmation that the plan to woo my friends could work. It needed a few tweaks, sure, but I had a glimmer of hope that I might find a soul mate in time, even if it wasn't the person I truly wanted.

CHAPTER 14

"It has come to my attention," I said a few days later at dinner, "that we're all still a little . . ." My nose twitched, and I wiggled my hand. "Jittery."

We'd continued with the tradition we started our first night in the castle, taking dinner together in one of the council rooms.

Rion looked up from the hunk of meat on his plate. "What do you mean?"

"Nervy."

"I have no idea what you're talking about." Lila munched on an apple. "I'm neither of those."

"Right, and you didn't almost stab someone when they entered your room to deliver you lunch yesterday."

She shrugged. "They should've knocked."

"They did. And announced themselves. And the way they tell it, you leapt at them from the bed, yelling like a banshee, knife raised above your head. They had to use a serving platter in self-defense."

"I was trying to take a nap."

Bethany tilted her head. "In the middle of the day?"

"I needed something to do. I'm bored." A dagger appeared

in Lila's hand, and she used the point of the blade to clean under her nails.

"So you decided to stab someone?" Matt asked, incredulous. "Lila, you do realize that's the definition of tense."

"Agree to disagree," she said.

"Anyway," I cut in. "Like I said, we're all a bit on edge. I mean, we spent months evading people who wanted to kill us. We almost died like six times. Our reactions to the stress of that are valid. That said, we have to stop scaring the servants."

Meredith cleared her throat. I cast a glance in her direction. She stood by the wall, a wine pitcher clutched in her thin fingers. She bit her lip and nodded vigorously.

"See?" I pointed at her. "We're frightening people."

Bethany placed a hand on her chest and feigned innocence. "I've done nothing of the sort, Arek. I have been the pinnacle of professionalism since we've arrived."

"Didn't you accidentally charm one of the stable hands into walking repeatedly into a wall?"

"Who said that was an accident?"

I narrowed my eyes and straightened my crown. "Bethany."

"Fine! She looked like the woman who tried to poison us with the stew that one time. Remember? In that town? Rion threw up for *hours*."

Ugh. I wish I could forget. It was days after we'd met Rion and had fulfilled the part of the prophecy about finding all the quest members. The failed poisoning was the first targeted attempt on our lives. Somehow Barthly had found out about the prophecy and discreetly tried to have us murdered via poison. Rion slurped one spoonful of the tainted stew, and that was the end. Luckily, the assassin wasn't that great at their job.

Otherwise, Rion would've died instead of just becoming violently ill. His vomit tipped the rest of us off quickly enough that no one else was affected, but the whole situation sobered us to the fact that we were in real danger, and our adventure turned from a jolly fun time into a serious quest.

"Well, was it?" Sionna asked. She'd remained quiet until then, casting glances around the room, especially at Meredith, the only servant in there with us. She seemed unusually distracted.

"No." Bethany scowled. "It wasn't."

"So." Matt drew out the vowel. "You overreacted to a perceived threat."

She flipped her hair off her shoulder. "And?"

"And there's no shame in it," I said, poking at a potato. "We're all experiencing it. I can't sleep. Sionna almost killed Matt on the stairwell the other day."

"What?"

"Seriously?"

"Matt, are you okay?"

Matt shot me a withering look, and I smiled widely at him. At her name, Sionna startled, wincing as she knocked her knee against the table. Her apparent edginess was a stunningly perfect example of what we were talking about.

"It's fine," Matt said. "It was a misunderstanding. Though I agree with Arek. We're all on edge despite having been relatively safe for a few weeks now."

"And since we're in a holding pattern until we receive word from other kingdoms and the populace, we should make sure to keep busy."

Meredith again nodded vigorously from the corner where

she stood. The wine sloshed dangerously in the pitcher, threatening the pretty butter color of her dress as strands of her blond hair fell from her long braid to frame her face.

Sionna knocked over her goblet.

"Sorry!" She righted it quickly so that only a few droplets colored the tablecloth. She dabbed at the mess with her napkin, then cleared her throat. "What were you saying?"

Matt's eyebrow went crooked, but he answered. "Arek is taking a really long time in announcing that we're going to hold a feast and that you're all going to be so busy planning it that you won't have time to accidentally scare the servants."

According to the records that survived of the time period before Barthly, including the princess's diary, feasts were commonplace celebrations. And what better thing to celebrate than a new king? Not to mention it would give me a backup selection of people to woo if none of my friends panned out. Matt and I had come up with the idea after we'd left the tower as my fail-safe option, and I was on board as long as I didn't have to plan it.

Bethany's head snapped up. "A feast?"

"You are the one who said that the castle is empty."

"Because it is!" Bethany's eyes sparked with excitement. "We need to invite all the lords and ladies of the lands and the surrounding kingdoms to the castle. And we need to send personal couriers as a gesture of good faith."

Sionna tapped her mouth. "And hope they don't kill the messenger?"

Matt huffed.

Bethany continued as if she didn't hear them. "And we'll have a masquerade ball after," she said with a gasp.

"Um . . . what?" I had a sinking notion that this was about to get out of hand. "Uh . . . wait. I was just thinking a feast, like lots of food," I said.

"Because you're thinking like a peasant."

I blinked, feeling vaguely insulted.

Bethany continued spreading her hands in front of her as if framing a painting. "Imagine it," she said. "The whole throne room decorated and filled with people in pretty dresses and flowing capes and masks and dancing. Soft candlelight. Lots of wine. Beautiful music filling the halls." She squealed in delight.

"Lots of pockets to pick," Lila added.

Matt shot Lila an unimpressed look. "No."

"As the mistress of finances in this court, I think it's my duty to know what is in other people's pockets," she said primly, a perfect imitation of Bethany.

Matt rolled his eyes. "Again. No."

Lila crossed her arms. "You're no fun."

"As much as it pains me to say this, Matt is right," Bethany said with a sigh. "The point of the ball is to build good relationships and trust, which we can't do if we're stealing." Lila grumbled under her breath. "But!" Bethany continued brightly. "There'll be plenty of chances for other types of fun at the party."

"And plenty of darkened corners for assassins," Sionna added. "A masquerade is dangerous. We don't have the security forces yet to hold anything that elaborate."

Matt and I exchanged a glance. We hadn't thought of that.

Bethany frowned and crossed her arms, mirroring Lila. "Wow. Way to get my hopes up and then dash them, Sionna."

"We'll still have a feast," I said. Bethany pouted. I sighed. "A ball, then. A celebration. But I guess we'll have to wait until Sionna says we're ready." I hid my grimace. Matt wasn't as successful. Postponing the feast completely undermined my plan, but Sionna had a point.

Sionna nodded.

Rion, who had remained quiet during our discussion, tapped his fingers on the table. "This does bring up another issue that has been on my mind."

"What's that?"

"Maybe you could focus on strengthening your fighting skills, Arek. Sword fighting. Archery. Hand-to-hand."

Bethany smirked. "Oh, *burn*, Arek."

"Bethany, don't you have somewhere to be?"

"No. I don't."

I pressed my lips flat. "Rion. I have kingly duties that preclude me from adding anything else to my own plate."

"You said you're not sleeping," Matt said gently. He touched my arm. "It might tire you out."

"Maybe. I'll keep it in mind." I would, but wooing was on the forefront of my mind and that would take up much of my time. Especially if I was going to find someone to bond with me in less than three months. Ha!

"Rion's not wrong about keeping our skills sharp," Matt said. "We shouldn't be complacent just because we're behind these castle walls."

"Do we all have to do this?" Lila asked. She twisted in her seat to stare at me. "Are you commanding us, *sire*?"

I would never get used to being called "sire" by these people, even if it was sarcastically. At least this time I withheld my flinch. "It's not a command. It's a strong suggestion."

She waved the knife lazily and leaned back in her chair, balancing on two legs. "Fine."

"Sionna?" I propped my head on my hand and affected my best cute face. She ignored me, focused on her plate, mutilating a potato. She'd been unusually distracted and quiet for a conversation about sword fighting. "Anything to add?"

Her eyebrows drew together in introspection. "I don't know how to dance," she muttered.

"Okay. What does that have to do with—"

"I do!" Meredith blurted.

Sionna snapped her head up and turned her intense stare toward Meredith in the corner. Meredith flushed so deeply, I thought she'd broken a blood vessel.

"I'll teach you! If you'd like."

Sionna's stern expression morphed into something soft and affectionate. Twin spots of red bloomed across her cheeks, and her dark eyes shone brightly.

"I'd like that."

What the fuck just happened?

"We can start tonight! After dinner, of course." Meredith moved quickly from her place by the wall. She plonked the wine pitcher down at Rion's elbow. "I'll meet you in the sitting room in the servants' quarters. I mean, if that works for you?"

"I'll be there."

Meredith scuttled out of the room in a flurry of yellow skirts and blond hair. She slammed the door in her haste hard enough to rattle our silverware; then the room was left in awed silence.

"What the spirits just happened?" I demanded.

Bethany burst into laughter. Lila joined in, wrapping her hands around her middle. Rion, Matt, and I looked at each other in complete confusion.

"Sionna has a date," Bethany singsonged.

Sionna blushed to her hairline while Lila's face stretched into something inhuman as she grinned with all her teeth.

"Wait? You and Meredith?" I pointed at Sionna, then to the place where Meredith routinely stood at our dinners. "Is that what just happened?"

"Yes. I mean, maybe? I hope."

I slumped back in my chair. "Huh."

"What? Does your kingship not approve?"

"Huh? What? Oh no, I mean yes, wholeheartedly. Go for it. Enjoy your . . . dancing." This was a massive kink in my plan. I'd have to cross Sionna off my to-woo list.

Bethany snorted and rolled her eyes. "Yes, enjoy your dancing with the lovely Meredith. We'll all be waiting for details at our next meeting."

"Oh hey, we're not . . . We don't need to . . . We're happy for Sionna, but details are not necessary."

"Speak for yourself," Lila said. "I want to know everything."

"Same here. I'm living vicariously because spirits know there's no one here that has shown any interest in all this." Bethany gestured to her figure, which I must say, did look lovely in the tailored blue dress.

"Don't worry, Bethany," Matt said, raising his goblet. "I'm sure you'll be beating suitors off with a stick once we have visitors from the neighboring kingdoms and the new knights and military arrive. You're beautiful." He threw his head back and gulped the wine down. Ugh. And Matt said he wasn't good at flirting. A pang of jealousy lanced through me, followed quickly by hurt that Matt would do so right in front of me while most likely knowing my feelings.

Bethany giggled. "Matt, if I didn't know any better, then I'd think you were coming on to me again."

Lila pursed her lips and made a rude noise. "As if Matt—"

"Stop," I said, raising my hand. "Okay, let's just, change the subject or eat in silence. Anything to stop talking about this."

The whole conversation made my stomach squirm. I was honestly a little disappointed that any chance I had with Sionna was gone, if I ever even had a chance at all. Truth be told, I really was happy for her and her date with Meredith. It was cute. And I was a little relieved. Except now I had to start the wooing process over.

"Aw, poor Arek." Bethany placed her chin in her hand. "If you're lonely, I know someone who would jump at the chance to—"

"Bethany," Matt interrupted, voice sharp, and throwing a truly nasty glare in her direction.

Wait, I wouldn't mind hearing more about someone who might be interested in me, but knowing Bethany, it was probably some kind of backhanded compliment or pointed barb. She and Matt had a weird relationship of being fond of sniping, so of course he'd be the first to jump in any verbal fray with her. "Matt," she replied evenly, a little grin playing around her mouth. "Are you volunteering to help me with planning the ball?"

"No." He matched her smirk. "I'll spend my time reading and researching in the library. Basically, finding all the information I can about magic in an effort to keep us all alive."

"Fair enough," she said.

We lapsed into silence as we finished our meals. Sionna was the first out the door, Bethany on her heels. "Don't worry," Bethany said, pushing Sionna's hair back behind her ear. "We'll do a quick stop at your quarters, throw on a different outfit, and maybe apply a little makeup."

Sionna gestured to her body. "What's wrong with my outfit?"

"Oh, babe," Bethany said. "Nothing. It's wonderful if you're trying to kill people. But this is a date, and you want to impress Meredith a bit, right?"

"Oh, I want in on this!" Lila vaulted out of her chair, jumped over the width of the table, planted her foot on the edge, did a flip, and landed right by the door.

"Show-off," I muttered.

She slipped out behind Bethany, only to stick her hand back in and make a rude gesture in my direction.

"Well," Rion said, dabbing the sides of his mouth with his napkin, "at least they aren't trying to stab anyone?"

I lifted my goblet. "Always looking on that bright side, Rion. I appreciate that." Drinking down the last of my wine didn't ease the sinking of my stomach. Wooing Sionna was off the table. That left me with Bethany, Lila, and Rion—and not much time to explore a relationship with any of them before I'd have to announce a betrothal.

I'd have to up my game.

Chapter 15

Staring at the canopy of my bed had become an annoying habit that I could not seem to break. I didn't understand why I couldn't sleep. I had a room with all the comforts afforded to a king, but even though my body was exhausted, my mind would not shut off.

Giving up, I reached for the princess's journal and picked up where I left off.

The picnic in the forest beyond the outer wall and the lower town was her idea. Bringing our horses and bows for hunting was mine. The bandits who attacked us were an added surprise, but I had always been taught how to defend myself. Between the two of us, we fended them off. After those who could run away were screaming, and those who couldn't were knocked out, she swooned into my arms. I caught her and lowered her to the forest floor. My heart pounded in fear that she'd been hurt, but it had been a ploy. She grinned at me when I panicked and tangled her hand into my hair. Drawing me down, she—

The knock at my door jolted me into action, and I leapt out of bed.

I could hear someone turning the handle, so I reached behind me to the nightstand and where my magical sword leaned. I grasped the hilt and whipped it in front of me.

Matt let out a squeak.

"Matt!"

"Is that a sword, or are you just happy to see me?"

I allowed the tip to drop and let out a breath. My heart pounded, and the sudden adrenaline rush left me shaky. "What are you doing here?"

"You should really lock your door."

"I thought I did."

"I know we grew up poor, but you should at least know how doors work."

Brushing past him, I pushed the door closed and engaged the bolt lock. I rested my sword against the wood, balancing the tip on the floor.

"Were you asleep?" Matt asked as he sauntered into the room. He jumped on the side of the bed, bouncing on the edge.

"You know I wasn't."

"I think you should take Rion up on the sword training."

A week had passed since Rion had utterly betrayed me and said I needed to work on my sword skills, but the insult still stung.

"I think I have bigger things to worry about," I said, pointing to the diary.

"I think that if you come across someone who is a better swordsman and wants the throne, then you won't have to worry about getting bonded."

I opened my mouth, then shut it. "Fair point." I crossed to the table along the wall that somehow always had a fresh bowl of fruit and a full pitcher. I poured myself a goblet and took a swig of the room-temperature water. "What brings you by?"

"So Sionna and Meredith, huh? That sucks. Not for them. I

think it's nice. But for you. What are you going to do?"

"Move on to Bethany."

"Really? You won't even mourn for what could have been?"

I squinted at Matt. His cheeks were a bit flushed and his eyes glassy. "You're awful mouthy. Are you drunk?"

He raised a finger. "No." He hiccupped. "But Rion and I did drink a lot of wine."

"Rion, huh?"

Matt closed one eye and stared at me. "We tried painting and drinking wine to relieve stress." He held up his hands as if a frame. "The more we drank, the better our pictures became."

"Makes a weird kind of sense."

"My painting still sucked, so I'm probably not that drunk."

Shaking my head, I refilled the cup. "Ah, not drunk, but solidly tipsy." I crossed the room to the bedside. "Here, you should drink this, or you're going to have a headache in the morning."

Matt took the goblet. I crawled onto the bed next to him and went back to my pillow.

"What's your plan?"

"Bethany said that she wanted a gallant person to rescue her and she wanted to swoon into strong arms. I have to figure out a way for that to happen, but it's doable."

Matt kicked his legs up on the bed. He toed off his boots and squirmed until he was leaning on the headboard, his hip right next to my head. He crossed his ankles. It was so reminiscent of how we were before all this happened; it was as if nothing had changed between us. His loose posture highlighted how easy it was for him to return to how we were before my awkward attempts to feel him out, while my whole being trembled from his proximity.

"We could hire bandits."

"We're not hiring bandits."

Matt frowned into the goblet. "I think I want you alive rather than dead. So as much as it pains me, I think we might have to hire bandits."

"Since when am I the responsible one in this friendship? And pains you? Why? Because you think it's deception?"

"Sure. That's it."

"Okay," I said, drawing out the vowel. "Finish that, and lie down. I'll not have you wandering around the castle this inebriated."

Matt laughed, but he did as I said and downed the cup. Which further solidified the fact that he was more on the side of drunk than tipsy. He set the goblet on the nightstand and scrunched down until his head was on the pillow. My heart ached. I was very aware of the scant inches between us, and I longed to reach out, to curl into his side as I'd done a thousand times before. Instead, I stayed still, not wanting to encroach on his space, but the warmth of his body seeped into the sheets and was both a comfort and a torture all along my side.

He clumsily pawed at my face, his fingertips running over my eyes. "Close your eyes," he said on a yawn. "Sleep."

My mouth went dry. "Easier said than done." The words came out as a whispered croak. Matt didn't seem to notice.

"I'm here. You can always sleep when I'm around."

He wasn't wrong. Even when we were boys, we spent more nights together than apart. Since we moved into the castle, it was the longest we'd gone without sharing a bed.

"I do have many kingly things to do tomorrow."

"Don't we all."

With a forced chuckle, I pulled the blanket over the both of us. "You're a mess, Matt. Go to sleep, and we'll talk in the morning."

"That's my line," he said around a yawn. "But okay."

His soft snores were the lullaby I needed. I stared at the canopy for a moment, drumming my fingers against my chest as I allowed my thoughts to quiet, and focused on the deep and even breaths of my best friend. I closed my eyes and fell asleep quickly.

I woke the next morning to a loud knocking. I opened my eyes and immediately shut them against the spears of sharp sunlight penetrating through the shutters. Squinting, I rolled to my side to snark at Matt, but found his space empty. I ran my fingers over the wrinkled sheets, but the heat of him was gone. The only evidence that Matt had even been there was the water goblet on the nightstand and the rumple of the blankets.

A strange feeling of loss pierced through me at his absence.

"Sire," Harlow called through the door. "Rise and shine. We have much to do today."

"Coming," I called as I disentangled from my blankets. Instead of heading to the door, I went through the small servants' quarters attached to my room and into the garderobe. Harlow's agitated knocking continued, but I ignored him as I relieved myself. Once done, I tottered to the door.

"Hold your horses, Harlow."

I opened the door to find Harlow on the other side. And as usual, he appeared as if he'd just sucked all the juice from a lemon.

"Good morning."

Harlow brushed past me into the room, a large amount of fabric draped over his arm. "Today is your first day of petitions, and you must be dressed for the part."

"Petitions?" Running my hands through my hair, I yawned again, my eyes crinkling. The crust of drool near my lip cracked. I ran the sleeve of my nightshirt over my face, earning a potent look of disdain from Harlow.

"We've discussed this, sire," he said, draping the pile of clothes over the foot of the bed. "Once a month the common folk are invited to the castle to petition the king to settle disputes or ask for assistance. It's your first public appearance as ruler of this land. It's an important day."

As he opined, the door to my quarters swung open, and a servant entered carrying a large tub. He sat on the floor next to the fireplace and more servants spilled into the room, carrying buckets filled to the brim with clear water. Within minutes, my fire was stoked to life, the tub was full, and the servants disappeared as quickly as they had come.

"Bathe, sire. I will return shortly to assist you with dressing."

"I can dress myself, Harlow."

He snorted. "Hardly."

"Wait!" He paused at the door. "Are the others going to be there with me?"

"Of course, sire."

"And are they having the royal treatment this morning as well?"

"I've ordered baths and regalia for them all."

Snickering, I shucked my nightshirt. "Excellent. Thank you."

He bowed and left.

The bathwater was cool despite sitting right next to the fire-place. It didn't have the steamy warmth that Matt was able to magic. But it was clear, at least, and the soap the servants left smelled like a deep spice. I scrubbed everything, even behind my ears, and the bottoms of my feet. Once I was satisfied, I stood and stepped out of the tub, wrapping myself in the drying sheet Harlow had left behind.

Shivering in the cool morning air, I had goose-pimply skin as I rifled through the clothes looking for a tunic. Or trousers. Or something vaguely familiar to anything I'd ever worn before. A feeling akin to panic shot through me as I realized that the kingly garb Harlow had brought were robes. And not just robes, but a cape with furs and gold chains and laces and puffed sleeves.

Oh no.

The door swung inward so hard, it smacked against the wall and startled me. I dropped the ermine I had pinched between my fingers as Lila scrambled through the doorway in a tornado of fabric, hair a mess, and ribbons trailing behind her. She turned, leapt at the door, and threw her body against it. The sounds of thuds hitting the other side of the wood echoed in the small space.

"What the fuck, Lila?"

"They're after me."

Alarmed, I clutched the towel tighter around my waist and lunged for the hilt of my sword. Once in my hand, I ran to the door and leaned against it, keeping the threat on the other side.

"Who?" I demanded.

"The maids!"

I blinked in confusion. "The maids? Why are you running from the maids?"

"They're trying to torture me!"

I took in the ribbons and the fabric hanging off both of Lila's arms and the wildness of her hair that looked to be an abandoned hairstyle.

"Are you wearing a dress?"

"Torture!" she yelled. "This is cruel and unusual. I protest!"

Adrenaline left me in a wash, and I slumped against the door. "Lila."

She grabbed a handful of the bright red fabric and shook it in my direction. Her poufy skirt lifted to show off a pair of pale, skinny legs encased in her regular soft calf-high boots.

"A dress! How am I supposed to run in this? And listen to it." She twisted her waist and the fabric swished. "Does this sound quiet to you? Do you think I could sneak up on anyone in this?"

I hid my face behind one hand to hide my grin. Spirits. I thought there was an assassin. Instead, it was a rogue in a red dress.

"Why are you naked?" Lila demanded.

"Because I just took a bath."

A solid knock sounded throughout the room. It was so forceful, I felt the wood vibrate against the back.

"Don't you dare open it. Those maids tried to do something to my hair." She waved her hand at the frizzy rat's nest on the top of her head.

"Like brush it?"

She bristled. "I brush it every night and braid it. That should be plenty!"

"Hold this." Sighing, I handed her my sword.

She took the hilt in her hand and raised the tip

threateningly at the door. The neckline of the dress slipped to show off her sharp collarbone.

"Scared?" I teased.

"No. Just . . . wary."

Another knock.

Stepping around Lila, I grabbed the handle and creaked the door open. Peeking around through the small crack, I spied Matt, and the tightness in my shoulders eased at the sight of him.

He stood in the hallway, surrounded by a gaggle of maids. I could barely see the arms crossed over his chest from the amount of fabric that swathed him. His staff poked through the crook of his elbow. The robes were floor-length and dragged behind him like a train. They were a deep blue with silver trim, and his hair was squashed against his forehead by a truly hideous puffy hat with a magnificent silver plume. He tapped his foot, looking extremely displeased.

"I thought I was clear on the subject of robes."

I couldn't help it. I burst into laughter.

"Oh my spirits," Lila said. "What happened to you?"

"Me?" Matt's voice pitched high. "What happened to you? Is that a dress? And red? I've never seen you in anything other than black, green, or brown."

Lila jabbed her finger in the direction of the three maids huddling together. "It was their idea." One of them squeaked.

"What is going on here?" Harlow appeared from around the corner.

Stifling my chuckles, I managed to regain a semblance of self-control. I scratched the back of my neck, my torso stretching. The maids erupted into giggles themselves, and Lila rolled her eyes. She smacked my stomach muscles. "Put those away, Prince Charming. You'll make them swoon."

"Huh?"

Harlow's face scrunched as if smelling something unpleasant. "Sire, you are naked in the hallway."

Another bout of laughter threatened, because the feathers from Matt's hat had fallen into his face, and Lila's dress was barely hanging on to the angles of her frame, the maids were indeed about to faint, and Harlow . . . Well, Harlow's disapproving expression was the best thing I'd seen all morning.

"It appears," I said, smile stretched so broad across my face that I'm sure I looked borderline deranged, "that we're having difficulty with our apparel."

"I am *not* wearing a dress."

"If she doesn't have to wear a dress," Matt said, pointing at Lila, "then I'm not wearing robes."

I shrugged and the edge of the towel slipped below my navel. "Sorry. I, too, will have to decline the robes."

Harlow choked, his sallow skin deepening to red tinged with purple. "You must reign with a modicum of decorum." He gestured to the three of us standing in the hallway—my nudity, Lila's near nudity, and Matt's beautiful angry face. "This is inappropriate. Borderline scandalous. The rumors will spread like wildfire that the king, the mistress of finances, and the trusted mage were all found in disarray in the hallway."

Lila barked a laugh. Even Matt, who had remained stone-faced throughout the encounter, huffed in amusement. I raised a hand to placate Harlow, and the maids tittered, and okay, I could see his point.

"Harlow, I promise I'm taking this seriously. Really!" I said when he made his lemon face. "But until a few weeks ago, we were peasants. I've never worn a robe, and I don't want to be worrying about tripping on the dais. I think Matt might strangle himself with all that fabric, and that feather is just going to make him sneeze. We don't want him to accidentally set something on fire because he sneezed, do we? And asking Lila to wear a dress will only end in murder. Hopefully not mine, but we can never be too sure."

He sniffed.

"That's a joke," I clarified. "She would not murder me. I'm fairly certain."

Harlow did not look amused.

Okay, time to try that diplomacy I'd heard so much about. "I'll wear my best trousers and tunic, and I'll even wear the cape."

Matt snickered. I stepped on his toes.

"The purple cape with the fur lining?"

"Yes, if that's what I need to do."

He nodded sharply and clapped his hands. "That will do." He turned on his heel and addressed the maids. "Escort the mistress rogue to her quarters and assist her with finding appropriate attire, and send a different outfit to Lord Matt's quarters."

"See?" I said, clapping Harlow hard on the upper arm. "No harm done in allowing people to express themselves how they want."

He grumbled about decorum and tradition, but I ignored him. If breaking tradition meant that Matt and Lila were comfortable, then so be it.

CHAPTER 16

The cape was a bit much, but I endured the swish of fabric as I strode to the throne room. At least I was afforded trousers instead of the robes, though they were soft and tighter than I was accustomed to. Luckily, the cape covered my backside, as I had a growing fear that the trousers might split when I sat on the throne.

Harlow insisted on the deep brown color and the tightly laced white tunic, which would have lasted about a day in my old village. My sword and sturdy brown boots completed my kingly ensemble. As did the gold crown. Somehow Harlow had managed to position it so it smoothed down some of my hair, which had a tendency to stand on end. Not as bad as Matt's cowlick, but close.

I felt like a peacock. A very unprepared peacock. No. A turkey dressed as a peacock. A turkey that might end up on a dinner table because, once everyone saw through the ruse of it being a peacock, they'd want to eat it. Great. Now I was strangely hungry.

Why had the universe chosen me for this?

Rounding a corner, I pushed open the side doors to the throne room and walked across the stone floor to a ribbon of carpet, which stretched the length of the room, from the dais to the doors that led to the outer atrium.

The others were already there. Matt stood to the right of the throne, looking much more like himself in plain tunic and trousers, his staff firmly held in the curl of his hand. The unimpressed downturn of his mouth couldn't hide his ridiculous beautiful face or the magic that emanated from him.

Sionna and Rion stood to the left, radiating intimidation. Rion looked every inch the knight in armor that had been polished to an eye-piercing shine. Sionna had returned to her leather armor, a style close to what she'd worn the entirety of our journey, though this version was newer, cleaner, and more ornate.

Lila stood on the lowest step beneath Sionna and Rion, shrouded in her green hooded cloak. Her hair was completely tucked underneath the hood, and I wondered if in her rebellion she'd refused to brush it.

Bethany was on the step near Matt, harp in hand, wearing a dangerously low-cut dress the color of plums, looking beautiful and poised and charismatic. Though nothing stirred in my middle when I looked at her like it had for Sionna, she would be a wonderful partner to help me rule the kingdom. Yes. Cunning and smart. Diplomatic and charming. She was a good choice to be next on my to-woo list. Maybe too good for me. But definite monarch material.

"You look like gaming pieces," I called as I walked closer. "Or like those markers on the map in the war room. Are we playing a game of strategy?"

They *all* glared. Which was amazing. I rarely managed to

annoy the whole set at once. Chuckling, I stepped onto the carpet.

"All hail King Arek!"

I startled and tripped, clutching the fabric of my tunic over my suddenly pounding heart. "What the spirits?"

"Protocol," Matt said cheerily in retribution, tipping his head in the direction of Harlow, who stood by the door at the back of the hall. "All hail King Arek," he responded in deadpan. He bowed. The others followed suit.

"Okay, let's not do that again."

"It's tradition." Bethany winked. "Or so we're told."

"Well, we're breaking tradition. And starting our own." I recovered and finished my walk to the throne, whacking Lila in the face with my cape as I spun grandly before sitting down on the throne. I wish I'd checked to make sure the blood stains had been scrubbed off. My first order of business after this was to have the whole thing replaced with something less menacing. "You lot are not required to bow in my direction. Ever. I feel like we know each other too well for that."

Bethany snorted. "A little too well," she said, lips quirking. "For example, I shouldn't know about your little mole that sits right above—"

"Okay, that's uncalled for." Witty too. She would be able to match me quip for quip. Yes. A good plan. I glanced at Matt, and the little smirk he wore dropped away. Yep. An . . . excellent plan.

"Fired, you're all fired." I rolled back my shoulders. "Now, serious faces on. Pretend we know what we're doing and have everything in control." I placed my arms on the rests of both sides of the chair and faced the large empty room. "Harlow, you may allow the petitioners to enter."

Harlow threw open the doors.

I don't know what I expected. But the lone butterfly that entered, fluttered around a bit, then left was . . . not it.

"Um . . . Are the people invisible?"

Harlow stuck his head out the door and looked around. "There are no petitioners, sire."

"Why?"

"I believe they did not come."

"Thanks for the observation. I can see that they did not come. My question is why."

"Ha!" Lila pointed her finger at Harlow. "You made me almost wear a dress for nothing."

"Harlow," Sionna said calmly, "did petitioners visit during the previous reign?"

"Yes. For several years, until—until . . . they became too frightened," he said with a shake of his head.

"That makes sense," Matt muttered.

"How would they know to show up today?" she continued. "Did we alert them?"

Harlow swallowed, his throat bobbing. "It's . . . tradition."

A headache bloomed behind my eyes, and I rubbed my forehead. "Tradition," I said. "I'm guessing we didn't actually put it out there that petitioners were welcome to return to the castle on this specific day, did we?"

"The fifth day of the third week of the month has always been—"

"When was the last time a petitioner braved a visit to the castle?"

Harlow's forehead crinkled. "Around six years ago, sire."

"And what happened?"

"They were eaten by the moat monster."

"Are you serious?" I threw up my hands. "The last petitioner was eaten by the *moat monster*, and we're wondering why no one showed up today?"

"It's tradition."

Frustrated, I stood. "We're making our own tradition. We dressed in these ridiculous clothes," I said, grabbing a handful of the purple cape. "We even took *baths*. We are meeting people today."

"Arek—"

"Follow me. If they won't come to us, then we'll go to them."

"Sire!"

"Field trip!" Lila yelled.

I didn't look behind me to check that everyone followed, because I was certain they would. I could feel them right there, protecting me as they had for the past nine months. We might be dressed like chess pieces, but we were still that ragtag group of assholes who had taken on the darkest and vilest regime in five lifetimes and lived to tell the tale.

"Bethany," I said as we exited the castle and walked through the keep toward the outer wall with the drawbridge beyond. The heavy wooden doors were thrown open, and the portcullis was raised, and the drawbridge stretched across the deep moat, which lay between the castle wall and the path that led to the village. "Magnify my decree."

"Oh, I love it when you give commands." She winked.

"Bethany."

"On it." She lifted her harp and plucked on the strings. The air reverberated with her magic and brought life to my words.

"Citizens of the kingdom of Ere in the realm of Chickpea," I called. "King Arek—"

"The Kind," Sionna said, dark eyes shining as she elbowed me in the side.

"The Kind," I added, rolling my eyes. "Decrees that the fifth day of the third week of the month is a day of petitions. Visitors are welcome to the castle to petition the king and his council regarding any matter and may request the resolution of disputes. The castle will be open until sunset today." I looked over my shoulder at the group. "Sound good?"

"Perfect," Matt said. Rion nodded, his chain mail clinking together.

"Okay, Bethany, send it out."

I would never get used to Bethany's power, or maybe I would if she did end up as my soul mate, but the sound of my voice echoing across the countryside—carried on the wings of song and magic—made me shiver.

"Now what?" Matt asked.

"We wait."

Gathered around the end of the drawbridge, we stood there like overdressed jerks. I rubbed the back of my calf with the toe of my boot, while using Matt's shoulder for leverage.

"How long do we wait?" Rion whispered.

"A bit," I said with all the confidence of someone who had no idea what they were doing. I hadn't the foggiest if anyone would dare approach the castle. "We need to give them time."

Other than being in the castle gardens, I hadn't been beyond the walls since we'd snuck in, and the view from the edge of the drawbridge was quite nice. The leaves had changed, and the breeze was stiff and wonderfully cool on my overheated skin. Maybe it was my imagination, but the overall atmosphere seemed lighter than it had been under Barthly's reign. The red and gold leaves glowed in the sunlight, the grass was greener, the sky bluer, and even the moat—which had been dark as pitch when we crossed it last—had lightened from black to murky brown. Maybe Barthly's death had brought in an era of renewal. Maybe his magic had been lifted and that was reflected in the changes of the earth and the sky.

Hands on my hips, I breathed deep.

"This isn't so bad," I said. "It's nice out here."

Lila crouched and placed her pale hand on the soil, digging her fingers in the earth. "It's wonderful."

Matt tilted his head back, and the sunlight caressed his features, highlighting the sharpness of his cheekbones and the faded freckles across the bridge of his nose.

Bethany tugged a lock of my hair. "Your hair is popping off in this light. It's the reddest I've ever seen."

"Because it's washed."

I squirmed as Bethany scratched her nails along my scalp, her knuckles knocking against my crown.

"Hallo?" a distant voice called.

I batted at Bethany's hand and faced the path. Across the drawbridge stood a small gathering of people, led by a man dressed in a plain tunic and a pair of work trousers. He clutched a straw hat in his hands, which he fidgeted with as he warily approached.

"Hello," I called back. "Welcome."

"Are you"—he fumbled forward—"King Arek? Sire?"

"Yes. I am King Arek."

His face contorted, eyebrows raising. "But you're so young, if you excuse my saying so."

"Not at all. Yes. I am young, but I defeated Barthly, uh, I mean, the Vile One, with my council here." I gestured behind me. "Which makes me the rightful ruler of this kingdom."

"You're all quite young."

"That, we are," Lila confirmed.

"She's a fae."

"Half."

"And he's a mage?"

"Full mage, yes."

Matt rolled his eyes.

"How do we know you're not like him?" A woman's voice erupted from the group. "We've heard the rumors, but you have a bard. You could be manipulating us."

"Yes, I have a bard, but she's entirely truthful. We're nice people. Well, we try to be. We're not perfect, but we're not evil. We're good, most of the time."

"Bang-up job you're doing on the oration here," Matt muttered. "Might as well tell them we'll only murder half of them."

"You're not helping," I whispered harshly. I pinched his arm. He stepped on my foot.

The delegate for the group inched forward. The heels of his boots thudded on the bridge. "And you'll allow us into the castle?"

"Yes. Just as my declaration . . . declared. I've been told it's tradition to allow the people of this kingdom to petition their king."

At my words, the tense line of his shoulders eased. He scratched his beard. "It is tradition. Or it was, before my time."

Before his time? The guy looked like an old glove. How was he younger than forty? Wow. Times have been hard.

"Well, it's back. And if you all would like to come inside, we have a very nice throne room where we can do the petitioning."

The man took another step on the bridge. He looked over his shoulder, nodded to the group behind him, then turned to face me. "Thank you, King Arek. I look forward to—"

A large white tentacle erupted from the moat, uncurled, wrapped around the man, and yanked him off the bridge and into the murky water below before any of us could blink.

"What the fuck?" Matt yelled. "What the fuck?"

"Henry!" someone shouted. "Henry!"

"Ah, crap." I pulled my magic sword from my scabbard, then ran to the middle of the bridge, tossing my crown off in the process. The tentacle appeared, the man in its grasp, screaming and soaked. I couldn't see what it was attached to, other than a bulbous, white fleshy membrane just beneath the waterline, but I knew I couldn't stand there and watch a peasant who had trusted me get eaten by the moat monster.

Taking a few steps back, I took a breath.

"Arek! Don't!"

I didn't listen. Sword raised, I ran to the edge and jumped.

Chapter 17

I knew the cape was a bad idea.

The icy chill of the water was a slap when it hit my skin. It stole my breath and my muscles clenched. The cape's chain snapped hard across my throat in a chokehold as the heavy fabric dragged behind me in the water. Thankfully, it broke after a few hard tugs, otherwise my ill-advised leap would've led to my ill-advised death.

Beneath the surface, the water was murkier than it had looked from the bridge, but even through squinted eyes, I was able to behold the moat monster in all its terrifying glory. Face-to-face with it, I realized two things. One, it looked like a giant version of the creature depicted in a framed painting in the castle with a caption that read: *Octopus destroys sailing vessel.* Second, I realized that jumping into the water was probably an impulsive and questionable decision.

But as I was right in front of the octopus, I took a chance and thrust my sword in its general direction. Sound rippled through the water as it screeched. Yes! I hit something. Point for me! Except, that seemed to garner its attention, and despite my attempt to swim away, I, too, found myself wrapped in a fleshy appendage.

It yanked me upward. Breaking the surface, I heaved a breath, though there was almost no room for my rib cage to expand, and my inhale sounded more like a strangled yelp. Its tentacle squeezed me so hard, my bones creaked.

"Arek!" That was Sionna's voice.

"What were you thinking?" And that was Matt.

"What?" I yelled back. I swept my arm over my eyes, brushing my wet hair and the streams of water out of my face. "Don't like my plan?"

"Go for the arms!"

"Hold on!"

"Lila!"

"On it."

The octopus waved its tentacles, which—aside from making me extremely nauseated—put me in close range to the poor peasant named Henry, who looked as panicked as I felt. Once he was in reach, I stabbed my sword in the general direction of the arm that held him. The blade sunk deep into the flesh, and blue blood erupted in a spray from the wound. Wrenching my sword free, I struck again and watched in relief as the tentacle loosened its grip on poor Henry.

"When it releases you," I called as loudly as I could with the breath being squeezed from my body, "drop into the water and swim to the other side of the bridge."

Henry emitted a strangled sort of shout that I took as confirmation of the plan.

"Ready yourself." Using both hands, I yanked my sword from the wriggling arm.

But a second before I could strike, it whipped me around to the other side, my head grazing sickeningly close to the castle's outer wall. Grunting, I pushed my hand into the spongy flesh, trying to pry it off. It didn't work.

"A little help!" I yelled.

An arrow rocketed from the shore and struck the creature in the part of its head that had emerged from the water. Another embedded in a tentacle. I turned my head to see that Sionna had commandeered a bow and arrow from one of the villagers. Handy.

Roaring in pain, the monster rocketed me back within reach of Henry. Instead of spearing the tentacle, I raised my sword above my head, and used all my strength to hack at the arm. The newly sharpened edge of my sword—because I had learned my lesson, thank you very much—sliced through the appendage. Henry dropped like a stone into the water, disappearing into a frothy wave of ink. After a moment, I spied his head popping above the surface.

Okay, one problem down. Now, on to the second, which was that my stomach was becoming too well acquainted with my spine. I cried out as the tentacle around me tightened further, and the spectators on the beach responded in kind. Once Henry was out of harm and arm's way, I took stock of the situation. The monster had fully emerged from the moat, sitting atop a pile of rocks, all eight limbs flapping in apparent chaos. Lila jumped onto one of the waving tentacles, light-footed as she was, and ran up the length until she skidded across the globular head. Dagger in hand, she stabbed away at the corpulent mound, blue blood squirting in every direction.

Great. Vomit had now become a real possibility. Among the motion, the smell, and the compression, I was on the verge of sensory overload.

On the shore, Bethany used her harp to subdue the crowd and charm them away from the creature as Rion pulled Henry from the water. Sionna drew her sword and fought something in the short grass, but from my position that was worsening, I couldn't see what made her crouch into her warrior stance, her sword stained with the same inky blood as my own. Matt glowed with power, his staff in his hands—the jewel at the tip sparking with intensity that released in magical blasts at the creature.

"Arek!" Lila yelled. "Free yourself! Or you'll be crushed. Or eaten!"

Right. Truer words had never been spoken.

The monster was not holding me at an ideal angle for me to hack my way to freedom. My grip on my sword weakened with each second, my bare hands sliding along the blood-slick hilt. Strength fleeing, I opted to slice my way free. But as the edges of my vision darkened, and I struggled for each breath, I realized I wasn't going to get free on my own.

On the shore, Rion, Sionna, and Matt were locked in a battle with a swarm of smaller octopi creatures, which had crawled out of the moat and now threatened to overwhelm them. *There were baby monsters! How cute? No. Wait. Definitely not cute.* Not cute at all as they viciously suckered to Rion's armor, twined around Matt's legs, and covered Sionna with inky black viscous fluid.

Bethany's charms didn't work on magical creatures; we'd learned that with the pixie, and she stayed away from the battle, protecting the group of peasants.

"Arek!" Lila yelled. She balanced on a writhing tentacle. "I'm coming." She took a step, but Momma Monster didn't allow her far. Another tentacle whipped toward her. Lila jumped over it but caught the edge of her foot and tumbled into the water. She barely made a splash, but she didn't resurface.

Oh shit. Okay. This was bad. My innards were going to become my "outtards" if I didn't do something. Lila was in the moat. The others were swarmed. I was going to have a short reign if I didn't get out of this and help my friends.

With the last of my strength, I yelled, "Matt!"

He snapped his head up from where the little spongy bastards were climbing up his legs. His eyes went wide, and his face drained of color. Driving the end of his staff into a mini monster head, he shook it off before wedging the wooden tip of his staff under another to try and pry it from his body. As its tentacles released, his staff flung sideways and knocked into Rion's chest plate with a loud clang.

The creatures recoiled. The two that clung to Rion slithered to the ground. Even the momma's grip loosened slightly.

Matt paused, realization dawning. He lunged for Rion's sword, pulling it from Rion's grip. He smacked the flat of the blade against the hard plate on Rion's chest. Another discordant bang. Another screech and wriggle from the creatures.

Sound.

They were vulnerable to sound.

"Sound!" I shouted. "Bethany!"

That was all they needed. Bethany ran to Matt's side, strumming her harp. The blue jewel of Matt's staff glowed, and he spoke words I didn't understand, and I could barely hear over the sudden gathering of power. The wind picked up speed, and the atmosphere compressed. Matt slammed his staff to the ground, and a harsh clang emanated, which was made all the louder by Bethany's harp.

I'd never heard anything as deafening before. I could only liken the sound to when rocks broke off the nearby mountains and spilled downward in an avalanche.

I'm pretty sure it caused some serious hearing damage, but it worked. Thank fuck, it worked. The octopus writhed. Blood spurted from the wounds Lila and I had inflicted in an exceptionally gross display. Gross enough that maybe Bethany would vomit, then swoon into my arms. I'd be the hero, surviving the constrictive tentacle of the moat monster. But only if I did survive.

The noise continued, and finally, *finally*, its grip loosened, and it let me go. I dropped to the water. My feet hit first, and then I went straight under. Going from being barely able to breathe to not at all was traumatic, but not being able to see due to the thick ink underwater brought a whole other level of fear. The water was needles against my skin, frigid on my face and hands.

I fought what I thought was my way upward but was making almost no progress, and my lungs were starting to burn. Wonderful. I wasn't going to die at the hands of a monster. I was going to drown. King Arek the Kind, done in by his need for air.

An otherworldly creature appeared in front of me, clouds of blond hair swirling around her. Bright eyes peered at me through the darkness as she swam to my side, ducking under my arm and propelling us upward.

We broke the surface.

"You okay there, King Arek the Impulsive?"

I coughed and my chest heaved as Lila tugged me toward the shore. "Oh, thank the spirits, it's you. I couldn't handle a mermaid today."

She snorted. "This is foul. I did not sign up for this, by the way."

"Agreed. Agreed so much." I pushed my water-and-ink-soaked hair out of my face. "Ugh. This is a new level of vile." By Lila's expression, I must have looked like a ghoul.

"Just don't vomit."

Bobbing in the water, we paddled our way to the shore as the octopus thrashed and cried nearby, wriggling in pain from the assault of sound emanating from Matt and Bethany. Gradually, its thrashing slowed, and its limbs submerged in its death throes.

Upon seeing us in the water, Sionna abandoned her chore of stabbing the smaller monsters and ran to the edge of the shore. She waded in and grabbed my arm, yanking me upward, until my feet were back on solid ground. Sliding along the wet grass, I made it a few steps before my legs collapsed from under me. I rolled to my back and stared at the blue, cloudless sky.

"Arek!"

Matt lowered his staff, and it was all the opening that the octopus needed. In one last desperate assault, it swung a tentacle and smacked Matt across the torso.

The force of the blow flung Matt backward. His surprised cry rent the air as he flew, ceasing abruptly when he collided with the lone tree along the village path. A sickening crack echoed loudly among the gasps and the yells of the onlookers as Matt's body went limp.

Jumping to my feet, I staggered to where he lay unmoving, pushing past all who stood between me and him, my body shaking with fear. My heart stopped. My breath stopped. My brain stopped. The only things about me that carried on were my feet and the blood that oozed from my ears.

"Matt!" I yelled, my own voice muddled. "Matt!"

He groaned.

Relief washed over me as he twitched, rolled to his stomach, then pushed himself to standing. Miraculously, he'd held on to his staff, and he leaned hard on it.

"Ouch," he said, doubled over, clutching his stomach. He lurched toward me.

"Oh, thank the spirits, you're alive."

He smiled, tight-lipped, face pale as a sheet.

I grabbed his arm to steady him, though I needed steadying myself. My knees were weak with exhaustion and with the ebb of panic.

"Are you okay?"

He didn't answer.

"Matt?"

He raised his shaking hand and wiped the edge of his mouth, smearing blood across his cheek. The bright red stood stark against the paleness of his skin.

We both stared at the blood. "Matt?" My voice was small, even in the stillness between us.

He met my gaze and gave me a wobbly smile; then his eyes rolled backward and he swooned, right into my arms.

Chapter 18

I lowered us both on the ground, Matt's head pillowed on my forearm, the rest of him cradled close to my chest. My knees dug into the soft earth. The smear of blood streaked like a comet across his cheek. More stained the inside of his lips, and I hoped he'd merely bitten his tongue instead of the alternative. The alternative meant crushed lungs, or pierced organs. The alternative was snapped ribs, or a bruised heart. The alternative was death, and I couldn't live with that.

"Matt?" I tapped his cheek. His head lolled; the dark cowlick of his hair was almost indistinguishable from the ink stains on my once-pristine white shirt. "Matt?" I cupped his cheek with my cold and water-wrinkled fingers. His skin was warm on my palm, his breath hot on the pad of my thumb. "Come on, Matt. Wake up."

He didn't. His eyes remained stubbornly closed. Another small stream of blood trickled from the corner of his lips. A hard lump formed in my throat. My eyes pricked with tears. Dread settled like a stone low in my belly. "Matt, *please.*"

No response.

"Help," I said, barely a sound. I turned my head to where the others stood a few feet off. "Help!" I yelled, my voice surged upward, high and rattled. "He needs help! Please! Is anyone a healer? Anyone?"

I turned back to him, rested my hand on his chest as people rushed forward, chittering with high, panicked voices, their feet pounding on the earth. My hand lifted with his breaths and fell; though he wheezed and his breaths were unsteady, at least he breathed.

"Sire," someone said tentatively. I don't know who, and I ignored them. My eyes locked on Matt's slack face, urging him to wake, wishing for any sign that he would stir. I needed him to be okay. I needed him to wake up and smirk and provide biting commentary, tease me for worrying so much over him, push me away and call me a doofus. Please be all right. Please be all right. Please. Please. Please. *Sire.*

"Arek!"

Snapping my head up, I spied Sionna standing over me with Bethany, and another woman I didn't know.

"She's the town healer. Let her look."

"Yes," I croaked. "Yes. Please."

"Lower him, please, sire. I can gauge him much better if he's laid flat."

With trembling hands, I rested him on the ground and sat back on my heels. Someone placed a hand on my shoulder as the healer worked, and I craned my neck to find Rion standing behind me. His grip tightened. Lila stood next to him, clutching a heavy coat, her teeth chattering.

Right. I was freezing. My trembling was a mixture of exhaustion, fear, and being chilled from the moat. I wrapped my arms around my quaking frame to stop the shaking and to keep myself from falling to pieces.

The healer knelt next to Matt and splayed her fingers over him, hovering an inch above the rumpled fabric of his best clothes. She whispered words, and a glow radiated along her arms, gathered beneath her palms in bright spots of golden light. She moved them along the length of Matt's torso. His breath hitched, and my fists clenched. She then held her hands on either side of Matt's head and pressed the tips of her fingers to his temples. The glow swept over his skin, and he appeared lit up from the inside before the light disappeared beneath his clothes. Bethany watched with interest over her shoulder, eyebrows drawn, mouth pressed flat.

Bethany. I forgot about Bethany. This would've been a perfect situation to have her swoon into my arms after playing the dashing hero. There was gore, which she was notorious for not being able to handle, and there was death-defying heroics. I had almost died, twice, but emerged victorious. Maybe. I wasn't sure. What happened to the monster? Regardless, I had missed my chance, and well, I really didn't care. I couldn't care. Because Matt . . . Matt . . .

"He'll be fine."

"The blood?"

She touched a single finger to Matt's lip, the flesh dimpling. "It's from a wound on his tongue. Nothing serious. It's already closed."

The crowd released a collective breath. I pitched to the side, weak with relief, falling from my knees to sitting.

"He's deeply bruised and will be tender for several days."

I bowed my head and ran my hand over my eyes. I had to regain my composure. I had to face the group. I had to give orders and explanations. I had to rule. "Let's get him to the castle," I said, staring where Matt's hand rested in the grass. "We'll need a litter and—"

"Hey." Lila crouched next to me. She nudged my shoulder. "Look up."

Swallowing, I took a calming breath and peered upward at the crowd around me. Except, they weren't standing around me anymore. They ... knelt.

"What's happening?"

"I think they might be showing you respect." She shrugged.

"Oh." I licked my lips; they tasted like moat. I shuddered. "I think I should stand."

"Can you?"

"I don't know."

Rion gripped my arm and between him and Lila, I managed my feet. My back ached. Pain popped along the entire length of my body, but I addressed the crowd. "Please, don't do that." I held out my hands. "Seriously. I'm too tired for formality."

"You jumped into the moat after my partner." A huge burly gentleman detached himself from the group. "You saved him."

"I really didn't."

Lila nudged me again. "Take the compliment, asshole."

"I mean. Anyone would have."

Henry's partner shook his head. "No, they wouldn't have." He glanced at Matt. "And they wouldn't have been so concerned about their friend."

The urge to step between Matt and the crowd, to shield him from their gaze, was intense, but I stifled it. I wasn't sure I could manage it anyway without Rion's assistance. "Matt's my mage and my best friend. I wouldn't be here without him. The others here too. Bethany, Lila, Rion, and Sionna—they are the people who have stuck with me through everything. They're the reason we were able to defeat the Vile One." Speaking of, where the fuck had I dropped my sword?

"Then we are grateful it was you and your group of friends who freed us from his reign."

I resisted the urge to wave him off and say something flippant. But Matt was unconscious on the ground, and Rion held the lion's share of my weight. And yeah, I had literally jumped into a moat to save someone from a horrifying tentacle monster. This wasn't the time for flippancy and jokes. This was serious.

"Thank you. We'll do our best to live up to your trust."

He bowed his head. "Thank you, King Arek the Kind."

Oh *spirits.*

Before I had a chance to ruin the moment, a castle servant appeared carrying a litter. Among Sionna, Bethany, and the healer—they moved Matt carefully from the ground to the fabric stretched tight between two long poles. Henry's partner moved between the poles at the back, and another strong-looking fellow from the crowd grabbed the front. Between the two of them, they lifted Matt and moved steadily toward the castle.

Harlow directed them across the drawbridge—the healer, Sionna, and Bethany following closely behind. I watched them before attempting to move myself, as I wasn't sure my feet were attached to my body. Matt's name was an underlying drumbeat in my head, but the healer said he'd be okay. I held on to that. Held on to it so tightly, it was the only thing keeping me standing.

Lila and Rion lent me their support, and the three of us

stumbled slowly across the yard. Lila carried Matt's staff. We found my sword in a patch of grass.

"I see you had it sharpened," Rion said with approval.

"I learn." The blade was coated in viscous black. It reeked. Bile crawled up my throat.

The carcass of the moat monster sat half-submerged in the water, its babies strewn all around. The sight made me slightly sad, but then I remembered it tried to eat me, and all empathy drained out of me.

"What are we going to do with that?"

"I don't think we need to worry about it," Rion said.

The townsfolk were already picking up the smaller carcasses and tossing them into a cart. Another set of townspeople had looped a rope around a few of the tentacles that had flopped out of the water and started to pull.

"Nice," I said. "By the way, once we get out of eyesight, I'm passing out."

Rion's grip around my waist tightened. "Noted."

True to my word, as soon as we were through the open portcullis and around the corner, I gave in to the darkness lingering on the edges of my vision and swooned into Rion's arms.

Chapter 19

I wasn't allowed to visit Matt.

Apparently, inhaling cold moat water and octopus ink and then standing around in soaked clothes could make someone unwell. I developed a horrendous cough, which on the surface wasn't so bad, but the fact that I'd been wrapped in blankets and confined to my quarters was horrible. The cough left my throat raw and made my sore ribs ache. The healer wasn't sure if I was contagious, and she didn't want to risk Matt developing a similar cough with the state of his injuries.

I'd been given tea to drink to relieve the symptoms, but it didn't relieve my irritability.

I was on day three of my confinement, and though I'd been assured that Matt had awoken and was well enough to threaten to turn everyone into toads, my skin itched to talk to him. I hadn't seen him since he'd been carried away, limp and bloody, on the litter. I didn't like that it was the last picture of him in my head.

In my boredom, I half-heartedly flipped through the princess's journal. I'd come to the stunning conclusion that swooning was too dangerous. Bethany wanted someone to save her, but she'd done the saving during the moat-monster situation.

She'd protected the townspeople and amplified Matt's magic enough to help kill the creature. Matt was the one who had done the swooning, right into my arms in a moment that was a strange mixture of my deepest hopes and worst nightmares.

Logically, I knew I needed to continue with the wooing plan, but my heart said otherwise. Seeing Matt injured brought more clarity to the fact that it would always be him. No matter what happened, he would be the person who mattered the most. But my feelings didn't change the fact that I needed to find someone else or bad things would happen, so regretfully, I continued my research.

Skimming the pages of the journal, I found a passage that might be helpful.

She pretended not to know how to dance. I saw through her ruse. All noblewomen learned to dance at early ages to avoid committing a social faux pas at a royal function. But I promised to teach her, to show her the steps to the traditional dances. We met in the stable, the smell of fresh hay thick in the air, as thick as the tension between us. At first, I taught her how to stand, my hands skirting her waist, running along her arms to position them, correcting her posture, and supporting her as we moved. My body pressed along her back as we danced, the pants of my breath on the back of her neck. I kept time in a soft voice, 1-2-3, 1-2-3, one hand splayed along her front, beneath the tight lift of her bodice, the other grasping her elbow. Her ploy didn't last long, and soon she turned quickly in my arms and passionately slammed me against the wall of the stable. She kissed me like she couldn't breathe without my mouth pressed to hers.

I coughed and set the journal aside. The pulse of my blood ticked up and I couldn't have that, not with the sweat already tickling my temples from the tightness of the blankets.

A knock sounded on my door.

"What?" I sounded like a strangled, panicked goose.

"Arek?"

Sighing, I shifted the blankets and sunk into the softness of the mattress, tucking the journal underneath my pillow.

"Sionna? Come in."

She entered, her steps quiet, and she softly closed the door behind her. There was already a chair positioned at my bedside from when the others had visited. Sionna didn't hesitate to perch on the edge.

"How are you doing?"

"I'm fine," I said, waving away her concern, then promptly stifling a traitorous cough. "Seriously. I'm good. Another day, and I'll be back on my feet."

"That's good to hear."

"How's Matt?"

"Sore," Sionna said, but she smiled to reassure me. "Sleeping most of the day, thanks to the potions the healer made for him. But he's doing okay."

I breathed a sigh of relief. "So, not dead, then?"

"No, not dead." She smiled and brushed a wave of dark hair behind her shoulder. "And neither are you, despite leaping off a bridge at a monster."

I shrugged. "I just beat the rest of you to it."

"The townspeople will be glad to hear you're doing well. They've been worried."

"Probably because they want petition day to be rescheduled as soon as possible."

Sionna rolled her eyes. "Not the only reason. They're calling you 'King Arek the Brave.'"

"Thank the spirits! That's so much better than 'King Arek the Kind.'"

She shook her head. "I liked 'King Arek the Kind.' There is strength in kindness."

"There's strength in bravery, too."

"Well, there is also quite a large faction that are referring to you as 'King Arek the Young.'"

"Well, that's not a good one either. I'll have to get that one changed by living forever."

Sionna laughed and placed a delicate hand over her mouth.

"How's Meredith?"

Sionna sighed like the winter, dreamy and hushed. "She's wonderful. I . . . really like her."

Beaming, I reached out and patted her hand that rested on the bed. "I'm so happy for you."

"Really?"

"Of course, why wouldn't I be?"

"I thought you might be . . ." She trailed off and ducked her head.

Oh no. Oh *no.* It appeared that Sionna had noticed a few of my inappropriate boners when it came to her. Um . . . maybe she wasn't as unobservant in that regard as I had hoped. Well, no worries now. "What? Jealous? Of you or of Meredith? Because I have to say—"

She swatted my leg.

I laughed. "No, I'm very happy for you." A blush spread across my cheeks. "I was a village boy who'd never met anyone like you; of course I developed a schoolboy crush when we first met."

Her face scrunched.

"What?" I asked.

"You had a crush on me?"

"Yes. For a little bit. Not any longer. Wait? What were you referring to?"

"Uh . . ."

"Sionna? What did you mean?"

Squirming on the chair, she wouldn't meet my gaze. "Just that I'd found someone, and you . . . have not? That you are . . . alone."

"You think I'm lonely?"

"No!"

"Then what?" My insides went cold. "Have you talked to Matt?"

"Have *you* talked to Matt?" she asked cautiously.

I pointed at her. "He spilled, didn't he? About the magical soul mate law?"

She went still. "What magical soul mate law?"

Oh crap. "Nothing." What the spirits was she referring to? "What are you talking about?"

"What are *you* talking about? What magical soul mate law?"

"Is there an echo in here?" I shot back. "Why would I be upset about you and Meredith?"

She opened her mouth, then shut it.

We reached a stalemate where we stared at each other in confusion, but neither of us spoke. She cocked her head. I lifted my chin and crossed my arms. She leaned back in her chair and mirrored my pose.

After a moment of intense gazing into each other's eyes, I had to look away. "Sionna—"

"Magical soul mate law," she said, her tone brokering no room for argument. "Explain."

Well, what was the point of being king if I couldn't flex? "No."

She raised an eyebrow. "Arek—"

"I'm the king. I'm saying, drop it." I licked my lips. "Unless you want to explain what you were talking about?"

She narrowed her eyes. "Oh, look at the sun. I must go. I have new recruits to train." She stood and headed for the door.

New recruits? Huh? "Hold on, Sionna. Wait!" I sat up quickly, too quickly, and the cough I'd been holding back broke forth, tearing up my throat. Doubling over, I grasped for the cup of tea on my nightstand. She took it from my hand before I dropped it, and I flopped back on the pillows until the fit subsided. Once I was able to breathe, she wrapped my hand around the cup.

"Drink, Arek."

It had gone cold, but it soothed my throat as it went down. After a few gulps, I set the cup on the table.

"Recruits?"

"No one has told you?"

I shook my head, not trusting that I wouldn't erupt into coughs again.

"After your daring heroics, about a dozen people showed up at the gate the next day, asking to join our military. More came the following day. And more arrived today. They've been given quarters, their first stipend, and we've started training." Sionna beamed. "Rion is with them now, outfitting them with clothes, uniforms, weapons, and supplies."

"Wow. Really?"

She nodded enthusiastically, brown eyes shining. "We both agree they will begin as castle guards, to protect our reckless king."

"I am not reckless."

"Yes, you are, slayer of monsters."

"Matt and Bethany killed it. I only cut off a few of its arms."
She patted my head and smoothed the red riot of my bedhead.

"If you say so." She dropped her hand to my shoulder and
squeezed. "I need to go, but you should visit Matt."

I gestured at myself encased in blankets. "I'm not allowed.
I've been told to stay here."

She scrunched her nose. "I thought you were the king."

Closing the door softly, she left.

What had she meant about Matt? Had he said something to
her that would make her think I wouldn't approve of her relationship? Why wouldn't I? Meredith was cute. Sionna liked
her, and she made Sionna happy. That was enough for me.

I fell asleep thinking about it and woke hours later with
the sun on its way over the horizon. I'd missed lunch, and the
servant attending me had left it nearby on the table under a
polished dome. I wasn't hungry, but I was restless.

Sionna was right. I was the king. I could make my own
decisions.

Standing wasn't too difficult. Dressing was near torture
and left me winded. Instead of donning boots, I shoved my feet
into my slippers. I forwent the crown but grabbed a thick cloak
and wrapped it around my shoulders and pulled the hood up
to shroud my face.

Creaking the door open, I slipped out and crept down the
hallway. Once into the main residential wing, I realized I had
no clue which of the rooms belonged to Matt. We'd been living
in the castle for nearly a month, and I'd never seen it, and that
said more about me than I wanted it to.

Okay. I knew Matt. I knew the others. Based on the doors that dotted the hallway on either side of me, I should be able to figure out which was his. Rion's wouldn't be here, because he wanted to be in the knights' quarters, which were in another section of the castle. Lila wouldn't be here either, as she would be somewhere with plenty of light and windows. Bethany's would be the grandest. Sionna's would be strategic, so that would leave Matt's to be the . . . I paused in front of a humble door, set in the middle of the hallway.

I bit my lip. Oh, what the hells? I pushed the door open.

The room was tiny compared to my own. The bed easily took up most of the space, and a large dresser took the rest. Matt's staff was propped next to his bed, where he lay, stretched out in a nap. A chair was pulled next to his side, and there was a wad of bandages and a pot of salve on a small table nearby.

Closing the door behind me as softly as possible, I skipped the chair and instead settled on the edge of the mattress. Matt's dark hair fell into his face and curled around the shell of his ears. I brushed a piece that had slanted across his eyelashes to a spot that wouldn't annoy him when he awoke. He was wrapped in bandages from the top of his trousers to under his arms, where splotches of yellow and blue and even darker purple peeked out.

"Fuck, Matt," I breathed. "They didn't tell me you were this bruised."

He stirred, his eyes opening to slits. "You don't look suspicious at all."

Of course. I threw back the hood. "Better?"

He nodded. "I told them not to," he slurred.

"Why?"

"Didn't want you running out of your bed in the cold."

His words ran together, the first sliding right into the next, an effect of his drowsiness or the potions. But I understood him, and I rolled my eyes, though his own had fluttered shut again.

"Well, I wouldn't have." Lie. I would've been right here, shivering, and complaining, but right here.

"Liar."

Damn. He was good.

"Well, I'm here now, and there is this sliver of the bed that is unoccupied by your gangly body, and look, there are blankets and pillows and everything I need to be warm and take a nap."

"Feel free." He lifted his hand. It wobbled as if he had no bones, but his gesture was clear. He offered, and if he didn't feel awkward, then I wouldn't either.

I kicked my feet onto the bed and tossed my slippers. I tucked my feet under the blanket and grabbed the other that was folded at the end of the bed. I covered us both and snuggled next to him. His bed was cooler than my own, but Matt's skin was sleep-warm, and his breathing was even and deep, and though I'd woken only a few minutes before, I was ready to nod off again. Weeks of not sleeping well caught up with me in a moment.

"I'm sorry you're hurt." I didn't dare touch him or curl into him like I wanted, like we'd done so many times. "Thank you for saving me."

His mouth ticked lazily up at the corner. "You jumped off a bridge."

"I did."

"Don't do that again."

"I won't."

"Liar."

I made a noise through my nose, ready to defend myself, but all pretense of affront I mustered melted away when he frowned, and his forehead crinkled.

"Don't make me laugh," he gasped.

"I didn't say anything."

"You thought it."

"I did."

He huffed, then grimaced.

"Go back to sleep. I didn't mean to wake you."

Matt did not like to be ordered, but it was a testament to the intensity of his pain that he listened to me for once. He exhaled, and within one breath and the next, his features eased, and he fell into sleep.

I placed my head on the pillow next to his and watched him—his horrid, wonderful face, and his wild hair, and the freckles on his nose, and that one mole on the side of his neck, and that scar on his chin from when we'd played swords with hayforks and I accidentally caught him with one of the prongs.

We'd been through some frightening things, but seeing Matt thrown like a rock from a catapult had been the worst so far. Worse than the innkeeper's amorous son. Worse than the pixie who wanted to feed off his magic. Worse than the Vile One's followers who threatened us with knives and swords and poison and birds and dogs. Worse than the bullies in the village and the wizard who had promised Matt freedom and power and everything else he'd wanted on the flimsy premise of prophecy. Worse than Matt saying he didn't love me.

Watching him as the sun sank below the horizon, I fell asleep, and the image of him looking like death was replaced by one of him with rosy cheeks and parted lips, sleeping through the afternoon, whole and alive and beautiful. It was the best sleep I'd had in weeks.

CHAPTER 20

"**R**ion, then?"

Matt was more awake than he had been in days. Since the night I'd slipped out of my room, I'd visited often, staying as long as I could, eating meals with him, reading to him from books, and even neglecting a few of my kingly duties. It was the most we'd been together since Barthly's demise, and I enjoyed it, even if the specters of grievous injury and almost death loomed over us.

Propped on pillows, Matt picked at the eggs the servant had brought. They had laid a tray for us on the bed, complete with a pot of tea for each of us. His was for pain. Mine was for my cough, which had almost fully disappeared, as had the worst of Matt's bruises.

"That's the plan," I said around a mouthful.

"Swooning didn't work for you, then?"

I raised an eyebrow. "The only person in this room who did any swooning was you."

Cheeks flushed, Matt gave up on his eggs and picked up his roll. "That's not what a little birdie told me."

"What did Lila say?"

"That you passed out and Rion carried you to your room."

"She talks too much."

Matt snickered, then winced, hunching slightly. "Well, think of it this way." He tore off a piece of bread and handed it to me. "You did swoon into his arms. That's a bonus for your plan."

"True. Though I think it was less endearing and more embarrassing."

Making a face, Matt popped the rest of his bread into his mouth. "You cannot embarrass yourself in front of Rion. He is the literal embodiment of good manners and wouldn't tease a soul unless he was certain it was permitted."

"That is true." I tapped my fingers on my lips. "That probably doesn't make us a good match."

"Anything can happen."

"You're in good spirits."

"I'm sitting up. At one point I thought I was going to become one with the mattress."

"That would've been unfortunate," I said as I bounced on the edge. "I kind of like your mattress."

Matt swung his hand at me and missed my shoulder. "Ouch," he said, curling into himself.

"That was supposed to be my line."

"Shut up."

I mimed buttoning my mouth, and Matt shook his head. I wanted to ask him about his conversation with Sionna from the other day. But I didn't have the heart. Whatever it was, it was between them, and if Matt wanted me to know, he'd tell me. It was a surprisingly mature view of the situation coming from me, but I was king; I'd matured. A bit. Kind of. Well, I wouldn't hold a party in my honor quite yet for reaching adulthood. For one, I'd die, because I had no soul mate. And two, adulthood was still two months away. Two very short months.

"Explain to me again how you're getting close to Rion?"

"I thought you wanted me to shut up?"

Matt gave me his unimpressed Matt face. I smiled in spite of it. "Fine. The princess described in her journal that the lady pretended not to know how to dance to seduce her. I'm going to pretend not to know how to sword fight."

"You don't know how to sword fight."

"I know a little."

"Not enough to not get almost squeezed to death by a moat monster."

"Extenuating circumstances!"

"Right."

"Hey, I hacked Henry free. I beheaded Barthly. I have some skill."

"You have a talent for luck when swinging a heavy piece of metal at things."

I narrowed my eyes. "I feel disrespected."

Huffing a laugh, then wincing, Matt wilted into the pillows, tilting his head back. He stared at the ceiling and breathed. "Don't make me laugh."

"I'm not trying to. But on the subject of my amazing prowess with a sword, Sionna told me we have recruits to train because of the moat-monster incident."

Matt wheezed. "That's even funnier."

"Quit laughing," I scolded.

"Then stop telling me hilarious things."

"I only told you because it means we can start really planning for the feast and the ball and whatever else Bethany wants. Our contingency plan can move forward."

Matt's forehead scrunched, and the small smile that played around his lips disappeared, replaced with a frown.

"Matt? Do you need to lie down?"

"Never again, thank you."

"That's going to be difficult for sleeping, then."

Matt closed his eyes. "I'm good, just like this."

"Right. That's my cue." I carefully slid from my spot on the edge of the mattress, then stumbled. I caught the post of Matt's bed to steady myself as the feeling of pins and needles tingled along my right foot.

"What are you doing?" Matt asked.

"Nothing!" I slid my slipper off. My toes tingled and then shimmered, as if translucent. Gulping, I shook my foot and placed it on the ground. The carpet was visible through my skin. I blinked, then wriggled my toes. They solidified. Decidedly not freaking out, I released the bedpost and lifted the breakfast tray from Matt's lap and transferred it to the floor by the door.

"Are you stealing my breakfast?"

"I'm making you more comfortable." I took the bowl of cut fruit from the tray and set it on Matt's nightstand, in case he was still hungry. "Because you're falling asleep."

"I'm not."

"Liar."

"Arek?"

"Go to sleep," I said. I pulled the blanket from the end of the bed over his bandaged torso and carefully tucked the edges around him. I checked my foot again, then shoved it into my slipper. Nothing was amiss. Huh. I must have been sitting oddly for it to tingle as it did. And the shimmering, a trick of the light from Matt's stained-glass window.

"Be nice to Rion," Matt said, brow wrinkled. "He's a good man."

"He is. I'll be my regular lovable self. I promise."

Snorting, Matt smiled softly. "Ass."

"Disrespect, I tell you. I left your fruit on the table. I'll be back later today."

Matt's response was a snore.

Quietly, I left the room, closing the door behind me. Once in the hallway, I leaned against it and pushed my foot against the stone. It was nothing. A quiver of nerves. A refraction of light. My own fatigue and worry bleeding through.

But just in case, I needed to hurry and implement my plan to woo Rion. Before it was too late.

CHAPTER 21

"**I**'m pleased you requested to revisit your sword training," Rion said as I followed him from the castle to the knights' training grounds.

My cape swished behind me as I walked. My crown glinted in the bright sunlight. After the incident with the octopi, I'd avoided wearing clothing that was too tight or had laces, but as I was trying to impress a potential wooing partner, I'd asked Harlow for my best clothes in which I could move freely. Also, I planned to meet the new soldier recruits, and it wouldn't do well for them to see me in my regular tunic and trousers.

"Well, after the moat monster, I decided to take you up on your offer."

"Excellent. We'll start with these wooden training swords and gradually progress to steel."

Rion tossed me one of the swords. I barely caught it, then spun the hilt in my hand with a flourish. "Okay. So, how should we start?"

"Slowly," he said. "You've been ill recently."

I waved away the concern. "I'm *fine*." I stretched my arms above my head and twisted my body, warming up my limbs. "See? All healed and well."

Rion raised an eyebrow. "Are you certain?"

"Are you questioning your king?" I asked, winking playfully.

"No." Rion smiled. "Let's begin, then."

I never took Rion for a taskmaster. I'd pictured our session to be much like what occurred between the princess and the lady in the journal, but that was not at all what Rion had in mind. First, we practiced forms and grips and steps and parries and thrusts. Each time my form was deemed sloppy or inaccurate, Rion did not encircle me with his thick, bulging arms and gently guide my limbs into the correct posture or position. No. Instead, he used the tip of his wooden sword to poke and prod me until I maneuvered into the desired stance. I was going to have little bruises all over me by the time we completed this session.

"Lunge forward, Arek."

My muscles trembled, but I lunged.

"Farther." The flat of his blade pressed on the back of my knee and urged me forward. "There. Now hold."

My chest heaved. Sweat dripped down my spine. I ached like it was the first day of haymaking and I'd spent the day scything and raking. A month in the castle, and my body had gone soft. I gritted my teeth and followed Rion's instructions until my tunic was wet and my face was as red as my hair.

"Excellent, sire."

Sire? I straightened from my stance. "Rion, it's—"

"Let's spar."

He tapped the tip of his sword against the dirt, then dropped into a ready stance. I mirrored him. I attacked first, hoping to catch him off guard. It worked for a moment, before he knocked my sword away, then thrusted his own at me. I managed to knock his sword off course and danced away, laughing. The clacking of our wooden blades filled the courtyard, as did my laughter between quick breaths, along with Rion's instruction when I did something wrong and praise when I executed a move well. It was like a dance, a series of movements kept in time. My pulse raced. The rapid beat of my heart pounded in my head and in my jaw. After several minutes, Rion disarmed me with a flourish, and my wooden sword flew across the courtyard.

Hands on my hips, I beamed. "That was fun."

A smattering of applause came from behind me, and I turned to find we had an audience. Several of the recruits stood watching. I waved at them. They all froze, and a few quickly bowed.

"Excellent session, sire."

I squeezed Rion's shoulder. "And this is why Sir Rion is one of your instructors," I called to the group. "He and General Sionna are the two best fighters of this age."

Rion blushed.

"Same time tomorrow?" I asked. He nodded. "Great. See you then."

That night, my mood was high. After taking dinner with Matt and telling him all about our sparring, I soaked in a warm bath to try to lessen the soreness I'd inevitably be feeling the following day. Though I still took much too long to fall asleep, once I did, I slept well.

I went back the next day sans cape and crown. And again the next. And the next. And the next after that. Before I knew it, a full week passed, and we were firmly into the second, and Rion had yet to touch me during our sessions, except with the blade of the practice sword. But I found I didn't mind. I stopped messing up on purpose and enjoyed learning the craft of swordplay and the benefits of physical activity. I slept better. My mood was better. I found myself looking forward to working up a sweat after hours of sitting on a throne or studying or learning rules and etiquette. We graduated from wooden to steel swords and added shields, and soon Rion would teach me how to use a lance.

Today, though, he beat the stuffing out of my shield arm.

"Wait," I said, holding up my hand. "I need a minute." I staggered to the bucket of water we kept near the courtyard, dragging my shield behind me. I dropped it to the grass, then scooped a cup. I chugged it, streams of water spilling out of the sides of my mouth and down my neck, cutting a streak through the sweat and grime. Once it was empty, I wiped my sleeve across my mouth. Panting, I leaned on a wooden post, which Rion had once explained was meant to hold a practice dummy. My breath puffed out in visible gusts, and steam rose from the heat of my skin. "I'm exhausted."

"We can end for the day, sire. If you'd like."

"No." I shook my head, my hair wet with sweat. My tunic was soaked through with it. I'd rolled up my sleeves over my elbows for better movement, and my forearms flexed as I picked up my sword and spun it in my hand. "No. I want to spar again."

"You're getting better."

"I couldn't have gotten much worse."

Grinning, Rion crossed his bulging arms. He stood taller

than me, but only by an inch or so. His dark blond hair hung to his chin, though when we practiced, he tied it back with a bit of leather. With it out of the way, I could appreciate the strong line of his jaw, the trim of his beard, and the planes of his face. He'd only grown more handsome over the months I'd known him, and I could imagine us ruling the kingdom together. His steadiness and sincerity were good counterpoints to my impulsiveness and sarcasm. Except, he'd shown no interest at all. Not a scrap of it. All the touching between us came from my end, or came from a need, like helping me to my feet after he knocked me down.

"No. I don't think you could've."

Teasing! That was a good sign.

"Disrespect!" I wagged my finger at him, though my grin belied any genuine ire. "Blatant disrespect."

Rion ducked his head and bowed slightly at the waist, spreading his arms. "My apologies, sire."

Okay, that was cute. Was that flirting? Was Rion flirting with me?

"So," I said, cocking my head, trying to flirt in return, "what do you think is my next skill? I know I haven't mastered any-thing, but I'm better. What is the next level?"

Rion rubbed his beard. "If you can teach someone else."

That was not what I was expecting. My eyebrows shot up. "What?"

Eyes lighting up with an idea, Rion pointed at me. "Yes. That's perfect."

Each day, we'd gathered more and more of an audience as we practiced. I didn't mind. The soldiers needed to see that Rion was someone I trusted and that he knew what he was talking about, so they could be receptive to learning from him. Except, right now. I really cared right now because Rion scanned the crowd. He snapped his fingers.

"Lord Matt!"

I whipped around to find him, surprised to hear he was out of bed. He'd been able to walk about in his room the other day, but I hadn't known he was up for being out in the court-yard. I spied him in the crowd, leaning on his staff, dressed in a plain tunic but with a heavy cloak draped over his shoulders. The recruits realized who stood among them and whispered as they parted like a river around a boulder and he moved slowly toward us.

"It's the mage," one of them whispered loud enough for me to overhear. "The powerful one who destroyed the moat monster."

"I thought King Arek killed it."

"King Arek saved Henry, but it was Lord Matt the Great who defeated it."

The Great? *The Great?* How was he called "Lord Matt the Great" and I was stuck with "King Arek the Kind"?

Matt approached warily, eyes shining with amusement as he, too, heard the conversation.

"No," I said to Rion. "That's not a good idea. He's only just healed."

"Which means as his teacher you'll need to be gentle with him and ensure he doesn't hurt himself while completing the movements."

Matt lifted his chin. "I can hold a sword, Arek. Especially if it helps you learn to stay alive for a bit longer."

The crowd tittered. "He calls the king by his name," the loud one whispered.

Rolling my eyes, I crossed the field and grabbed a practice sword from the barrel. I wouldn't be able to teach Matt the same way Rion taught me, by pushing his body using the wooden sword, so I'd have to think of something else. Matt leaned his staff against the perimeter fence, shrugged off the cloak, and met me in the middle of the yard. I handed Matt the hilt, and he wrapped his spindly fingers around it.

"No, like this." I placed my hand over his and turned it gently into the correct position on the hilt. "You want to hold it like you're shaking hands with it. Act like you're meeting it for the first time."

Matt's lips quirked. "Well, nice to meet you, sword."

"You're ridiculous."

"Be careful there, Arek. You're on the wrong side of the pointy end."

Laughing, I stepped behind him. "Good point." I moved Matt's arm into the correct position, supporting his elbow in my palm and placing my hand in the middle of his back. "Okay. Now fix your feet." I nudged his leg with my knee. "Yeah, that one, move it forward a bit."

Matt shuffled his feet until they were more or less in the correct place. "Like this?"

"Yeah. That's good."

"Excellent," Rion said, observing from in front of us. He, too, held a sword and lifted the tip in Matt's direction. "Now I'm going to mime attacking from above, so move Matt into the correct position." Rion swung downward in slow motion.

Leaning in, I ran my hand down his arm and maneuvered his sword into the correct position to block. I grasped the jut of his opposite hip and gently tugged him.

"Matt, drop your foot back. No, other foot," I said, stifling an *oof* when he stepped on my toes. "Yes. Good. Keep your posture straight." Wrapping my arm around him, I pressed my hand to his chest to steady him. His heart fluttered like a hummingbird under my palm. The skin of his nape prickled, and I realized I had exhaled as Rion had taught me but right across Matt's shoulder and ear. Before I could mutter an apology, Rion's sword clacked against Matt's. Even as light of a hit as it was, Matt's arm rippled, and I rushed to steady him, grabbing his wrist to prevent his arm from falling.

"Good. Now deflect my strike and attack."

Matt's body was a block of warmth along my front. The weather had cooled significantly, but I had built a sweat during my practice with Rion and had shed my overclothes. Now, though, the moisture cooled against my skin and I shivered in the breeze. I squeezed closer, leeching Matt's heat, as I showed him how to repel the strike and then mount an attack of his own.

"Okay, step forward." My knee knocked into the back of his leg, and he stepped. "Now thrust your sword arm."

As he did, I supported his arm with my palm, running it beneath to correct his form, then resting it along his ribs.

Matt sucked in a harsh breath.

I snatched my hand back as if he was on fire. "Are you okay?" I asked, scared I'd touched one of his lingering bruises.

"Fine," he said. "I'm fine."

"Are you sure?"

He stiffened in my arms. "I'm not weak."

"Never said you were," I answered. "But you were injured."

"I think I'm done." Matt dropped his sword arm and stepped out of my embrace. Shivering from the sudden lack of his body heat, I hastily unrolled my sleeves, then wrapped my arms around my torso.

Flushed from his neck upward, Matt ran a hand through his hair. "I think I'll stick to magic." He jerked his head toward the onlookers. "But I think you'd find a willing volunteer over there to finish."

I didn't want to find a willing volunteer. I wanted . . . Well, it didn't matter. Matt was obviously not okay with us being physically close with an audience. He was fine when in our rooms; in fact he initiated it, climbing into my bed first, then inviting me into his when he was injured. And I was grateful that hadn't changed between us. But out here, in the face of Rion and the new recruits, he was uncomfortable, and I needed to honor that.

"I'm done for the day as well." I followed him back to his cloak and staff, not wanting our interaction to end on a sour note. "I'll walk you back."

He raised an eyebrow. "Who says I'm going back to my room? I said I was done playing with swords, not with my outing."

"Really? Where is Lord Matt the Great heading now?"

"Why? Is King Arek the Kind going to follow me around the castle?"

"Yes."

The group of soldiers erupted in whispers as they raptly watched the exchange with wide eyes.

Clearly amused, Matt fastened his cloak around his shoulders. "To the garden, then, *sire*."

I admired how he continued to make the honorific sound like an insult.

I collected my things, slipping on my jacket and fastening my sword belt with the heavy magic sword at my hip. I ran a hand through my sweat-slicked hair. Gross. I would need a bath later.

The gathered group moved out of the way as we stepped through them and left the courtyard. Matt carried his staff in one hand and huddled into his cloak, pulling up the fur-lined hood.

"Fancy," I teased.

He huffed. "Says the man who wears a cape."

"It was one time. Okay, twice," I said. "But I regretted it the moment I jumped into the moat."

Snickering, Matt led me through a maze of overgrown hedges and high grass and thickets filled with nesting birds. Several places amid the grounds had been neglected for years, and I made a mental note to hire gardeners for the spring.

"Where are we going?" I asked as I squeezed through a tight spot, thorns from a rosebush catching on the fabric of my jacket.

Instead of answering, Matt asked, "How have things been going with Rion?"

"Rion?" I asked. "Oh yeah, Rion. Wooing. Um. That man is made of stone. Not that I've been trying too hard. I mean, I tried, because I don't want to die." I should tell Matt about the weird moment in his room, when my toes had faded. But I didn't want to worry him. I still had six weeks until my birthday. I'd worry later. "But there's nothing there on his end."

"On yours?"

Shrugging, I sighed. "He's handsome. And he's nice. And he's a good friend. But he's not for me."

Matt nodded. He tapped his fingertips on his mouth. "Should I assume, then, you're moving on to Lila?"

"Yeah, I guess. Lila, though . . . She's secretive. We literally know nothing about her other than she's part fae, and she can steal the clothes off your back if you're not paying attention."

"We know more than that."

"Do we? Really?"

Matt waved his hand at an old, weathered door, and it opened inward. He led me through into a walled garden, which was somehow more tangled and overgrown than the others we'd walked through. And it was much, much warmer.

"Of course we do. She'll follow you into battle. She ran up the arm of a moat monster to save you. And she stayed." Matt paused at a close crop of flowers. "She was the first to suggest leaving, and yet, she stayed."

I tugged on my collar. The air was damp and hot, like when we'd have a brief rain shower on the hottest day of the year and the drops would turn to steam on contact. Vibrant plants crawled along the stone walls, shot into the sky, higher than anything I'd ever seen, casting the whole place in a green light.

"Staying is a low bar."

"Is it?" Matt's gaze was sharp. "Staying is the biggest act of loyalty any of them have shown. It's one thing to follow a prophecy that has an end point. It's another to stick around indefinitely, with no conclusive ending, not knowing what the future might hold, and not knowing what your role would be."

"I gave them roles. Remember?"

"And that was the smartest thing you've done thus far. Giving them purpose."

"Thanks for the compliment. But what does that have to do with Lila?"

"Lila has always been guarded. We don't know anything about her family or if she even has one. We don't know her motivations other than coin and riches. But we trust her."

"Yes. I trust her. She jumped onto a writhing beast to try to save me." I wiggled out of my jacket. "Why the blazes is it so hot in here?"

"It's spelled." Matt waved his hand. "When I first discovered it, the spell was weakening. I strengthened it to last for the next few years. Within these four garden walls, there will always be enough warmth to grow whatever we need."

"Really?" I said, voice pitching in awe. I left Matt's side and explored what I could. The area wasn't large, more the size of one of the dining rooms in the castle, but it was packed with herbs, flowers, vines, and everything imaginable. I trailed my hand along the stone, which was warm to the touch, and marveled at Matt's ingenuity. "This is amazing."

"Herbs and plants for the court physician to use in his potions and salves. Fruit trees in case we need them for the winter. And this . . ." He used the tip of his staff to move a leaf and reveal a bevy of small, bright red flowers.

"What are those?"

"Heart's Truth."

"I don't know what that is."

"I read about it in a scroll from the library. It's a rare flower.

The pollen urges a person to reveal what's in their heart."

My eyebrows shot up. "When did you find this?"

"Before the moat monster." He chewed his bottom lip. "I didn't want to use it, honestly. But you're running out of time. I had hope for Sionna, Bethany, and Rion, but I'd rather you not waste two weeks trying to woo Lila if she has no feelings toward you at all."

Bent at the waist, I studied the plants. Upon inspection, their bloodred petals were shaped like tiny hearts.

Matt pushed the tip of his staff into my chest. "Not too close. Unless you want to reveal your heart's desire to me."

I straightened. "Ha!" My laugh came out more like a panicked burst of sound than anything else. I tried to cover it with a cough as I skittered away from the plant but was unsuccessful if Matt's raised eyebrow was an indication. But wow. I did not want to touch that because soliloquizing to Matt about his face and his freckles and his . . . everything would only end in embarrassment and tears. I cleared my throat. "I'm sure you want to hear all about how much I want to stay alive. And about the pie we had the other night."

"I'll pass," Matt said dryly. "Anyway, I suggest you plan an outing for you and Lila. I'll prepare the flowers."

"And what? Slip it into her drink? Sprinkle it on her toast? Shove it in her face?"

"I'll think of something." Matt frowned. "You just need to be nearby to ask her the right questions."

"Fine." Hands on my hips, I marveled again at the ingenuity of the warm space. The vibrancy of the greens and the different colors of the flowers were beautiful. The thick crush of the humidity dampened my skin. The heat was welcome in comparison to the chill of deep autumn on the other side of the door. "This really is brilliant, Matt. An everlasting garden."

"I didn't think of it." He spun his staff in his hand, the point twisting the grass beneath the wood. "I only bolstered it."

"Still. You really are Matt the Great."

He huffed. "And you are Arek the Kind."

"Ugh. Stop." I rolled my neck and looked toward the sky. The weak sun spread a hazy light through the gathering clouds. "Not you too."

"I don't know why you don't like the name. It's much better than 'Arek the Terrible.' 'Arek the Ugly.' 'Arek the Despicable.' 'Arek the Repulsive.' 'Arek the—'"

"Stop. Please stop describing me."

Snorting, Matt knocked his shoulder into mine. "Dramatic. I'm not describing you, only giving examples of what you could be. Those are bad. Kind is not bad."

"It makes me look weak."

"Kindness is not weakness." Matt made a face. "After all we've been through, it would be easy to be cynical, turn our backs on everyone else and only take care of ourselves. Because who has taken care of us? Huh? Who, other than our parents, has ever cared about us? I was driven out of my home village because of the *rumor* of magic. You were chosen for a quest you never wanted. We have been chased and injured, terrified, poisoned, beaten, almost *killed*. Even now, you're facing down potential death."

Sighing, I crossed my arms. "Occupational hazard of being king, I guess."

"Yeah," he said, rolling his eyes, "not kind at all. Not selfless. Not even a little bit *completely* loyal to a people who didn't even know your name two months ago. Not the most generous king this land has had in an age."

"To be fair," I said, holding up my forefinger, "my kingly competition was Barthly, so not a very high bar to jump over. And second, I only put the crown on my head because you urged me to and because I thought there was a princess in a tower that would be able to take over after I reigned for a total of, like, an afternoon. It's not like I set out to suddenly be the person everyone looked at to fix things." Grinning, I elbowed Matt in the side, then remembered his injuries as soon as he winced from the contact.

"I know that," Matt snapped, all traces of humor gone from his tone and face. "If I hadn't told you to put that stupid crown on your head, you wouldn't be bound to the throne and you wouldn't be forced into a soul mate situation. You don't need to remind me."

I held up my hands. "Whoa. Matt. It's okay. I was joking. It was a joke. I don't blame you."

"Well, you should! You're right. I'm the one who told you to take the crown off Barthly's head and put it on your own. I even teased you about it. This situation is my fault. It's my fault."

"Matt! It's not your fault. It was a mistake."

"A mistake that is going to alter your life forever! Or end it!"

My pulse ticked upward. The humidity, which I had welcomed when we'd first entered the enclosed space, now felt claustrophobic. "Since when do I follow every order you give me? Huh? I could've chosen not to listen to you. I do that *all the time,* or do you not remember large swaths of our childhood? I'm an impulsive asshole. We both know that. Just because you said to put on the crown doesn't mean I wasn't going to do it and sit on the throne anyway. I probably totally was going to, just after it had been cleaned."

Matt's face was a thunderstorm. His knuckles were white from the grip he had on his staff. Red crept up into his cheeks and down his neck beneath his tunic. "Don't lie to make me feel better."

"I'm not!" My voice cracked. My shoulders shot to my ears. "I'm not lying. I swear."

Matt's expression was skeptical.

"Please don't feel guilty." That was absolutely the wrong thing to say.

"I don't feel guilty!" he exploded. "I feel stupid! I feel help-less! I feel stuck!"

I froze. I heard my heartbeat in my ears. "Stuck?"

"Never mind. I didn't mean that. I didn't mean any of it." He squeezed the bridge of his nose between his thumb and fore-finger. "I'm tired and sore. I'm not myself. I'm going back to my room."

Did Matt feel stuck in the castle because of me? Would he rather be somewhere else? My head spun.

"I'll walk with you."

"No!" He shook his head. "No. I'm fine on my own. I don't need your help." He swallowed harshly and turned his head away. His dark hair hung in his face obscuring his features. My heart ached. "Just make sure you have a meeting with Lila in the next few days. I'll have the pollen ready."

"Matt—"

He walked away, his back stiff. He left the spelled garden, the door opening and closing without his touch. I stared after him. It was such an abrupt shift from only a few moments before, and my whole body went cold despite the heat. I missed Matt so suddenly, it was like a lance through my chest. My fingers tingled. Mouth dry, I raised my hand and looked right through my palm.

Chapter 22

"Are you checking up on everyone, or am I a special case?" Lila asked dryly as she led me through the castle. Her dark cloak fluttered behind her as she stepped swiftly and lightly, heading from the throne room to one of the courtyards. She held a bundle of leather in her hands but didn't tell me what it was for, just that she'd need it during our outing.

"Just you." The words came out more biting than teasing, but that was more due to my mood than anything Lila had done or said. Since my altercation with Matt two days ago, we'd barely spoken, only to exchange information about the pollen and my date with Lila today. I wasn't sure what I'd done wrong. If anything. But he was mad at me and thus I was irritated with him.

"You don't trust me."

"I trust you fine when it comes to things like saving my life and doling out the correct amounts of coin. Otherwise, call me justifiably suspicious."

She flipped a lock of blond hair over her shoulder. "Fair enough." She squinted at me, not paying attention to where she walked, instead studying my face even as she moved with a preternatural grace through the corridors. "Are you okay? You look like someone stole your piece of pie."

I pinched my nose. "Did you steal my piece of pie?"

She pressed a hand to her chest and affected an innocent expression, something she surely learned from Bethany and which didn't quite work on her narrow features. "Me?" She grinned like a shark. "No. I didn't steal any pie. Why would I steal pie when I can ask Meredith's mother to make us a pie? She's amazing, by the way."

"And where exactly are we going? You haven't said."

"You'll see."

"Does it have to do with death and destruction?"

She tapped her chin and hummed. "No."

"It bothers me that you had to think about it."

"It bothers me"—she poked me in the chest—"that you're sullen. Does it have to do with Matt? He's been in a mood as well."

No shit. I was well aware of the fact that he's been in a mood. But the fact that Lila knew also bothered me. "Has he? I wouldn't know."

"Oh, then it *does* have to do with him."

"Not everything is about Matt."

"But this is."

When did Lila become perceptive? Sionna's influence, obviously.

"Can we get on with this, please?" Okay. This was bad wooing. Even I knew that. But I couldn't muster any energy toward Lila when all my thoughts were focused on Matt. His horrible, beautiful face and his stupid perfect magic and his snarky hilarious comments. It bothered me that he felt guilty over my predicament. It bothered me that he felt stuck here in the castle. Everything about him *bothered* me—how smart he was, how he cared about everyone, how he put himself in danger for my sake, how he followed me when I ran away, how he looked when the octopus smacked him and sent him airborne, how he'd cultivated flowers just for me, how he trembled when I held his arm as he thrust the practice sword, how the heat of his body against mine made my knees weak and my head spin. How he was the only one I wanted, but I was pretty sure he didn't want me.

Lila snapped her fingers in my face. "Where the hells were you?"

"Right here."

"Yeah, sure."

Looking around, I found Lila had led me out into a courtyard near the stables. She crossed the stone yard, flung open the doors, and disappeared inside the darkened building. The horses inside whickered, and a few small birds flew around the rafters. A large orange cat stretched on a bale of hay and flicked his tail, staring at me with bright yellow eyes.

"Lila?"

"Hold on."

I knew what happened in stables. Well, I had heard about what happened in stables in stories and bawdy tavern tales. I don't think that was what Lila wanted, but who knew. She had always been a mystery.

"Okay, Arek, meet Crow."

Lila stepped through the door and into the sunlight. On her outstretched arm sat the biggest fucking bird I had ever seen in my entire life. Its claws were as big as a bear's paw, and the middle appendage wrapped all the way around Lila's skinny arm, digging into the tough leather she'd donned on her sleeve. Its feathers were black as pitch, but its head was bare and pink, and its beak would haunt my nightmares. It was definitely not a crow, but a cousin to a vulture or other over-size bird of prey, something built to hunt and eat big things. Like cows. Or people.

"Crow," she said seriously. It turned its head toward her, its brownish-red eyes glinting in the sunlight. "Say hi to Arek."

Crow did not caw or screech. No, Crow hissed. Disconcerted, I took another step back.

"What the fuck, Lila? What is that?"

"It's my pet!" she said cheerily. "I found him locked in a cage in the castle. After a few days of visits and of hand-feeding him raw meat, we became friends. He lives in the stable now."

Oh my spirits. She'd found the Vile One's familiar or dismemberment minion or thunderstorm monster and befriended it. This bird demon was her pet. The terrifying vessel to the underworld was her *friend*.

"Lila, I am not sure if Crow is a pet."

"You're right." She touched her finger under his beak and stroked the feathers of his chest. He snapped at her, and she snatched her hand away in a movement so fast, her body blurred. She cooed. If that had been anyone other than her, they would've lost a finger. "He's a companion."

Bowing my head, I ran my hands over my face. "Oh my spirits."

"What? What's wrong?"

"Nothing! Nothing." I hastened to reassure her lest Crow

interpret that I offended her or him in some way and decided to peck out my eyes after eviscerating me with his talons. I gestured helplessly at the bird of death. "He's cute." He stared at me with his wide unflinching eyes, peering straight into my soul. I wanted to shrivel up and cry.

"Isn't he, though?"

I bit my tongue to keep every potentially disparaging remark to myself because Lila appeared so achingly pleased. Was nurturing a very large bird of destruction better than stabbing people accidentally when startled? I didn't know. How was I supposed to know? I was not prepared for this.

"Does Crow do tricks?"

Lila gasped, aghast. "Tricks? Of course not. He's not a jester. He's not here for your amusement."

"Oh, sorry."

"Just joking. Of course he does. Do you want to see him fetch?"

I didn't want to see anything less. "Sure."

"Crow," she said. He tore his gaze from me and looked to her, cocking his long neck to the side in an eerie approximation of a human. "Find a stick. Bring it back."

He hissed and spread his wings. Their total width was more than Lila's height. He flapped them and her whole arm bent under his weight when he launched into the air. He circled the courtyard several times, casting a terrifying shadow, then disappeared over the peak of the western tower.

"Um. Where did he go?"

"To find a stick."

"When will he come back?"

She shrugged. "When he finds one."

"Are you at all worried that he'll bring something back other than a stick?"

"Like what?"

"Like a small child!"

"He wouldn't do that. He's not evil."

"Are you sure? Because he appears to be evil incarnate. He looks like an ancient horror that came back to enact revenge. He's the thing that keeps children up at night. He's the creature that inspires cautionary tales."

Lila crossed her arms and lifted her chin. "He's a bird, not a malevolent being."

"Oh, okay then. I feel so much better. This has been enlightening, and I'm glad you've found a pet. But I can't not express my concern that you're harboring a murder bird."

Lila frowned. "Crow is not a murder bird." She raised an eyebrow. "Are you judging him on his appearance?"

"No. Of course not." Yes. Yes, I was. "It's just that he's not built for anything other than the killing of other things. He's an omen of destruction. He's a—"

A panicked screech interrupted my monologue. Perking up, I exchanged a glance with Lila, in which we both raised our eyebrows and had a moment of unspoken conversation. The yelling happened again, this time higher-pitched, and on silent agreement, we ran toward the commotion. I reached for my sword at my hip, and Lila brandished her dagger as we ran to the edge of the courtyard and darted along the outer path leading to a small grassy area. Skidding to a stop in a swath of cool shadow next to an outer building, I pulled up short.

A picnic blanket was spread on the ground. A basket and

two goblets sat on the cloth. Matt stood next to it, holding his staff with both hands, and fighting off an agitated and aggressive Crow. Crow had the tip of the staff—the end with the jewel—clutched in his massive beak and was wildly flapping his wings in an attempt to wrench it out of Matt's grip.

"I will blast you! Don't think I won't!" Matt tugged, but Crow held on with his supernatural strength. Each flap of his massive wingspan sent a blast of air that sent Matt staggering. "Let go, you overgrown turkey!"

"Crow!" Lila yelled. "Not that stick!"

Oh! Crow found a stick. A stick that happened to be Matt's staff, and he wanted to fetch it for Lila. If Crow wasn't so terrifying, I would've laughed until I cried, because this was frankly hilarious. As it was, though, I ran behind Matt, wrapped my arms around him, and grasped the staff, adding my power to the tug-of-war.

"Call him off, Lila!" I yelled, right into Matt's ear.

Matt startled. His whole body shuddered into mine, and his grip loosened in surprise. The staff slid through our joined hands a few inches.

Crow hissed in triumph, wrapping his massive talons around the neck of the staff.

Pouncing forward, the back of Matt's head knocked into my collarbone, but I grasped higher on the wood and yanked.

Crow hissed again, his red eyes wide and glinting. His talons scraped along the wood, leaving gouges. I cringed at the sound and at Matt's indignant squeak.

"Let go of my staff!"

The atmosphere went dense with magic, as if a storm gathered overhead. The jeweled tip burned as we struggled. Crow snapped his powerful beak, barely missing Matt's arm as he sliced through the fabric of his sleeve.

This was how I died. I knew it. I just knew it. I wasn't going to fade away because I couldn't find my soul mate. I wasn't going to die at the hands of the Vile One's angry followers. I wasn't going to fall asleep in my bed at an old age and not wake up. No. This was my death, at the claws of Crow, the horrific pet of one of my best friends. Or in the wake of a torrent of magical lightning when Matt became agitated enough to blast the feathers right off Crow.

"What are you doing here?" Matt yelled.

"Us? What are *you* doing here?" I shot back.

"Fighting this monster for my staff. What the hells is that thing?"

"That. Is. Lila's. Pet," I said through gritted teeth. My palms were slick with sweat, and Matt's staff was smooth with age and had nowhere to grip. My hands chafed with each tug Crow managed.

"Her pet?" The dense crush of magic that had gathered around us eased slightly.

Matt's eyes narrowed as he studied the bird. "Of course," he muttered.

"Crow! Drop it!" Lila stomped her foot. She stood between us and Crow, on one side of the shaft. She waved her arms in Crow's face.

Crow didn't listen to Lila's demands to drop the stick. Crow did decide that yanking backward wasn't working and thus pushed forward. The end of the staff rammed Matt in the stomach, and he doubled over.

"Just let it go!" Lila yelled, waving her hands.

"Who? Him or us?" I yelled back.

"You!"

"No!" Matt's twisted the staff back and forth in an attempt to wriggle it out of Crow's grasp. "I can't let the staff fall into the wrong hands."

"Trust me!"

Tired of toying with us, Crow screeched, an unnerving sound that sent a shiver down my spine. He clacked his beak. Ah crap. I released the staff. Matt whipped his head around and stared at me in betrayal as Crow pulled upward and Matt's feet lifted off the ground, the toes of his boots carving furrows in the ground.

"Let go!"

Scrunching his face, Matt shook his head. "No! Tell him to get his own staff."

"That's what he's trying to do." Lila lunged and grabbed Matt's arms. Her added weight rocked Matt back on his heels. His body jarred, and his knees bent so deep, he almost toppled.

"Hey, let go of him." Though I had released the staff, I wasn't going to stand by and watch Matt get injured again. I joined the fray, grasping Matt's tunic with one hand, and his staff with the other. Among the four of us, we fought, grunting and yelling at each other, or in Crow's case, uttering the deepest and most unsettling guttural sounds.

"Why won't you listen to me?" Lila yelled.

"Who are you yelling at?" I steadied the group, neither tugging nor pushing, just holding, my heels digging in. The blanket beneath us twisted around Matt and Lila's feet. The picnic basket tumbled to its side. The silver goblets rolled.

"You again!" she shot back, and gave a harsh pull.

Matt stumbled forward. His foot landed on one of the goblets just as Crow gave a well-timed tug and hiss. Matt's foot slid right from underneath him, and he went from standing, to falling, to flat on his back from one breath to the next. Without his grip on the staff, I let go, as did Lila. Crow took off, carrying the long stick through the sky in victory.

"Matt!"

Lila knelt next to Matt and placed her hand on his shoulder. "Don't worry. He'll bring it back. I promise. We're playing fetch."

Grumbling and panting, Matt rolled to his side, and accompanying his cursing was the sound of breaking glass. He froze, then sat up quickly, knocking his head into Lila's, before jumping to his feet, flapping the fabric of his tunic and patting down his torso.

"Oh shit. Oh shit."

He spun in a circle. As he frantically searched, a puff of red pollen wafted from his pocket right into Lila's face, then floated upward.

Red. Pollen. Heart's Truth.

I slapped a hand over my nose and mouth and quickly backed away, out of the vicinity of the powder. I stared in horror as both Matt and Lila inhaled—Matt due to the exertion of fighting the murder bird, and Lila, unaware of the Heart's Truth. The pollen flew up her nose, and when Matt sucked in a breath, it went right into his mouth.

He shoved his hand into his pocket, pulled out bits of

broken glass, and held the remnants of a vial and sparkly red particles in his palm.

"What's that?" Lila asked as she stood. She bent over Matt's hand, brow furrowed.

Matt raised his head and stared at me, his face void of color, his expression as close to terrified as I'd ever seen it.

"Matt?" Lila asked. "Arek? What's going on?"

We both stared at her.

"Why are you looking at me like I have something on my face?" She waved at her nose. "Do I? I had a strawberry scone earlier." She rubbed her sleeve across her mouth, and the pollen smeared over her upper lip. "Did I have frosting on my face, and you didn't tell me? What kind of friends are you?"

The worst kind, Lila. The absolute worst.

Crow circled above us, Matt's staff clutched tight in his claws. Lila stuck out her arm, and Crow swooped down, dropped Matt's staff on the twisted blanket, then landed elegantly on the leather along her forearm.

"Good job, Crow." She rubbed the bird's back. "See, I told you he'd bring it back."

Matt's eyes were saucers. He grabbed the basket and shook the remnants of the glass and pollen into it, before snapping it shut. He wiped his palm on his trousers, leaving a red smear across the fabric. Shaking his head, he looked to me and clapped his clean hand over his mouth.

"Seriously, what is wrong with you two? Did we step in something?" She lifted a boot and checked the bottom. "Matt, what were you doing out here anyway . . . ?" She trailed off. Her eyes glazed. Her pupils blew wide, and her mouth fell open on an exhale.

"Matt," I said, speaking through my fingers, knowing he would soon succumb to the pollen as well. "Take your staff and run to your room. Go!" I snapped when he looked about to protest. "Before you reveal anything you don't want to. I'll handle this."

Matt didn't wait for any further approval. He grabbed his staff and took off at a dead run. Once he was safe, I dropped my hand and slowly stepped toward Lila, though Crow eyed me like I was a deer mouse, or maybe a deer. It was hard to tell. He could totally eat a deer if he wanted.

Lila dropped her arm. Surprised, Crow fell in a hissing tangle of black feathers. It should've been hilarious. But it wasn't, because Lila clutched her cloak, right over her heart, and her features twisted in pain.

"Lila," I said, as if talking to a spooked unicorn. "Lila, can you hear me?"

She opened her mouth; her bottom lip glistened. She stared at me, or through me, her bright eyes hazed. *"Rion."*

"Um. No. It's Arek." Oh shit. Oh shit. Oh shit. This was worse than I thought.

She shook her head. "No. *Rion.*" A tear fell down her cheek. "Rion."

I stopped short. Wait. What? Lila's heart's truth was . . . Rion? I blinked. "He's in the training courtyard."

She took off as if shot from a catapult. Lila had always been faster than the rest of us, light on her feet, and able to move without a sound. Now she was a blur. She left me standing there with Crow on the picnic blanket.

Yeah. No.

I ran after her. Crow took off behind me and dogged my

heels like a ravenous hell bird. Though I was fairly certain he was not after me but after his master, his friend, the person who freed him and fed him. Huh. Maybe he was her pet and not a freewill murder fowl.

Thanks to Rion's training regimen, I was not out of breath when I reached the courtyard, but I was several yards and seconds behind Lila, who skidded across the stone toward Rion before I could even yell his name. At least I was there to explain it all after the fact and witness the inevitable destruction.

"Lila!" I called.

She didn't listen. She blew past the phalanx of soldiers training, her blond hair a comet trail, her feet light as feathers. The group didn't have a chance of stopping her, even if they'd noticed, but she went untouched and undetected until she abruptly stopped right in front of Rion.

If Rion was caught off guard, he didn't show it, except for the barely perceptible twitch of his face and the clench of his jaw, but it was so subtle, only his close friends would have noticed. Undoubtedly, Lila did.

"Lila? Is something wrong?"

I was not near as quick or silent, so the training soldiers all turned when I jogged between them, zigzagging through the line, trying to catch up to Lila and stop whatever was about to happen. Crow was an omen behind me, his huge wings smacking unsuspecting guards in the backs of their heads and the sides of their faces. I skidded to a stop once on the grass beside the pair of them. Crow careened past me, then took off high into the sky, circling.

"Lila?" Rion prodded.

I grabbed Lila's arm. "She's not herself, Rion. There's been a mistake with a certain pollen. Heart's Truth? Have you heard of it before? Well, Matt and I found some, and we were playing around with it, and the vial broke in Matt's pocket. Lila was accidentally doused. She needs to sleep it off," I babbled. "She'll be fine tomorrow."

"Arek, what is going on? Is she all right?"

"She's fine," I lied. "So fine. I promise." I tugged on her arm. "Come on, Lila. Let's go steal something. It'll make you feel normal. Better! Feel better. Not normal. You are normal. Well, you're not normal."

"I love you."

Rion's eyebrows shot up. I smacked my face.

"I love you, Rion," Lila said again. There was an openness to her face, to her body language, to her aura, that I'd never seen before. Even her cloak was thrown back, her hood fallen, her shoulders bare. "I've loved you since you saved that rabbit from the snare."

"What? What rabbit?" I asked.

"We were starving, and he caught one for our dinner. But then he let it go. It was the moment I knew." She swallowed. Her eyes shone. I remembered that night. My stomach had been eating my spine with hunger, and the others were in the same boat. We'd caught a rabbit. A single rabbit. But Rion accidentally released it. Well, that's what he'd said. Apparently, he let it go. I jabbed my finger at him. "You let it go for her?" She tipped her face up to Rion.

"You knew I didn't like seeing it in pain. You knew the others would be angry with you. You let it go anyway. It struck me, that you cared so much."

"Like lightning," I said softly. That's what Lila had told me that day, weeks ago, about how love would feel for her. Like getting struck by lightning. Instantaneous. In a moment.

Rion's cheeks flushed. He removed his glove with his teeth and tossed it on the ground. With the gentleness of nobility, Rion tucked a lock of Lila's hair behind her pointed ear. He cupped her cheek and caressed his thumb over the line of her cheekbone.

"I care for no one more than I care for you."

Suddenly, I was in the middle of a tale of romance and chivalry. I didn't know how it happened. Well, I knew how it happened. Pollen was what had happened.

Crow landed on the practice dummy at the edge of the yard and tucked his massive wings close to his side. He craned his neck and also watched the exchange, but with a knowing glint to his eyes. The terrified gasps at his appearance from the trainees validated my general unease about him, but I couldn't begrudge him his presence. He, too, was Lila's friend, if new to the circle, and he should be able to witness the love story blossoming in front of us.

I released Lila's arm and took several steps away. Just in time, too, because Rion bent his head, and Lila stood on her tiptoes and they kissed.

A light applause followed from the trainees along with a few hoots. I couldn't hold back my own smile, but I refrained from yelling my support and politely clapped. I couldn't forget I was the king to these people. I nodded my head in kingly approval while my own heart lurched.

Happy for my friends, I was suddenly aware that Lila had been my last chance at a friendly resolution to my predicament. I was screwed. I still wore a crown. I was still magically attached to a throne I wasn't exactly keen on. And I needed to bond to a soul mate, or I was going to fade away. My stomach churned. My time was short. My options few. My feet tingled.

Then my legs gave out.

Chapter 23

ionna and Bethany stared me down with the mother of all disapproving expressions. They'd been given the abbreviated version of events when the recruits hauled my uncoordinated ass into the castle and placed me in my chair in our council room. They didn't know the whole story, but they knew something was up because there was no way Lila would ever willingly run into someone's arms and confess her love.

Speaking of, Lila and Rion were not present. Neither was Matt. Matt and Lila had locked themselves away until the effects of the Heart's Truth wore off while Rion had uncharacteristically abandoned me to my fate with the two very scary women who currently had their arms crossed and were staring at me like I was an ant who had ruined their picnic. "You can start explaining at any time," Sionna said, jabbing her finger at me.

"What makes you think I had anything to do with what happened?"

Bethany narrowed her eyes. "Because we know you."

"That's mean, Bethany."

"And the fact that everyone saw you chasing Lila," Sionna added. "Who then confessed her love to Rion. In front of a crowd. Of people. While being chased by you and a vulture."

I raised my finger. "That's Crow. Her pet. And he was not chasing her in a malicious way. He adores her."

"Arek." Sionna's tone teetered between murderous and long-suffering. I decided to cut my potential losses.

"Lila may have inhaled a pollen that changed her demeanor for a few minutes."

Bethany's mouth fell open. "A pollen? Like a lust pollen?"

"It wasn't a lust pollen."

"How the hell did she inhale a lust pollen?"

I threw up my hands. "It wasn't a lust pollen. It was pollen from a plant called Heart's Truth. It had nothing to do with lust."

"Fine." Bethany's voice was hard. "Do you want to explain to us why you doused our friend, our rogue, our mistress of finances, with Heart's Truth?"

"Point, I did not douse Lila. The vial broke."

Eyes narrowed to slits, Sionna stalked forward. "Do you want to explain to us why you had a vial of Heart's Truth in the first place?

"Not really?" My voice pitched high. I tugged at the collar of my tunic. I wished I had my crown because it might remind them of my position of authority. Okay, I doubted that. Bethany had less esteem for my position than I did, and while Sionna had respected it previously, she was *angry*.

Bethany scoffed. She tossed her hair. "You have so much explaining to do right now, Arek. I don't know where to start."

"Um. Let's not. And say we did?"

"Our tolerance for your jokes grows thin, *sire*."

Ouch. Sionna was not playing around. That bit of humor she'd shown on the stairwell weeks ago was nowhere to be found, and yeah, I got that. I'd basically assaulted one of our friends. I'd made two of our friends lock themselves away because they feared interacting with anyone while still under the influence of the flower. I understood I'd made a mistake. But I was desperate. Don't desperate times call for desperate measures?

I slid down in my chair. "I made a mistake. I'm sorry. I'll apologize to Lila when she feels better."

"You mean when she's not drugged?"

Ugh. Okay. "I really am sorry. It was a bad idea. Matt and I should've never—"

"Matt?" Sionna placed her hands on her hips. "Matt's involved?"

"Um. No. He's not. Forget I said his name at all."

Sionna slapped the table so hard, the silverware rattled. She leaned in, baring her teeth, her muscles taut, every inch the deadly warrior we'd needed on our campaign.

"Start speaking plainly, King Arek, or there will be a coup right here, right now."

I shivered. Effectively cowed, I turned my head away and stared at the tapestry on the wall. "Fine. You want the truth? I'm dying." At their gasps, I amended. "I mean, I'm fading. Fading. Dying. I don't really know the difference. I imagine the result is the same." I couldn't meet their gazes. I picked at my fingernails. They were solid and real, thank goodness. "It's a magic law, and Matt and I have been trying to combat it, but so far we've failed."

"You're lying," Bethany accused. She grabbed her harp from where it rested next to the bowl of fruit on the table. She waved it at me threateningly. "I can charm you. I can make you talk."

"I'm not lying!" I stood quickly, but my legs shook, and I sat back hard in the chair. "Okay. This is the truth. When I put that damned crown on my head, it bound me to the throne. I'm stuck here. I can't leave. I'm King Arek, now until forever or until I die, whichever comes first. Which will be the dying if I don't find someone with which to bind my soul."

Sionna's hard expression didn't waver, but her eyes narrowed slightly. "The soul mate law," she said flatly.

I nodded. "The soul mate law," I confirmed.

"I think now is the time to explain."

"I am explaining. I thought I was anyway. You can ask Matt, when he's not magically compelled to act on his heart's truth."

She exhaled through her nose. "Arek, I'm your friend, but I could pummel you right now."

"I know. If I could kick my own ass, I would. But look, it didn't end horribly, did it? Lila and Rion had been mutually pining after each other this whole time." My shoulders went up to my ears. "Did you know? Did any of us know that?"

Sionna and Bethany exchanged a glance. "No," Bethany admitted. "They're both stoic to a fault. I didn't know."

"I didn't either."

"Okay. Happy ending and all that. No, the ends don't justify the means, and I will be profusely apologizing to our friend, and I will allow her to keep the murder bird, even if it frightens the living light out of me, but I had a reason."

Bethany sighed. She pulled out a chair and sat down next to

me. Sionna did not follow suit, but she straightened from her impressive forward lean of intimidation and instead rested against the wall, her ankles crossed.

"What do you mean you're fading? What does that mean?" Bethany asked, brow furrowed.

I rubbed my hands over my face. "When I sat on the throne, a wave of magic washed over me and basically tied me to the throne for the rest of my life. I tried to abdicate, and the magic almost killed me. The only way to transition the power of that throne is through death."

"That doesn't explain why you were in possession of Heart's Truth. And around Lila at the same time. And why there is a bird named Crow. Or why there was a picnic blanket and goblets near the stables."

"There's a lot to unpack there," I said.

"Arek," Sionna said warningly.

"Fine. No, it doesn't explain any of that. But one of the conditions of being king is that I have to soulbond with someone. I have until my eighteenth birthday to choose someone, otherwise I'll fade away and the throne will open for someone else to take my place."

Bethany's eyebrow arched, and her lips twitched. "And you thought Lila might be your soulbond?" She barely held in the laughter. I didn't blame her. In hindsight, the whole plan of trying to woo my friends was just an extreme effort in avoidance of the problem.

"No, not really. I just wanted to see if Lila held any affection toward me to see if it was worth my time to try and woo her."

"Woo her?" Bethany did break into laughter then. "*Woo* her? What, are we in a romance scroll?"

239

"Hilarious," I said. "I'm dying."

Her grin fell away, and she winced. "Sorry."

"Anyway, she's not. No, I am not trying to woo any of the rest of you, at least not anymore."

"Not anymore," Sionna said, words measured, the pauses significant.

"I know it sounds silly, but I didn't want to be with someone who I didn't know. I never wanted to be king. And I don't want to be tied to someone who doesn't know me. I only had three months, much less than that now. I thought I'd start with my friends. I thought that if any of you had an inkling of affection toward me, we might be able to make something work. Lila was my last hope."

Bethany and Sionna exchanged a glance. I couldn't tell what it meant.

"So you tried wooing Lila, me, and Sionna. . . . What about Matt?" Bethany asked carefully. I hesitated before answering. Did she know how I felt? Did *both* of them know how I felt? The thought was both terrifying and oddly relieving. The idea of *finally* being able to share my secret with someone was tempting. It'd been so hard not having anyone to talk to. But then I imagined a concerned Bethany or Sionna going to Matt to discuss my feelings within the context of my current situation. Even if it was well intentioned, it was the perfect way to make Matt feel obligated to soulbond with me to save my life, and I just couldn't risk putting him in that position.

"Matt's been in on all of this since the beginning."

"And?" she prompted.

"He knows it all. Matt was the one who found the Heart's Truth. He planned for me and Sionna to be trapped in the tower together, though that did not work out. The tentacle monster was an added bonus that we did not plan, but it didn't work either because you didn't swoon into my arms. And I really did need the sword lessons with Rion despite him not touching me the entire time we trained together, and now I know why." Once it was all out, and Bethany and Sionna looked at me with more pity than disgust, I wilted. Falling forward, I buried my face in my crossed arms. "I'm screwed."

"You could've just asked us. I don't know why you kept it a secret."

Groaning, I lifted my head. My chin dug into my forearm. "I knew the minute I said anything that the lot of you would feel obligated to stay. I didn't want you to feel like you had to. I know in the beginning we were all enthusiastic about ruling this kingdom, but it's fucking hard. We have our whole lives ahead of us—why would you want to be stuck here with me in this drafty castle? What if you decided you wanted to leave and go be with your families?"

"Again," Bethany said dryly. "You could've just asked."

"Ugh."

Sionna crossed the space between us. She patted my head. "We're your family, Arek. We wouldn't leave you."

And that was the fear, right there. That they would leave, and I'd be left here without them, with no friends or family, and no way to abdicate other than death. Damn perceptive Sionna.

I don't know what happened. Maybe it was that it was finally out in the open among us. Maybe it was that Sionna and Bethany were irritated with me, or that I couldn't quite feel my feet other than the constant pins and needles. But I dropped my face into my sleeves and broke beneath the crushing weight of all my fears, my stress, my obligations to a kingdom I didn't want to rule.

I couldn't hold back. I sobbed, my face stinging with warm rivers of tears. I cried out everything that had been pent up inside of me since I'd chopped off the head of a bad guy. The sleepless nights, the pain of Matt's rejection, the responsibility of the throne, the pressure of finding someone to bond with me for all eternity—all of it came out in a hiccuping torrent. The humor and the flippancy finally cracked, and beneath it was a mess of a boy who wanted to go back to a simple life and never be chosen in the first place.

My whole body shook with each wracking sob. I clenched my fists, the fabric of the tablecloth bunching in my fingers. The small space where I'd tucked my face warmed with my gasps, and my sleeves dampened with my tears.

I didn't register Bethany's arms around me until she tightened them fiercely and whispered soothing noises into my ear. Sionna's nails scratched along my scalp. She tugged my hair between her fingers, a rhythmic motion that calmed the churning of my stomach.

"It's okay," Bethany said. She rubbed my back. "It's okay, Arek. It'll be okay."

My heart ached. My shoulders heaved. I couldn't stop, despite trying to. "I'm sorry," I wheezed. "I'm sorry."

"You're fine," Sionna said. "You're fine. We'll figure it out. Together."

"She's right. We're a team. We're your family. We won't let anything happen to you."

Their assertions calmed my mind, but the tears kept

pouring. The dam had broken, and there was no stopping the deluge.

"I hate to say this," Bethany said, talking over my head to Sionna. "But I think we may need the guidance of a responsible adult."

"Agreed."

Oh spirits. "Not Harlow," I managed.

Bethany laughed kindly. "No. Not him. I was thinking someone a little more nurturing."

"On it," Sionna said. I heard the door open and close, and then I was left alone with Bethany.

"You know," she said thoughtfully, "I could always charm someone into giving you a chance. I couldn't make them fall in love with you, but I could at least make them go on a date. That would not be a problem."

I snorted through my clogged nose. "No thanks."

"Yeah. I wouldn't want that either."

Bethany stayed with me until I regained my composure, distracting me with tales from the castle and silly stories about her time in the tavern. She kept one hand on my shoulder; she strummed her harp with the other. Her words blurred together. The thoughts clamoring in my mind quieted, and my hitching breaths evened.

When Sionna returned a few minutes later, I was limp in my chair, my eyes half-lidded, my face covered in tears.

"Oh, the poor dear." Matilda, the cook and Meredith's mother, followed Sionna into the room. She crossed the space and rested her hand on my head. "Is the king okay?"

"I charmed him a bit," Bethany said. "To help him calm."

"What's wrong?"

"He's had a hard day," Sionna said. "Bethany and I aren't quite the nurturing types. We're out of our league here. And Matt isn't available to step in."

At the mention of Matt's name, the knife in my gut twisted. Another wave of tears threatened, and I scrunched my nose, turned my face into my arms.

"Nothing a warm meal, hot bath, and good nap won't solve." She gripped my upper arm. "Come along, dearie. Let me take care of you. The lot of you are so young to be doing all you've done. It was only a matter of time before the stress became too much."

I stood, and, thankfully, my feet and legs seemed to remain solid. My head ached from crying. My eyes were swollen, and my face heated. She led me from the council room to my chambers, Sionna and Bethany trailing behind.

The next hour passed in a blur. It was nice to just follow Matilda's orders, to not have to think for a bit. By the end of the process, I was tucked into bed, the curtains drawn, and I fell into an exhausted sleep.

Chapter 24

It was well into the evening when I was summoned for dinner. I'd slept heavily until Harlow knocked on my door. Checking the mirror, I had creases on my cheeks from the pillow, and my face was puffy from sleep and sobs. At least my head didn't ache as badly as it did before. Though I was slightly embarrassed by the fact that Matilda had to intervene after my meltdown and that Sionna and Bethany had witnessed it. Oh well. I hoped they wouldn't tease me over the whole situation, but I wouldn't know until I showed at dinner.

Taking a breath, I straightened my clothes and left my room.

When I arrived at the council room, everyone was already present, save Matt. His usual seat by my side was empty, but the others were there. I ignored the pang of hurt at Matt's absence and the swell of relief that followed when I realized I didn't have to face him quite yet. Lila sat next to Rion, looking decidedly more like herself than the last time I saw her. The only difference was that her fingers were tangled with Rion's next to their cutlery.

I sank into the chair at the head of the table. The group was quiet, and they all watched me with varying degrees of sympathy and annoyance, and I was not going to survive that.

"Hi," I said. "Can you all not look at me like I'm a lamb that's going to be slaughtered and eaten, please?"

Lila cleared her throat. She lifted her chin. "The situation has been explained to me, and though I'm livid with you over the pollen, I understand why you did it." Her grip on Rion's hand tightened. "And the consequences of your actions weren't overly horrible."

"I'm sorry." I dipped my head, ashamed. "I'm very sorry, Lila. I don't deserve your forgiveness, but thank you for offering it."

"There will be retribution," Lila said, mouth sliding into a small smirk. "When this is over and you least expect it, I will be getting you back."

I managed a half-hearted chuckle. "I'll take it." I sighed. "I owe you all an apology. I should've told you all about everything. I shouldn't have tried to . . . influence your feelings about me. I should've involved you in the decisions. Thinking that I could use the princess's journal to guide my own situation was foolish."

Bethany's eyebrows shot up. "You did what?"

"The princess's journal. She wrote all about how she and her lady had fallen in love and the situations that led them there. I thought I could try it out on my own and see if it spurred any feelings between me and all of you."

"That is the most romantic thing I've ever heard," Bethany said, eyes wide, her hands clasped to her chest. "Seriously, Arek. That's like next-level. If I didn't view you as my very annoying brother, I might have been swayed."

"Thanks," I said. "It was ridiculous."

"Barring the lust pollen—"

"It wasn't lust pollen!"

"That wasn't a horrible idea, Arek." Bethany shrugged when the others stared at her. "What? No, I'm not happy that Arek and Matt, the little goblin, kept it from us, but setting up romantic situations to gauge our feelings wasn't a bad idea. And Arek obviously backed off when he realized there was nothing between any of us except platonic affection."

I rubbed my brow. "Can we just move past it, please? I will never do it again. I've learned the errors of my ways."

"Well, you're going to have to do it again." Bethany pulled a pile of letters from a satchel by her side and dropped them on the table. "These are all the responses to the correspondence we sent out to our vassals."

"And?"

"They're not sending their children to squire until we show an act of good faith," Rion said. He glared at the potato on his plate. "They don't trust you."

"Why should they?" I asked, grabbing my goblet. I drank the water down, not realizing how parched I was from crying until the cool liquid hit my throat. "The last guy was awful. They think they're sending their kids to die or be ensnared into evil deeds by an evil overlord."

"We didn't start receiving recruits from the populace until after the incident with the moat monster," Sionna pointed out. "Only after your show of bravery saving the townspeople did they trust us enough to join our military."

"Exactly," Bethany said, gesturing at the pile of letters. "Which is why the feast and the ball is even more important than before. It will be our act of good faith for the lords, and when they all arrive, we'll find Arek a soul mate."

I blinked. Bethany said "we" as in they, as in my friends would find my soul mate. "What?" I impressed myself with my ability to be deadpan.

"What do you mean 'what'? You tried to trope your way into romance, and it didn't work. Now it's our turn to do it for you. And we'll find you a soul mate. You don't fade away. You start a period of peace that lasts a thousand years. And we die as heroes."

Lila pointed her fork in Bethany's direction. "This is not a bad idea. I like it. We can vet all the potential soul mates for Arek, so he doesn't waste time."

Bethany snapped her fingers. "Exactly."

This was not the turn of events I expected. Yes, the ball was my contingency plan to find a soul mate, but I did not predict that my friends would want in on the action. Did I want to bond with a person who Bethany thought would be perfect for me? Or Lila? I looked forlornly at the empty chair next to me. "What the fuck is happening?"

Frowning, Sionna took a gulp from her goblet. "Where is Matt? He should be part of this conversation."

"I don't know. I haven't seen him since the courtyard."

"I talked with him." Bethany glanced toward Sionna, her levity gone, her expression serious and weary, tired in a way that looked sorrowful. "He agrees with our plan."

"Oh. Oh." She looked down and swallowed. "That's good, then."

I didn't know the context of their interaction, but I didn't like it. My gut churned. There was a secret there. One that involved Matt. Another pang followed by tingling in my right hand.

Glancing down, I noticed my thumb was translucent. I tucked my hand into my sleeve to hide it. I reached across the table with my left hand and clumsily speared a piece of ham for my plate.

"So," I said, ignoring the unease in my stomach, "we could send for any of your families that you wish as well. We could invite them to the feast."

"That's a wonderful idea, Arek." Sionna lifted her goblet in my direction. "I'll send for my mother and sister."

"And my brother," Rion said.

Lila shrugged. "I have no one."

"Neither do I," Bethany said.

"You have us." I nodded at them. "You have us." I stared at my plate. "It's decided, then. Alert the staff. I'm sure we'll need to air out rooms and gather enough food for a party. I . . . don't have much time, so we should plan for as soon as possible."

"Agreed," Sionna said.

The others nodded.

"Good." I tucked into my dinner, my right hand hidden in my lap. I glanced at my side, my stomach sinking at Matt's empty chair.

Chapter 25

After dinner, I went to my chambers and retrieved the princess's journal and flipped through the pages. My thumb had solidified, thankfully, and I used it to parse through the yellowed pages. There was nothing about soul mates other than her writings about her lady. There wasn't much about ruling, either, other than advice on deciding as fairly as possible during petitions and caution about making sure to know the whole story before making a judgment. There was a bit about relations with other kingdoms, but all that information was moot, since Barthly had destroyed any good ties the kingdom had with the others of the realm.

I didn't want to stay in my chamber alone, so I meandered around the castle until I found myself at Matt's door. I knocked and waited. I knocked again when there was no answer. Either he wasn't there or wasn't taking visitors. I tried the handle, but it was locked.

Well, if he wasn't there, he was in the library. I headed that way and upon entering, I spied him at the table near the large fireplace. The fire was lit, casting light and warmth in the room. Candles burned down to their holders sat on a table, and scrolls were spread across the wood. I recognized the prophetic parchment immediately.

Matt looked up at my entrance.

"Hey," I said softly.

He dropped his head. "Hey," he said in response. He sighed heavily, his shoulders lifting and falling.

"I see you've recovered from the Heart's Truth."

The corner of Matt's mouth twitched. "I see Lila didn't kill you."

"It was a near thing. She has promised retribution, though. I see a prank in my future. Something grand."

"Knowing her, you better nail down your belongings or they'll all go missing."

I nodded. "Good idea." Ambling farther into the room, I studied Matt. The flickering light from the candles and the fire threw his features in sharp relief. The straight line of his nose, his cheekbones, the jut of his chin, and the delicate curve of the shell of his ear. His eyes darted as he read, ever studying, ever analyzing, ever learning.

I joined him at the table. "What are you looking at?"

"Everything," he said, shaking his head. He pushed his hair out of his eyes. "These are all the documents I could find about the magic laws."

"And?" I couldn't keep the hopeful tone out of my voice. "Anything new?"

"No." He grimaced. "I've read and read and hoped for a loophole, but it all reads the same."

"Once I put the crown on my head and sat on the throne, I became the king for now and ever, until I die, or someone comes along and usurps me."

Matt nodded. "Kills you. Yes." He picked up the book of laws. "And the king needs a soul mate. Or he will fade or wither or disappear. Still unclear on that part."

I wasn't. I flexed my hands, then ran my finger over the wrinkled prophecy. "You don't think the answer is under that wine stain?" I asked.

Matt's lips twisted into a frown. "No. It's not." He sounded so sure for someone who claimed he didn't know what was written beneath, but I didn't question him. I trusted him completely. If he didn't think it important, then it wasn't.

I held up the princess's journal. "It's not in here, either. I've read it over and over." I dropped it on the table, next to the parchment. Though I'd read the prophecy, experienced the prophecy, sometimes it didn't feel real at all.

Matt glanced sideways. "I'm sorry."

"For what?"

He shrugged. "For everything. I don't know." He flopped into the nearest chair. "For the situation. For being difficult and moody."

"You're always difficult and moody. You have been the entire time I've known you. It would be disconcerting if you weren't."

"Well, you've been a sarcastic ass for the entirety of our relationship. Glad to see that's not changed with your sudden nobility."

"Such disrespect," I said, knocking hard into Matt's arm. "I thought we were friends."

"We're best friends," Matt said, smiling slightly. "Forever."

"Good. I couldn't bear it if we weren't." I bent over the parchments, studying them in the low light. "I'm sorry too, you know. For everything. For dragging you on this quest in the first place."

"You didn't drag me. I gladly followed."

"You didn't have to."

"I did," Matt said, pointing to the prophecy. "You needed a mage. It said it right there."

"I could've found one."

"No, you couldn't have." He dropped the book in his hand and knuckled his eyes. "I heard about the others helping to vet potential soul mates during the ball. It's a good idea."

"Is it?"

"Yes."

I flexed my thumb. "I guess it might not be so bad to be bound to someone. In the grand scheme of things, it's a fair trade-off for living. Being happy is a bonus. Right?"

Matt grunted. "Make up your mind, Arek. One moment it's how much you don't want to choose a soul mate, and the next you're hanging curtains and planning on ruling for the rest of your life."

"Hey." I lifted a finger. "That's not fair. This is life or death. My life or death. And life is my preferred option, thank you. But if I'm facing down death, I'm going to do what I can to survive."

Sagging in the chair, Matt pinched the bridge of his nose and closed his eyes. "I know. I'm sorry. I'm not in a good mood."

"Ha!" I clapped my hand on Matt's shoulder. "Right in character for you, then. Come on. I think the others are playing a game in the throne room. Something with dice. I could use your magic to cheat."

"No thanks. I think I'll stay here and continue to look, just in case."

"Oh. Maybe I'll stay here with you, then?"

"No." Matt pushed my shoulder. "Go be with the others. Have fun. You'll just distract me anyway and make me grumpier than I already am."

I snorted. "I don't think that's possible."

"See? I'm already annoyed."

"Funny," I said. "Are you sure? I . . . wouldn't mind sitting here with you. I'll be quiet. Or you could read to me? Maybe hearing things out loud will help reveal something that could solve all my problems."

Brow furrowed, Matt caressed the spine of the book of laws. "You'd rather be here with me reviewing this information than be with the others playing a game?"

"Like that's a question. Of course I'd rather be with you." I snapped my mouth shut, worried I'd overstepped, but Matt merely shrugged.

"It's your castle. I'm not going to kick you out of the library." He cleared his throat. "Here." He passed me a book titled *Contract Magic: Promises, Oaths, & Declarations*. "I've read it cover to cover. It's dry, but maybe hearing you read will make something stand out." I flipped through the faded pages. "You could work on your literacy anyway." He stood and pawed through the documents on the table.

I licked my lips and cracked open the book. "Chapter One: Spoken Contracts."

A few hours later, Matt snored from his slumped position in his chair, an open book on his chest and a scroll loosely rolled in his hand. Gently, I took the book and the scroll from his grip and placed them on the table.

I touched his shoulder to rouse him.

He flinched. "Arek?"

My heart twinged. "Yeah."

"You shouldn't have stayed." He dropped his leg to the floor.

Well, that hurt, but I couldn't help but poke at the wound. "Why?"

"It'll be harder later."

Oh. Later, when I'm bound to someone else. When I won't be able to spend time with the person who means most to me in the world. Matt was . . . pushing me away. "Come on," I said, proud my voice remained steady. "Time for bed."

He yawned wide. He stood, but instead of following me toward the door, he went to the couch near the wall. He grabbed the blanket from the back and crawled onto the cushions. Tucking himself in, he didn't even kick off his boots and was out like a light within a moment.

Huh. Taking it upon myself, I wrangled off his boots and tucked his feet under the blanket. I blew out the candles and banked the fire. I left the mess of documents as it was, for us to continue to review in the morning, then closed the door softly when I left.

I'd thought Matt was handling things better than the others, better than me, but maybe he wasn't. Maybe he was just better at hiding it.

CHAPTER 26

A knock on my door roused me from a fitful sleep. I blinked awake in time to see my door open and Bethany waltz inside dressed in more fabric and frills than I had ever seen on an outfit.

"Morning," she said, beaming. "You should probably be awake and dressed by now."

I groaned and flopped back onto the pillows. The sunlight pouring in from the high window marked the time as mid-morning. "Probably," I said, rubbing the sleep from my eyes. I felt fatigued. The tingling sensation that preceded the fading of my body parts had spread overnight. That coupled with the anticipation of the feast and the ball and the rest of my life had made it almost impossible to sleep.

Bethany took a seat in the chair at the table. "The first of our guests should be arriving today."

"Already?"

"Yes. We only have three days before the masquerade, Arek."

"Huh. I guess I should greet them when they get here."

"That would be a good idea. Unless you don't want to. You are the king. You could delegate."

I shrugged. "Harlow would have a stroke if I didn't show to greet the first noble guests that the castle has seen in decades. Like you said, I am the king. Somehow. Unfortunately for both me and the kingdom."

She looked away and tugged on a ringlet of her styled hair.

"Is something wrong?"

Bethany wrinkled her nose. "You know, you're really oblivious."

"Well, I've never been accused of being overly smart."

"You're smart." She leveled an intense gaze at me. "When it comes to making quick decisions, you're a genius. You don't give yourself enough credit."

I sat up straighter because this conversation felt like one for which I wanted to be upright.

"Are you trying to flatter me, Bethany?"

She rolled her eyes. "Arek, I love you as a brother, but you test my nerves so much, all the time."

"Part of my charm."

"Right. Anyway, I don't know if anyone has said this to you, so I'm going to be the one to do it."

Yikes. I readied myself for the harsh truth incoming.

"You're a great king."

What? I scrunched my nose. "I couldn't be much worse than the one before me."

"Will you stop? Take the compliment. You're a great king. You make sound decisions. You're an excellent leader."

I opened my mouth to protest, but she held up her hand.

"Just listen. I know we each played our role in defeating Barthly. They were literally spelled out for us in that prophecy. I happened to be your bard, which I loved. I loved using my talents to your benefit. Sionna was your fighter. Lila was your rogue. Rion was your protector. And Matt was your magic."

"And I was the chosen one who had to make it to the end. I know this."

"*No.* That's where you're wrong. The whole time you thought all you had to do was survive. That living was all you were good for, and that was your only purpose."

My hands fisted in the sheets. "Yeah. You guys had to get me to the throne room with the sword in my hand. All I had to do was swing."

Bethany shook her head, her auburn hair swinging in her face. "Arek, you are so much more than the guy who swung a sword. You led us. Your quick thinking got us through so many tough situations. Your ability to delegate and recognize the strengths in others was our best asset. I mean, you were able to get two disparate personalities in Rion and Lila to not only work together, but fall in love."

Crossing my arms, I raised my eyebrow. "I am not responsible for those two falling in love."

"No, but you did bring them together. You brought all of us together."

"It was the prophecy."

"Arek, you *are* the prophecy." She picked up the crown from its place on the table. The jewels glinted in the sunlight. "You are the person to usher in the thousand years of peace."

"And?"

"And we all just want you to be happy."

I picked at a loose thread on the quilt. "What if being happy isn't part of the prophecy?"

"Then it's a shit prophecy."

I laughed. "No lies detected."

"Arek, accept that you're king. That you're a leader. And for spirits' sake, listen to your heart about this soul mate business. I think you're making it much harder than it needs to be."

"What do you mean by that?"

She pressed her lips flat.

The door opened, and Matt poked his head inside. "Hey, I received a message from one of our guards that a retinue will be here in about an hour." He gave me a once-over. "You should probably get dressed, sire."

Ah, I was "sire" again, but of course, said in a tone that was a total insult. I really needed to learn how he did that, so I could return the favor.

"Lord Matt," I said, using his title though it didn't have the same bite, "would you fetch Harlow for me? I believe I shall need a cape for this meeting."

Matt snorted and closed the door.

Bethany sighed.

"What?"

She rolled her eyes, then stood and waltzed out of my room.

It was time. My crown had been shined to a high gloss, as had my boots. I wore a cape over a fitted and laced tunic and a pair of fine trousers. Matt stood to my right in formal robes, which had made me laugh with delight when I first saw him. I quickly stopped when he pinned me with a classic withering glare and reminded me he'd found the spell to turn people into toads.

Sionna and Rion stood to my left, shining in armor. Bethany and Lila stood on the lowest step. To my despair, Crow perched high in a window, overlooking the scene with his hooked beak, death claws, and aura of gloom.

Don't screw this up. Don't screw this up. Don't screw this up.

Swallowing, I tugged at the high neck of my tunic, then adjusted the drape of my cape. I crossed my legs, then uncrossed them and settled my feet flat against the floor. I clasped the arms of the throne, then placed my hands in my lap, then decided that one arm on the throne and one in my lap would look the most nonchalant.

"Stop fidgeting," Matt said, voice low. "You'll do fine."

Okay. I went with sitting like a statue, which wasn't unnatural at all. My back was so straight, I could have been used as a measuring stick.

"Announcing the Lord and Lady of Summerhill, William and Eliza, and their family," the page called as the two finely dressed individuals entered the throne room, followed by a large crew of children and servants.

The lord bowed and the lady curtsied.

"Welcome to the castle," I said stiffly while doing my best impression of Harlow. "We're pleased you've traveled so far to attend the feast."

"It's our pleasure, King Arek." The lord addressed me, returning my stilted language. He eyed me with thinly veiled suspicion and disbelief. "We have brought our household members, including our eldest two children who may be interested in squiring with your first knight."

Two young adults strode forward, both of them about my age, and both of them taller and bulkier than me. For a moment, I thought they were going to charge the throne and throw me off, but instead they paused, cast a vaguely disconcerted look at Matt and his staff, then kneeled.

"Oh, don't do that," I said quickly, waving my hands. "Please. That is not necessary."

They exchanged a glance and stood. I gestured to my side. "This is Sir Rion and General Sionna. They will be deciding who becomes a squire. I suggest observing a training before the feast."

"Yes, sire," they said in unison.

"Until then, please make yourselves at home. The castle staff will show you to your chambers and take care of your needs."

They bowed. "Thank you, sire."

After a few bustling minutes, the group was escorted out of the throne room and into the guest wings of the castle.

I let out a breath. "How many of those do we have to do?"

Bethany looked over her shoulder at me. "About twenty more."

"Twenty?"

"Over the next three days."

"Shit."

"Do we have to be at every one?" Lila asked, plucking at the green cloak she wore. "This is itchy. And I don't think Crow likes being inside."

"I don't think I like him being inside," I muttered. The murder bird shifted on the window ledge as if he heard and understood. "I mean, yes? I think. We've met the first family all together. Won't subsequent ones feel slighted if we're not all here?"

Harlow cleared his throat. "King Arek is correct."

A ripple of collective grumbling surged through the group, which I did my best to ignore.

A page walked into the room and stepped smartly onto the ribbon of carpet. "Announcing the Ladies of Winterhill, Lady Petra and Lady Gwenyth, and their family."

We all snapped to attention, resuming our positions, and I mustered my best smile.

Three days later, the castle was teeming with people. I couldn't so much as walk from my chambers to the council room without being bowed to or curtsied at or called "sire" by anyone I passed. I had to wear the crown at all times, and it weighed heavy on my brow. I couldn't be silly, or make faces, or run around in an untucked tunic with my hair untamed. I couldn't slurp my soup for fear of one of the guests seeing or hearing. I couldn't even spar with Rion without half a dozen people clapping each time I did something remotely skillful. It was madness, but it also meant we had succeeded in filling the court with people who acknowledged me as king. It was a win, even if an annoying one.

I was relieved to find several potential suitors my age among the visiting nobles. One of the Summerhill young adults, who engaged Sir Rion in deep discussions about chivalry and shared the same gods as him, was quite striking in appearance, and they had glanced meaningfully in my direction a few times. Though I wouldn't say no to a dance during the masquerade, and while I may have harbored an inappropriate thought or two while alone in my chambers when considering them as a potential soul mate, my heart didn't thump wildly the way it did when I thought about Matt. Though I had to remind myself that the level of feelings I had for Matt wasn't a realistic standard for week-long courtship.

One of the Winterhills passed me in a hallway and slipped a note into my pocket about scheduling a midnight rendezvous, and while I was flattered, I didn't have the heart to engage in a moment that might not possibly go any further than one night. I knew the feast was a mission of my life or my death, but even with that knowledge, my focus was more on getting through to the other side of the chaos.

I also thought about Matt constantly—how he'd muttered my name before he curled up on the sofa in the library. How I'd only seen him at announcements, demonstrations, and in passing since the arrival of our guests. I missed him.

It was weird to miss someone who was within reach. But I did. I missed him fiercely. And it hurt to think about how this was just a taste of the future. A future where I was bonded with someone else. And while Matt would technically still be in my life, it wouldn't be the way I wanted. It was one thing to think about all of this as a concept, but experiencing it was vastly different. I wondered if the ache would fade in time or if it would always feel this sharp, this immediate.

Despite my heartache and the fact that my attention was split between so many things at once, I hadn't screwed up royally yet. Yes, there was skepticism from our visitors. There was wariness. There was disbelief. There was concern. But I hadn't experienced any outright hostility, and none of our guests had tried to point a sword or dagger in my general direction.

Having the others around me helped, since they were an

intimidating group. People frequently stared at Matt's staff and Bethany's harp, as many remained wary of magic in the aftermath of Barthly. I did my best to assuage our guests' fears by having Matt and Bethany give demonstrations. For the awe of the crowd, Matt made plants and flowers grow, and Bethany charmed everyone she met, even without magic.

With all the successes, I still needed a moment alone to gather myself before the big event.

"Sire," Harlow said, popping into my chamber and right into my musings, "the feast will begin shortly. Do you need any assistance preparing?"

"No, thank you, Harlow. But please check on the others."

"I will, sire. Your costume for the masquerade is in your wardrobe for when the time comes."

"Thank you."

He bowed, a tiny smile lighting up his otherwise dour face. "May I have a moment, sire?"

"Yeah, sure. What's up?"

He stepped fully into the room and closed the door. "I wanted to say . . . Well . . . The servants are all very happy to see the castle full." He clasped his hands behind his back. "We've waited for peace, and I feel it's finally here. And it's your doing."

"Thank you. Well, not only mine." I reached for my cape, which I admitted I'd inexplicably grown fond of, and flung it around my shoulders. "I couldn't have done it without the others."

"Yes, of course, sire. I'm thankful for them as well."

"Me too." I took a breath and spread my clammy palms down my clothes. I mustered a smile. "How do I look?" Spreading my arms, I slowly spun.

"Like a king."

"Well, that's good at least. One less thing to worry about." I followed Harlow out my door and clapped him on the shoulder when I passed. "Now, let's throw a feast, shall we?"

CHAPTER 27

I'd never been to an event this rich, much less presided over one. I'd been to harvest festivals when the last of the crop had been gleaned. I'd been to wakes when the village lost one of its members. I'd been to celebrations when two people desired to bind themselves to each other. But I wouldn't categorize any of those as feasts.

This was a *feast*.

There was enough food to feed a small village for months. I tried to quiet my feelings of guilt by reminding myself that this was an effort of goodwill and would benefit everyone if I could pull it off.

"Kind of sickening, isn't it?" Bethany asked, leaning over to whisper in my ear, as everyone shuffled in and took their seats, curtsying and bowing to me before they did so.

I nodded.

I sat in the middle of the head table, which looked out over all the guest tables. Bethany was on my immediate left and Matt on my right. Lila and Rion were next to Matt and Sionna and Meredith next to Bethany. Standing off to the side was Harlow, who raised his eyebrows and nodded meaningfully toward the guests. Right—I was supposed to make some sort of welcome speech. The tables were buzzing with chatter and laughter, so I stood and cleared my throat. Almost immediately, the attention of the room shifted toward me. In the span of a few seconds, the crowd had quieted.

"Thank you all for joining us for this winter feast," I said, indicating the massive spread. "I'm grateful we can now begin to heal the wounds that the previous regime inflicted upon our great kingdom and realm. My council and I will endeavor to ensure that peace will grow across the land and that kindness and friendship will be the rule instead of the exception. Now . . ." I grabbed my goblet and raised it to the crowd. "To new friends."

"To new friends," they chorused.

I drank from my goblet of water and set it down. "Let's feast!"

I sat just as someone from the crowd yelled out, "Long live King Arek the Kind!"

"Yes! Long live the king!"

"Long live the king!" my friends echoed.

I suppressed the scowl that I wanted to give them all and smiled instead. After the cheers died down and everyone tucked into their food, Matt leaned on my shoulder.

"How long did you practice that speech?"

"Days!"

He laughed.

"What? I wanted to sound kingly, so I practiced. Did it sound okay?"

Matt's soft smile made my middle thrum. "It was amazing." He downed his own goblet and reached for the pitcher of wine and filled it to the brim. "You're amazing," he added.

I looked away quickly, my face hot and my throat suddenly tight. I forced a smile and clinked my cup to his. "Glad you finally caught on," I said with as much self-importance as I could muster.

Rolling his eyes, he focused on his meal, dishing a huge helping of mashed potatoes onto the fine pewter of his plate. "Ass."

Laughing, I took the spoon from his hand. "Jerk."

"Glad you finally caught on," he parroted, smiling around a mouthful of carrots.

I ducked my head to hide my giggles. And as we passed the meal together, laughing at each other, I cataloged every moment, every joke, every flash of Matt's smile. Because as much as I wanted this to be my future, Matt by my side presiding over every feast, it wouldn't be. And the bittersweetness of that knowledge seeped into the spaces between us.

A chorus of "Long live the king!" rang out amid the crowd and snapped me back to the present and out of my maudlin thoughts.

Bethany and Lila had hired a troupe of jugglers to dance through the aisles as everyone ate, entertaining the smallest children, while musicians played several tunes and a group sang. I ate my fill, keeping to water because I was not about to make a drunken fool of myself, and sat back to watch the scene unfold before me.

"Not bad," Bethany said.

"You did a good job."

"I did, didn't I?"

I held up my goblet, and she clinked hers against mine in celebration. "To you," I said.

"To me," she agreed.

Once the food had been consumed and the dishes cleared, it was time for the masquerade ball. The servants pushed the tables out of the way, and the crowd dispersed to don their costumes.

I managed to extricate myself from the crowd without too much bowing. Slipping to my quarters, I took a moment to myself and breathed. I tossed my crown to the table and ran my hands through my hair.

Shrugging out of my cape, I hung it over the back of my chair, then opened the wardrobe. I hadn't looked at my costume ahead of time, but I should've. Harlow was lucky there were so many people in the castle. It would be untoward for me to kill the steward in the midst of a peaceful celebration.

The jacket was bright green. My mask was also green, with small purple accents and with a large green feather attached to the side, which plumed over my head like a peacock. Oh my spirits, I was a peacock.

I tugged the lapels of the jacket and shook my head. Oh well. Not much I could do about it right then, and I couldn't stay in my room and hide. That wouldn't do, especially if I was to find my soul mate in the throngs of eligible people.

Closing my door behind me, I made my way to the party. I hadn't lingered in my room, but the musicians had already started by the time I made it back to the grand hall. I stopped in the entranceway and marveled at the work the servants and my friends had put into the evening.

Matt had spelled a few balls of light to float in the air to illuminate the room with an ethereal glow. The entertainers roamed the area. Servants carried trays of drinks. Ribbons and flowers were strategically placed about the room.

Most importantly, though, was that the citizens of Ere celebrated. They mingled and talked and laughed. They drank wine and ate sweets. They swayed with the music, their capes and dresses twirling in bright swashes of fabric. They were *happy*. Probably for the first time in forty years, they were able to relax and have fun, and that felt bigger than any treaty or trade deal or political connection.

The atmosphere was festive and beautiful. For a moment, I was proud. Proud of all we'd accomplished. We'd provided aid, resurrected diplomatic relationships, and restarted the kingdom on the path to healing. We'd done good work. And even if I faded away in the next week, I'd take this as my legacy.

"Arek."

I turned at my name. "Isn't the point of a masquerade anonymity?" I asked as Bethany looped her arm through mine and dragged me to the dance floor, where several couples were already dancing. She wore a maroon dress and a black mask with purple flowers. Sparkles and glitter adorned her cheeks.

She huffed at me. "As if everyone doesn't know the green peacock with the red hair is King Arek the Kind." She spun me around and clasped my hand, guiding my other hand to the indent of her waist. We moved to the music—a waltz, I thought. I was kind of bad at it, but Bethany led me around the room. "Now, I know for a fact that in a few moments the eldest child of Lord Summerhill is going to cut in. Their name is Gren and they're gorgeous and they want to squire for Rion. They beat the stuffing out of the other recruits, and it was hot."

I raised an eyebrow. "That doesn't sound good for morale."

"Are you kidding? It was amazing to watch."

I spun her, and she laughed, her auburn hair trailing behind her, and when I yanked her back to me, a little too hard, she crashed back into my arms. I laughed.

"We're not good at this," I said.

"Speak for yourself; I'm amazing at it."

"Well, I'm not good. How about that?"

"I think you're fine," a voice said. We halted midstep, and Bethany smirked at me knowingly. "May I cut in?" the person asked.

This must be Gren.

Bethany curtsied. "Of course." She stepped on my foot as she passed by me. "Have fun," she whispered, then winked.

Gren was taller than me, bulkier too, but they didn't lord it over me when they stepped into my space.

"You'll have to lead," I said.

Gren grinned. "I can do that."

Gren was excellent at firmly guiding me into the correct position as we moved around the floor. We didn't talk, except to exchange pleasantries, because *Would you bond with me to keep me from dying?* wasn't the greatest conversation starter and would probably have Gren running in the other direction. But it was nice to be in the moment—to feel their grip on my side, and the pounding of my heart, and the stone floor beneath my boots, and the pulse of the music in my veins, and it was almost enough to distract me from wishing I was dancing with Matt instead. By the time the song ended, my face was flushed. I forgot to let go, until Gren stepped out of the cage of my arms.

"Oh, sorry."

Gren's mouth ticked up. They bowed.

I bowed in return. "Thank you for the dance."

"You're welcome, sire."

I smirked. "The hair give it away?"

Gren shook their head. "No. You just stand out."

"Oh." My mouth went dry. "So do you."

Gren's laugh was low and throaty, completely different from Matt's. It was nice. Nice enough that I had the vague flash of wanting to hear it in my ear, but my thought was cut off.

"Okay, you've had your turn." Lila knocked her hip into Gren's and physically moved them out of the way.

Stunned, Gren's smile dimmed. "Oh yes, my apologies. Another dance later in the evening, then, sire?"

"Yes. That would be lovely."

Lila made a face visible through her mask and grabbed my hand. "Yeah, later." She pushed a lock of her blond hair that had tangled in her own mask over her ear. "Okay, Arek. Have I got the soul mate for you."

"Really. Do tell."

The music started again, and Lila pulled me along. "Yes. Her name is Petal, and she is from the Autumnhill family. She likes birds and embroidery."

And that was how my night went. I danced with Lila, then Petal, and then Rion, and then someone whose name I couldn't remember. I danced again with Gren, and I shivered when they dipped me backward at the end of the song. I danced with another individual Bethany brought over. Halfway through the masquerade, I had danced with most of the populace within marrying age. It had been fun, and almost enough to soothe my heartache, but not quite, because as much as I liked

Gren's brown hair, the color wasn't quite the right shade, and though Petal's fingertips were warm when she caressed my hand, they were too smooth, missing the familiar callouses.

During a pause in the music, I took a much-needed break. Excusing myself from the dance floor, I meandered over to a tray of water. I grasped a cup from the servant and took a long gulp before ducking into an archway next to a tapestry.

"Arek!" Sionna whispered.

Startling, I nearly dropped the cup. "Sionna!" I said, clasping one hand over my heart. "What the hells?"

She peered out from behind a tapestry. Meredith peeked over her shoulder, her chin digging into Sionna's shoulder. "Hello," she said, smiling wide. Meredith tittered.

"Why are you hiding behind the tapestry?"

"My mother is here," Sionna said, as if imparting a secret. "I forgot how much I don't get along with her." Then she giggled.

"Are—are you drunk?"

"No," Sionna said, swiping at the air. "Nonsense."

"She totally is," Meredith said, laughing. "It's the best."

"Great."

"It's fine," Sionna said. "I have loyal guards placed all around the room. Don't worry."

That was good to know. "Okay. Well, have a fun time. I'm going to dance some more, I think."

Sionna clasped my arm. Her voice dropped into a serious tone. "Have you found your soul mate yet?"

"No. I don't know. I mean, there were a few prospects. There was this person named Gren—"

"I know who your soul mate is," she said, nodding. "I found them."

I blinked. I'd assumed Bethany and Lila were the only ones trying to set me up with someone. But Sionna must be in on it too. The three of them must have had a side bet.

"Go on."

She pointed down the length of the room, to a darkened corner. "They're down there. Look for the red mask with a beak."

"You're drunk."

"I'm serious."

Well, it couldn't be any worse than the handsy lady who grabbed my ass a few dances ago. "Okay. I'll go talk to them."

"Be nice."

"I'm always nice."

Meredith laughed like a chicken. It was not at all cute. But Sionna must have thought it was adorable because she turned and kissed Meredith on the tip of her nose.

And that was enough for me. I could handle drunk antics, but cute ones were my limit. Sionna may be tipsy, but she wouldn't steer me wrong. She hadn't in the past, even when I had annoyed her.

I left the space by the tapestry and wove through the crowd, ducking out of the way of eager dance partners, bowing in apology as I sidestepped them, until I made it to the darkened corner. Sure enough, someone stood there, a thin figure in a sharply cut red jacket, black trousers, and black boots. They wore a red mask with a beak, but the dark cowlick on the crown of their head was a dead giveaway.

Matt. Sionna had sent me toward Matt. My heart lurched. Why? Did she know about my feelings for him? Did the rest of them know? Was this a joke? No, Sionna would not be that cruel, but if this was a push toward him, then she couldn't have known he had rejected me. The misunderstanding didn't stop that stubborn flame of hope from flaring back to life, though, enough that I found myself saying his name.

"Matt."

He turned on his heel and wobbled. "Arek." He drew out the second syllable.

"Oh my spirits, are you drunk too?"

"Me? *Pfft*." He teetered. "You're a peacock."

"I am. That doesn't change the fact that you're tipsy."

He snorted. "S'not true." His words slurred together, the syllables banging into each other.

I laughed. Because Matt was drunk. Very drunk. He held a goblet, and the wine spilled over his hand as he moved.

"Matt, how much have you had?"

"All of it."

"All of it?"

He nodded. "Yes."

My general and my mage were sloshed. My bard was busying thrusting eligible people at me. What a night.

I took Matt's hand. "Come on, we should get you water and a place to sit before you fall over. Or spell something by accident and cause a political incident."

Despite his level of inebriation, Matt's grip was strong, and he halted me from pulling him through the crowd.

"Dance with me."

I paused, unsure and confused. "What?"

"Dancing." He waved his hand. "That thing you've been doing a lot with people."

"I'm aware." I licked my lips, my mouth dry. Saying I was

conflicted would be an understatement, but Matt offered and I . . . wanted. "You want to? With me?"

Tipping his head to the side, he squinted at me through the eyes of his mask. "Dance with me, sire."

I swallowed. Well, I had danced with everyone else. Why not Matt? "Okay, Lord Matt."

His eyebrows shot up in a dare. I wasn't sure I should even try to move him to the dance floor, so I merely adjusted my grip on his hand and loosely grasped his hip, guiding him into position. He was remarkably malleable, probably due to the amount of alcohol. If he happened to cut himself, I'd be able to catch a buzz from his blood.

"Are you going to lead, sire? Or should I?"

"The better dancer should, I believe."

"Excellent. Follow me."

I laughed. "You? Do you remember that harvest festival where you almost fell into the bonfire?"

He pouted. "Fine."

"Besides, you're barely standing."

To say he was unsteady was trivializing. I couldn't let him hurt himself, so I wrapped my hand around his waist, spread my fingers across the small of his back to support his ungainly body. It brought us close, so close that I could see the brown of his eyes and the sweep of his lashes in the colored light of his magic floating above us. Luckily for us, the next song started, a slower tempo that wouldn't require me to sweep Matt across the floor.

I took a step, he followed, and within a few beats, we danced and spun around the cramped space, the crowd making way for our awkward endeavor. Even with Matt stepping on my feet occasionally and the stumble we took into a table, it didn't feel awkward. It felt *right*, like Matt belonged right there with me amid all the chaos.

For all Matt's inebriation, within a few moments, his gait evened and matched me step for step. I spun him, and it was graceless, but he let out a breathy laugh and smoothly stepped right back into my arms. Smiling, I pulled him closer, until there wasn't anything between us but fabric and air. His breath hit my chin, and he smelled of wine. His grip on my hand was firm, his other arm curled around my shoulder, his fingertips dug into my jacket, blunt points of pressure. I was a prisoner to the moment, aware of him on every level, where he was pressed against me, where he wasn't, where I wanted him to be. Despite how painful it would be later, I was unwilling to let go.

My heart pounded. My entire being yearned for him. It was a kind of magic, being this close to Matt, seeing the dimple of his cheeks, the mole on the side of his neck, the scar on his chin, the pulse of his throat. My gaze dropped to the red bow of his mouth, the way it tipped toward me, and my whole body flushed.

"You're a fine dancer, sire." His eyelashes fluttered. He ducked his chin and looked away, and I wanted him to look back to me, to look at only me.

"Stop calling me 'sire.'"

"It's your title."

I rolled my eyes. "You don't care about titles."

"No," he said, and then his gaze was back on me. He licked his lips. "I don't. I care about you."

"Yeah?" I asked, my voice low and breathless, so achingly

full of hope that I couldn't hide it even if I wanted. "You do?"

"I always have." His forehead crinkled. "Before everything."

He abruptly stopped dancing, and I stuck in my spot. He curled his hand around the back of my neck, then pulled me to him.

He kissed me. He kissed me in the middle of a crowd, pressing his mouth into mine, insistent, and inelegant, and the best thing that had ever happened to me.

I froze, and then I kissed him back, because *this was Matt*. Matt was kissing me. I tightened my hold on him, crushing him to me because I never wanted to let him go. This was everything I had wished for since I'd fulfilled the prophecy, and it was happening. Maybe . . . maybe I'd get my fairy-tale ending. Maybe a happy ever after was written for me after all.

I was only vaguely aware that the music stopped. Someone pulled on my arm. I shrugged them off, because I wasn't going to stop kissing Matt for anything, but it was Matt who broke away.

His lips were red. His face was pink. His eyes were wet. "Oh shit," he said, pressing his fingers to his mouth. "Oh shit." Then he turned on his heel and ran.

"Matt!"

Bethany tugged on my arm, and I whirled on her. "What the fuck, Bethany?"

She narrowed her eyes. "You were making a scene," she hissed. "And now you're making a worse one. But go after him. I'll deal with this."

The "this" was a bunch of gossips and whispers and people holding their hands to their mouths in scandalized fashion.

Oh. Yeah. The king probably shouldn't make out with his mage in the middle of a masquerade. But whatever, Bethany would fix it; she could charm a snake out of its skin if needed.

She pushed me before I could make the situation any worse by speaking, and I took off running after Matt. The halls outside the throne room were also crowded, but with smart individuals who took their trysts out of the view of the general crowd. Noted. Next time. Kiss Matt in the hallway.

If there was a next time. There better be a next time. I desperately hoped there would be a next time because I loved him. And maybe, just maybe, he loved me too.

Or maybe, a voice of doubt whispered to me, he was just drunk and overwhelmed, and maybe he didn't mean it. He could be embarrassed. I shook my head, trying to dispel those thoughts. Whatever it was, I had to find him.

The plume of my feather bounced and smacked me in the head as I ran. I ripped off the mask as I skidded to a stop in front of the doors to the library and threw them open.

Matt stood by the table, head bowed, mask thrown on the ground. His shoulders shook.

"Matt."

He whirled and wiped his sleeve over his face, hurriedly scrubbing away the evidence of his distress. "Hey," he said, his face red with wine and tears. "Uh . . . sorry." His voice was scraped raw.

I held up my hand and crossed the distance between us. My hands trembled as I touched his face and crowded close to him.

"Hey," I said. "Are you okay?"

"No," he said, face crumpling. "I'm drunk."

My throat clogged. "I know you are. It's okay." I wanted to cry. I wanted to take Matt to my room and kiss him until my lips went numb and we fell asleep tangled in the blankets. I wanted to tell him I loved him. I didn't want him to be sad. I wanted him to be okay.

"I shouldn't have done that," he said, looking devastated.

I sucked in a harsh breath. Fear and worry swirled in my stomach. "Why?"

Tears leaked out of the corners of Matt's eyes. "Because I *can't*. No matter what Bethany says."

It was like being stabbed. I'd been stabbed once; well, not really stabbed—grazed by a knife in a fight. We'd run into a few followers of Barthly on the journey, and one managed a lucky strike to my side, before Matt had blasted him with magic, and Sionna ran her sword through him. He'd only given me a flesh wound, but it had bled fiercely and hurt like a motherfucker.

This was worse. This was much worse. Fuck, Bethany must have meddled and asked Matt to at least try to be with me in order to help keep me from fading. Knowing that Matt had tried, yet couldn't follow through, hurt worse than his first rejection. It hurt us both, and I hated it. I hated the situation. I hated that Matt couldn't feel for me the same way I felt for him. I hated that he'd tried to force himself to. I hated every tear that slid down Matt's flushed face.

I swiped my thumb over his cheek and wiped one away. "You don't have to do anything you don't want, Matt. Please don't do anything you don't want, even if you think it would make me happy."

His eyes fluttered shut. "King Arek the Kind," he said on a breath. "Always saying the right thing. Doing the right thing. Utterly unselfish."

"Not true," I said. "I'm a horrible brat. I'm selfish. I'm the worst. I drugged our friend to see if she liked me."

Matt chuckled through his tears. "Poor judgment."

"I have so much of that." I rocked back on my heels. If there was one thing I could try to give to Matt in this moment, it was a way out. "You're drunk."

"I am."

Matt stepped away from me, and I felt the loss of his warmth keenly. If Matt's kiss was the best thing ever, this was the worst. He crossed the room and rummaged around in a basket that was haphazardly left by the couch. It was the one from that day with Lila, the picnic Matt had orchestrated that went terribly awry due to her death bird. He yanked out a bottle and held it up.

"What are you doing?"

"Sharing a drink with my king," he said, his voice tinged with bitterness. Then he softened. "With my best friend."

Matt grimaced as he popped open the wine. Then he drank straight from the bottle, gulping it down as rivulets of red ran from the corners of his mouth. When he stopped, he scrubbed his sleeve over his face, then staggered toward me. He offered me the bottle, and I took a swig. It was sweet, a fruit wine, something Lila would've liked. Spirits, Matt was always so attuned to everyone, paid attention to the smallest details.

I handed it back to him, and he took another drink as if fortifying himself.

"Now I'm very drunk," he said, and his legs shook. He took a step and stumbled. Instinctively, I grabbed him, wrapping my arm around him, hauling him close. My fingers flexed against his side. His shoulder knocked into mine, and he tucked his face close to my neck, his breaths as whispers over my skin.

"We should get you water before you pass out," I said, my voice choked.

He shrugged limply as his eyes started to droop.

"You'll care when you wake up tomorrow feeling like you've fallen down a hill."

Manhandling him, I half carried, half dragged him to the couch. I dumped him on it as gently as I could, but his limbs flailed. Curling up on the cushions, he tucked his hands beneath his head as I draped the blanket over him.

"I'll fetch you water."

I straightened, but his hand shot out from beneath the blanket, his fingers wrapped around my wrist.

"Stay."

His eyes were already closed. He was on the verge of passing out. A glass of water wasn't going to help him. I needed to return to the masquerade and dance and mingle and find someone willing to be my soulbond. It was a matter of life and death, but even with a broken heart, I couldn't deny Matt.

"Okay." I sat on the floor next to the couch in front of him and clasped his hand in both of mine. "I'll stay."

A small smile graced his lips. "Thank you, sire."

I swallowed down my tears. "You're welcome, Lord Matt. Sleep now."

He did.

I stayed on the cold hard floor for a long time, watching the rise and fall of Matt's breaths. I tucked his hand back by his side and adjusted his blanket. Occasionally, sounds from the masquerade faded in through the door, but eventually they quieted. I tipped my head back onto the cushion, next to Matt's legs, and my arms flopped to my sides. My fingers grazed the cover of a familiar book.

The journal. I'd left it with Matt forever ago. He must've been reading it. I picked it up and flipped through, landing on a page that looked like it had been well-handled.

When he started amassing power, I knew there would be little time for us to prepare. Rumors came swiftly of a dark mage, one who would see the downfall of us all. Our prophets had seen the end of my family's line, but we didn't realize it would come so soon. While my father and sisters prepared for battle, I pushed my lady away. She wanted to stay by my side, but I wouldn't allow it. Couldn't allow it. Because I loved her and knew her staying would also be her end. I couldn't bear the thought. I loved her so fiercely, I only thought of her safety, her happiness, and I would not be the cause of her death. I let her go. It was the hardest thing I'd ever done, but I let her go and faced my destiny on my own. My one regret was that I did it harshly, and she left the castle in tears. If I ever get out of here, I'm going to tell her I love her.

It was the passage Lila had read that first night while the flames from the funeral pyre lit up the sky. The princess missed her chance to tell her beloved that she loved her. She pushed her away instead, pushed her toward a better future. I slammed the book closed. I didn't want to think about regret, not with my lips still stinging from Matt's kisses.

Throat tight, I looked to Matt's sleeping face. His beautiful, horrid face, and his plump awkward lips that I had kissed. I slid the journal away from me, and it knocked into the leg of the couch. I turned and buried my face into the cushion near Matt's hip and shuddered. I closed my eyes to banish the thoughts that passage formed in my mind. But I couldn't.

The princess never told her lady of her love, lost her chance due to circumstances beyond her control. I did not want to suffer the same fate. Even if tonight had made it clear my sentiments wouldn't be returned, I wanted to say it plainly for once. No second-guessing. No innuendo. No hedging around the truth. I'd tell him first thing in the morning, when he woke up. But for now, I wanted to get out my feelings, record them, so I wouldn't forget their strength in the light of day. With my days ticking down, there was no time for regret or embarrassment.

Fortunately, we were in the library. I found a quill, a pot of ink, and a scrap of spare parchment among the mess on Matt's table. In an attempt to make some room, I pushed aside some of the history books and scrolls, uncovering the prophecy laid flat on the table. I smiled to myself, thinking how a simple piece of parchment had led both of us here, to this castle, to this moment. Who knew where the next words I'd write would lead us. But I was finally ready to find out. *Dearest Matt,* I began, then poured all my feelings over the page, my months of yearning, my years of affection, my fondness for his dry wit and his sharp mind and his cowlick. I wrote of my previous plan to tell him about my feelings toward him when the prophecy ended, and then when it didn't, my fear that he'd feel obligated to bond to me if I told him the truth in the light of my circumstances. And lastly, the hope I felt when he kissed me at the ball tonight, but my understanding that he didn't feel the same way. When I was done, I signed it *Love always, Arek* with a flourish. I put down the quill and wiped my ink-stained hands on my trousers.

With all that completed, I still didn't want to leave him. I'd have a horrible neck ache in the morning, but I chose to sit on the floor and rest my head on the couch. I would undoubtedly endure a lecture from Harlow tomorrow about skipping out on the masquerade and abandoning my guests, but it was a small price to pay to be at Matt's side.

Chapter 28

A frantic knocking launched me out of sleep. I rubbed my sore neck and cursed. Sunlight streamed in the windows like a blade. I groaned and held up my hand to block it, though it didn't help much.

"Ow, ow, fuck," Matt said, pulling his blanket over his head. "What the hells?"

Oh yes. Matt. He drank. We danced. We kissed. I chased him. We fell asleep. He was hungover and hating life.

I loved him. He didn't love me.

"Why does it taste like something died in my mouth?" Matt asked. He squinted out from the cover of the blanket. His eyes were bloodshot. A crease from the cushion ran across his cheek. His hair stood on end.

"You drank all the wine in the castle."

"Oh," he said. He smacked his lips. "Oh."

"Yeah."

He rubbed a hand over his face. "What else did I do?"

I rolled out of the way of the sun and sprawled on the stone, my face luckily in a shadow. "What do you mean what else?"

"I remember the feast. I remember dancing . . . What happened after? How did I get in here?"

My body went cold. My stomach sank. "You don't remember?"

He groaned low. "Oh spirits, did I dance on a table? Turn someone into a toad?" He made another miserable noise. "My head. My brain is leaking from my ears."

"You . . ." I swallowed. "Don't remember dancing with me?"

The knocking came again, louder this time, insistent.

"With you?" Despite the sun, he fully emerged from beneath the blanket and gingerly sat up. He turned a shade of green and clapped a hand over his mouth, swallowing several times. I squirmed away, just in case, but he kept himself together. "No," he whispered. "We danced?"

He watched me warily. When I considered how I was going to handle my confession this morning, I hadn't factored in the possibility that Matt might not remember that we'd kissed. And as another round of aggressive knocking started and Matt scrunched his face in pain, telling him all that had happened in a rush while he tried not to vomit didn't seem the best option. Later, then. We'd have to talk later, but right now, the easiest solution was to tell a shortened version of the truth.

"Yeah. You stepped on my feet in the most awkward dance in the history of this kingdom, and then we came in here to escape the masquerade. You drank more, then passed out."

He wilted in relief. "Oh, thank the spirits."

My heart cracked a little more.

The knocking continued. "Come in," I yelled, hoping to break the weird tension between us. Groggy, I was not in the mood for any of it.

Harlow cleared his throat as he strode into the room. "Sire," he said, cutting me off. "Your guests are waiting for you to join them for breakfast."

"Are you serious?"

"As a heart problem, sire," Harlow said dryly.

Ugh. Why was sarcasm the thing that Harlow picked up from his interactions with me? "Where?"

"In the formal dining room."

I stood and staggered. My legs tingled, and I couldn't tell if my feet were just asleep or had disappeared altogether. That could be a problem.

Matt groaned like he was dying and rolled to his side, turning faintly green. "Please don't mention food," he whined.

"Stay here. Let Harlow take care of you." I rushed past Harlow, my gut swirling with emotions. "Matt needs water. Maybe some wine. Definitely a painkiller."

"Of course, sire." Harlow cleared his throat. "Might I suggest you return to your chamber and change before meeting our guests?"

I looked down at myself. I wore the costume from the night before. My shirt was untucked and wrinkled. I knew my hair was a mess without glancing in a mirror. My face flushed in embarrassment.

"That bad, huh?"

Harlow hummed. "To put it bluntly, yes."

"Right." I was about to complete a walk of shame in my own castle. And not even really a walk of shame at that because Matt and I hadn't done anything beyond kiss. *Matt.* I stared at his pinched face as he gamely tried to ignore the sun and Harlow and the task of waking. Yes, we'd talk later. After he felt better.

"Sire," Harlow prompted.

"Yes! Going." I shook myself out of my thoughts and placed all of it—Matt, my feelings, the soulbond—aside. I had to go be king.

Breakfast was awful.

I sat at the head of an exceedingly long table full of nobles, most of whom were half-asleep. The few who were awake watched me with sharp gazes, and I was thankful Harlow had laid a set of clothes out for me on the bed. The last thing I needed on this already horrible day was to commit a social faux pas that undid the progress we'd made with the court.

As it was, none of the guests spoke, everyone exhausted from the grand feast and ball. Based on their appearances, I wondered how late the party had gone and why breakfast had been scheduled for so early the next day. Definitely an oversight.

Once the food had been served, the room filled with the sounds of chewing, the scrape of utensils against plates, and the occasional snore. At least the food was good.

Of my council, only Sionna had made it to breakfast. The rest of the group was conspicuously absent, but I couldn't blame them. If I wasn't king, I would not have roused myself either. But I was grateful for the chance to speak to Sionna alone. I needed to know why she had pushed me toward Matt the night before, what she had thought might happen. Best to ease into it, though. I wasn't sure whether I'd be able to keep my composure if I had to endure any direct questioning from her, and I needed to in front of the guests.

"Where's Meredith?" I leaned over to her and asked, my voice low.

"Summoned to the kitchens this morning," she responded.

"And your mother and sister?"

Sionna pressed her lips together. "If I'm lucky, on their way home."

I snickered.

She nudged me with her arm. "How's Matt?"

I intentionally kept my tone light. "Hungover. I've never seen him that shade of green before."

Sionna muffled a laugh into her palm.

Thank the spirits for convenient segues. "Speaking of Matt," I started. "Last night, why did—"

"*Psst*, sire."

I swung my head to the sound and spied Meredith in the doorway. She looked pale and twitchy, which seemed to be the normal state of folks the morning after a ball. What worried me, however, was how she frantically beckoned me to her.

I cocked my head to the side. Sionna had noticed as well, her eyebrows knotted.

Well, I better find out what crisis awaited me. It couldn't be more awful than this painfully awkward breakfast. I stood, my chair scraping loudly in the hall, alerting everyone to my imminent departure and startling those who had fallen asleep in their chairs.

I cleared my throat. "Apologies. I have business to attend to. Please continue to enjoy your breakfast."

Then I turned on my heel and strode out, Sionna right behind me.

"Merry?" Sionna said, voice gentle once we cleared the other side of the door. She took Meredith's hand in hers. "What's wrong?"

Merry. How disgustingly cute.

"I think I've done something wrong," Meredith said, eyelashes wet.

"That's okay. I do things wrong all the time," I said, forcing a smile. "And I'm the king, so it's not like we can't fix it, whatever it is."

Meredith didn't take comfort in my words. In fact, they seemed to upset her more.

Sionna shot me a glare. "Just tell us what's wrong."

"I was in the kitchens. And I was summoned to the library to take Lord Matt some water and wine, since he was . . . not feeling well."

My whole being went cold. This was about Matt. "Is Matt okay?" I asked slowly, vaguely terrified.

She didn't answer. She bit her lip as she looked to me with wide eyes. "I'm sorry."

I sucked in a harsh breath. "What happened?"

"We were talking, and he seemed really distracted."

I tensed.

"I mentioned how wonderful the ball was and how much fun everyone had and about all the wine we'd drunk. And I told him I was happy for him since you and he—" She winced.

My knees went weak. I staggered and leaned on the wall, the back of my head thudding against the stone.

Sionna grabbed my arm, steadying me. "Arek? What am I missing?"

I rubbed my chest. "He didn't remember. When he woke up this morning. And I didn't tell him."

"Oh, Arek," Sionna breathed.

Meredith's face crumpled. "He became upset, and he wrote a note. He told me to wait an hour before I gave it to you. He made me promise. But I—I didn't think it should wait that long. So, I waited half the time."

She reached into the pocket of her apron and shoved a note at me. I took the piece of parchment from her with trembling hands and unfolded it.

> Arek,
> I'm sorry. I can't.
> I need time and space. I'll return when I can.
>
> Your friend,
> Matt

Oh. No. No. He couldn't leave. He wouldn't leave. He wouldn't go when he knew I couldn't follow. Would he?

"Arek," Sionna asked. "What does it say?"

I didn't answer. I crushed the parchment in my sweaty fist and pushed away from the stone. I ran. Dodging servants and guests, I sprinted through the castle. I had to explain. I had to tell him the full truth. If he wanted to go after that, I wouldn't stop him. But I didn't want to be like the princess. I didn't want to live the rest of my life in regret. With Sionna on my heels, I burst into Matt's room. He wasn't there. His staff wasn't propped by the dresser. His satchel wasn't hung around the bedpost. His blankets were rumpled. I crossed the small space and flung open the wardrobe. Clothes were missing, as was the heavy cloak he wore.

I met Sionna's worried gaze. "Matt's gone," I whispered.

He had left. Matt had left. *Fuck.* Tears sprang to my eyes. My heart sank. I stumbled, dizzy, out of breath, and knocked into the bed. His stupid note was still clutched in my hand, and I tore it up. I ripped it into a dozen tiny pieces because I'd fucked it up. I ruined our friendship. I shouldn't have kissed him. I should've kissed him sooner. I should've said something ages ago. I shouldn't have said anything at all. I should've pushed him away in the library. I should've held him closer. Anything would have been better than wallowing in this interminable pining, this half-life of waiting for magic or fate to thrust me in the right direction. I was finally ready to take charge, but it was too late. And I lost Matt for it.

Breath hitching, I felt my anxiety spike. The only person I'd ever wanted, my soul mate, had ridden off into the sunset, and unless I found a replacement in a few days, I would be the shortest-reigning king in a century.

A tear slid from the corner of my eye.

"Oh, Arek," Sionna said, wrapping her arm around me. "It will be okay."

"I hope so."

She squeezed me. "I know it will. Don't give up."

I swallowed the lump in my throat and nodded to placate her. I followed her from Matt's room and into the hallway. I made it only a few steps, and then the world spun beneath my feet. I staggered. My whole body tingled. Not just my hands or my feet, but my entire being trembled and wavered. I stumbled to my knees.

"Arek?" Sionna's voice was far away, like hearing a sound through water.

She grabbed my arm.

"Arek?"

I didn't respond. Instead, my world tilted. A stabbing pain pierced my head, and I pitched to the side. Between one breath and the next, I passed out.

Chapter 29

I woke up in my room.

I had flashbacks to the day I tried to abdicate. This time, the pain wasn't as immediate or acute. It still sucked, though.

I rolled to my side and groaned, my muscles cramping beneath my blanket. Okay, never mind, this was just as bad. Ow.

"Arek?"

"Bethany?"

Her hand cupped my cheek, and I pried my eyes open to her concerned face. "There you are, you jerk. How are you feeling?"

"Like I was beaten with a stick."

"Good to know your flair for the dramatic wasn't bruised when you collapsed."

I made a face. "Not funny."

"No," she agreed. "Not at all. Lucky that Sionna was with you. She kept you from braining yourself on the stone."

"Nice. I can always count on Sionna. How long have I been out?"

"Most of the day. It's past dark." She wrapped her arm around my shoulders. "Can you sit up?"

"Yeah, I think so." That was a lie. I had no idea. Everything trembled.

She eased me into a sitting position and stacked pillows behind me. "Stay still and don't do anything stupid."

My hands shook when I took the cup she handed me, and I splashed a bit as I drank. I was exhausted. My spirit was thin, stretched out, like I was hollowed. Insubstantial. I *felt* translucent. I didn't think it would happen so quickly. I still had a few days left, but magic apparently was a fickle bitch.

"Uh . . . Who knows I passed out?"

"Oh, everyone," Bethany said with false cheer. "The healer from the town checked you over and said you passed out because you hadn't eaten." Her brow furrowed. "But I know you had breakfast, so that can't be true. But too little sleep, too much drinking, and too much dancing last night could've just as easily been the culprit." She said the last part with snark.

"Those are all things I've done," I confirmed with a nod.

Her expression was the pinnacle of unimpressed. She cleared her throat. "You also had a shock to your system, finding that Matt had left. That probably didn't help."

I avoided her gaze and picked at a loose thread on my blanket. "Yeah. That . . . might be true."

Bethany studied me. "The rumor is that he's left the castle on a special errand for the king."

I bit my lip. Matt. Matt. Matt. My thoughts were merely a litany of his name, and my heart beat in rhythm. *If I ever get out of here, I'm going to tell her I love her.* He'd left. But maybe—maybe it was better this way? Maybe, since he obviously was going to reject me, *again*, it was better if we had space from each other. It would be too difficult to see him every day when I was bonded to someone else, like picking at a raw wound.

"Arek?" Bethany poked my arm.

"Huh?" I was hoping Sionna must have come up with a rumor to hide what really happened.

She crossed her arms. "Arek, we all know the special errand is bullshit. Sionna told us. She said he sent you a note, and then you ran to his room and he was gone. Matt would never leave. Matt would never leave *you*. Especially after you two kissed last night."

Thinking about him hurt. Remembering how his kisses tasted hurt. Feeling phantom caresses of his fingers hurt. "Can we not talk about it right now?"

Bethany arched an eyebrow. My exhaustion and desperation must have come across in my voice because she acquiesced easily. She bit her lip. "Fine. But after you've rested, we're talking about it."

"Fine." I'd have to tell the group at some point. They were Matt's family as much as they were mine, and they had a right to know why he left. And that he said he'd return; we'd do our best without him until he did. I might be dead by that point, depending on how epically I had ruined everything at the ball.

"Arek? I think you should rest."

"Huh?"

"You're drifting."

"Oh."

With encouragement, she got me to drink the last sip of water in my cup. She rearranged my pillows, and I flopped onto them with a contented sigh. Bethany pulled the blankets to my chin, then tucked me in.

"Don't tell another soul that I fluffed your pillows."

"Never," I agreed.

Warm and exhausted, I drifted to sleep.

Chapter 30

I slept until the late morning the following day, and only stirred when Harlow roused me to sit on the throne and say goodbye to several of our guests who were departing. Despite the awkward kissing moment at the ball, the feast was a success in that several of the noble families left their children at the castle to squire and train to become knights. Gren was one of them, as was Petal.

I sat on the throne and did my best to project nobility. Sionna was the only member of the council there with me, the only one who hadn't made up an excuse to skip out. I didn't blame them. Despite sleeping for an entire day, I was tired to my bones and wished for the comfort of my bed.

"I wish we could stay longer," the Lord of Autumnhill said, bowing in front of the dais. "But we must travel before the first snow."

"I understand. Thank you for coming. Know that the castle will always be open to your family."

"That is very generous, King Arek," the lord said, sweeping his hand to the side. "Our family will take you up on that offer in the spring. Until then, please—" He snapped his mouth shut when he straightened, staring at me with oddly oriented eyebrows.

"Is—is something wrong?" I asked as the lord's face lost color and his expression became one I could only describe as vaguely horrified.

"Your ear," he whispered.

My body had tingled for the majority of the day, and though I noted the increased buzzing in my ear, I thought it was another unfortunate side effect of being exhausted and having to sit through several meetings with lords and ladies. Apparently, it was not.

"It's gone."

"What was that?" Oh, poor timing of that question. "Gone? Surely, you jest. Hilarious, my lord." I cleared my throat and nonchalantly tried to block my ear under the guise of adjusting my suddenly crooked crown.

Sionna stared at me with wide eyes. She gave an almost imperceptible shake to her head.

"No, sire. I do not." His voice wavered, like he was afraid to contradict me.

Okay. I could use that.

"Are you questioning your king?" I asked as Sionna moved from her position beside me, where Matt usually stood, and blocked me from view.

"No, sire. I am not."

"Good. I believe it's time for your retinue to depart."

"Yes, sire."

"Have a good journey." I waved my hand and noticed it, too, was translucent. I shoved it back by my side, between my hip and the throne, and hoped my sleeve would hide the fact that my palm was see-through. "I hope to see you in the spring."

"Yes, sire." The Lord of Autumnhill peeked around Sionna's imposing figure, frowned, shook his head, then left the room.

"Are there any more?" I asked Harlow.

He nodded. "Yes, several."

"Shit."

Sionna whirled on me. "What is happening, Arek? Why can I see through your ear and your hand?"

"Well, it seems that I'm fading. Just like the law said I would."

"Shit!" she echoed.

"Exactly."

"You're suspiciously calm," she said, hands on her hips. "You've known."

"Oh yeah. It's been happening for a while."

"Arek!"

"Look, we have—" I swung my head around to Harlow. "How many?"

"Five more families, sire."

"Five more of these to get through," I said, addressing Sionna. "Help me, and I'll explain everything."

She narrowed her eyes. "Harlow, summon Bethany."

"Yes, General."

A few minutes later, Bethany appeared, harp in hand, wearing a tight bodice and dress, and looking as beautiful as she did the night of the masquerade. She swiped a finger along the line of her lips, cleaning the smudged lipstick.

"This better be good. Petal and I were . . . uh . . . talking."

Great. Another prospect gone. But yay for Bethany. Get it.

She paused at the base of the throne, her bright gaze sweeping over me, and I saw the moment she noticed my missing ear.

"Arek!"

I held up my hand. "Okay. Yes. I'm fading. I'm aware. I need you to hide it."

"Hide it?" She waved her hand at her own face. "How do I hide that you're translucent?"

"I am?"

"I can see the throne through your neck!"

"Well, that's not good, is it?" I snapped back.

Sionna placed her hand on my shoulder as I slumped forward. I tried to catch my forehead with my hand, but that didn't work, since my hand was fairly missing. I ended up falling forward and nearly braining myself with my knee.

"Ugh."

"What do you want me to do exactly? I'm not Matt. I can't fix you magically."

"No, but you can charm the people here into not seeing it."

She tossed her hair. "Oh yes. That I can do." She strummed her harp. The strings reverberated, and the magic in the room grew.

"But we're going to have a talk after this is all over."

"I've already endured one of your talks."

"You're getting another one," she yelled, voice pitching into a shriek. "Because this is not okay!"

She strummed a particularly vicious chord on her harp, and the magic shimmered in the air, vibrating along my skin.

"Yes. Fine. Okay. Let's get through this."

"Are you ready, sire?" Harlow called from his place by the entrance. "The guests are waiting."

"Yeah." I squirmed on the throne, gripping the arms so tight that my knuckles—or what was left of them—turned white. I swallowed. "Yeah."

Harlow opened the door.

We made it through all five families, despite the Summerhill family being exceptionally chatty, specifically about how awesome Gren was at fighting and diplomacy. Each time I thought I'd been caught missing an essential body part, Sionna stepped in the line of sight of the lord or lady who made the confused or horrified face, and Bethany's strumming increased in frequency and sound.

By the end of it, I was so thoroughly exhausted that I wanted to take a nap on the throne. Head tipped back, my eyes slid shut, and I went boneless.

"Arek!" Bethany said, fingers tapping relentlessly against my cheek. "Come on. Wake up."

Groaning, I cracked open one eye. "One more minute."

"No."

Rousing, I yawned so wide that my jaw cracked. "Sorry. M'tired."

"Maybe we should let him rest." Sionna threw my arm over her shoulder and lifted me off the throne. My legs tingled, but I was fairly certain it was just from sitting so long that they'd fallen asleep. I looked down, and yeah, they were there, mostly.

"And waste more time?" Bethany shored up my other side. "We can't wait any longer. We only have four days. We have to find Arek someone to bond with or he'll die."

Sionna pursed her lips. "One of us will do it if we can't find someone."

"You mean me," Bethany said flatly. "Rion and Lila have each other, and you have Meredith."

"Will you two quit talking as if I'm not standing right here? Thanks." We walked toward the exit, though "walked" was a loose term. I was mostly dragged, since my balance had fled. "No one is sacrificing themselves to be my other half. I'd rather fade away than make someone give up their life and own chances at love."

"King Arek the Kind," Sionna muttered.

"Stop it." I snorted. "I'm not kind. I just don't want to be stuck with any of you longer than I have to be."

Bethany frowned, but didn't comment. Between the two of them, I made it back to my chambers. They all but tossed me into the bed.

I was asleep before my head hit the pillow.

"Hey, King Arek the Dumbass," Lila yelled as my door swung open with a bang. "Wake up!" She pushed aside the curtains. "You slept the whole day away, and now you only have three days until you become ether."

Pushing myself to sitting was a monumental task. I brushed my hair from my eyes and squinted at her in the light. "Go away."

"And let you die in peace? Never." She ripped open the shutters. "Besides, I'm not alone."

A line of servants followed Lila into my room. With a flurry of movement around the table along the wall, trays were set down, goblets filled, napkins placed, and then they danced out the door, only to be replaced by Rion, Sionna, and Bethany.

Sionna kicked the door shut with her heel. "How are you feeling?"

How was I feeling? Like spoiled meat. Like brackish water. Like I had worked very hard at shearing and chasing sheep all over the field, and had fallen down a rocky hill, then trudged home to sleep on the floor, and woke up with a sore body and without purpose.

"Awful," I managed. Apparently, my strength, motivation, and desire to live were affected by the fading too. I furrowed my brow. "Hollow."

"That is worse than we thought, then," Sionna said.

Rion filled a pewter plate with food, then brought it over to me. He perched on the edge of the bed. "You're really fading?" he asked softly.

I held up my hand, and Rion peered through it with wide eyes. "It's legit. I'm in trouble." I pinched a strawberry between my fingers and thought of Matt's garden. Then I thought of Matt, and my stomach somersaulted. "It started a few weeks ago with my fingers and my toes coming in and out. It wasn't a big deal, but then I started losing a whole hand or my feet. And now . . ." I gestured to my body. "I'm all fair game to the magic."

"On the practice field," Rion said, pointing a finger in my direction, "when your legs collapsed. While Lila and I . . ." He blushed. "When we kissed for the first time—"

"Yeah. That was the fading."

"You're a doofus," Lila shouted. She stood and slammed

her hands on the table. "Why didn't you tell us before? Why would you keep something this important a secret?"

I shrugged, hiding my surprise at Lila's vehemence. "There was nothing we could do. Not until I found a soul mate."

"Well, you obviously can't be put in charge of your own well-being. We're deciding. Right now!"

"Agreed," Bethany said.

I looked to Sionna for support, but she merely took a sip of her drink. "Gren is cute," she said.

"I vote Gren." Bethany nodded. "They're hot, and they have fighting skills."

"What about Petal?" Lila plopped into her chair. "She is demure and may be able to balance Arek's more obnoxious traits."

"His impulsivity or his deficits in communication?" Rion said calmly.

Ouch.

"I was thinking more along the lines of his tenuous grasp of self-preservation."

"She's also a great kisser," Bethany said, smiling.

Rion gave her an unimpressed glare.

"What? Oh, lighten up. It was just for fun."

"You lot are awful." I rubbed my temple, a headache building behind my eyes. "I wish Matt was here," I muttered. My soul ached at the thought.

"Well, he's not. He ran away because you found out he was in love with you. And we'll be talking about that as well." Bethany narrowed her eyes at me over the rim of her goblet. "Because you're not cruel, and whatever you did must have been awful for him to abandon us like this."

My brain grounded to a halt. *"What?"*

"Matt would have great opinions," Sionna said.

"No, he wouldn't. He has bias. He's in love with Arek, but obviously Arek doesn't love him back or he wouldn't be in this mess." Lila speared a piece of fruit with her fork. "He's too close to the situation to be able to think clearly."

Rion sighed. "Matt would want what was best for Arek and would pick someone worthy."

"Again, what?" They must be confused. He'd shown his disinterest at every turn. He'd made it clear he didn't want to be pursued. Hadn't he?

"Do you know how big of an incident it was when they kissed during the masquerade?" Bethany flipped her hair. "I did so much charming that night and the morning after. I should be called the department of damage control. You have no idea how many of those nobles showed up to try to seduce Arek and acquire a crown. It was a mess."

"What?" I said again.

Lila and Rion shared a guilty look. "We weren't exactly present for the last few hours of the feast," Rion said diplomatically. Lila's face colored. "But we did hear the rumors afterward."

"Hey, we did our part. I directed Petal toward Arek. Rion introduced him to Enzo and Rami. I sent anyone half-good looking over to cut in. We tried."

"Enzo wouldn't be a bad choice either," Sionna said. "I like Giada as well. She was very pretty and sweet. Oh, and also that Declan fellow, though he's a bit older. But sturdy. He would make good decisions and would temper the more irrational parts of our beloved king."

The three of them continued with their conversation, but I couldn't discern anything past what Lila had said.

"What do you mean Matt's in love with me?"

Lila rolled her eyes. Bethany made a noise of disgust in her throat. Sionna winced. Even Rion mumbled something disparaging.

"You didn't know?" Bethany asked. "Are you serious? How did you not know?"

"I have no idea what any of you are talking about right now."

"Arek," Sionna said. "He's pined for you this whole time."

Again. What? "Pined for me?"

"He really is oblivious," Lila said to the group of them. "I thought he just wasn't interested."

Sionna sighed. "Matt loved you well before I met you in the tavern. Before you started the quest. I imagine it began when you lived together in the village."

I swiped my goblet from my bedside table with a trembling hand and wet my suddenly dry mouth.

"He loves me." More a statement than a question now.

"Um . . . yes!" Lila made a face. "Since forever."

"Why didn't he say anything?"

"You're asking why Matt didn't profess his love for you? Matt, who must research everything before acting, so he might know the outcome in advance?"

"This whole time—"

"He thought you weren't interested," Sionna said bluntly. "He would rather have spent his life by your side in silence than risk saying a word and being sent away."

"I wouldn't have sent him away!"

"Then why did he leave?" Bethany asked.

I opened my mouth, then snapped it shut. "He said he couldn't. He wanted space."

"Uh-huh," she said primly.

I tugged on my hair. "You don't understand. I want Matt by my side. More than anything. Always."

Sionna frowned. "That might be true, Arek, but if you'd known Matt loved you, then you would have distanced yourself. The casual intimacy you two have developed over the years would've evaporated."

I slammed my fist on the headboard of my bed. "That's not true! Because I love him!"

Bethany gasped. "You *love* him?"

"Of course I do! He's *Matt*."

"So why did you attempt to woo us?" Rion asked, pointing among the four of them.

"Because I basically confessed to Matt, and he rejected me, okay? *Twice!* And, hey, why are you yelling at me when he's the one who left?"

"We're not yelling!" Lila yelled. "Okay, maybe I am. What do you mean he rejected you?"

I held up my hands, defensive in the face of Lila's vehemence. "The first time, I told him there was someone I wanted to confess my feelings for, and he cut me off and said that person wasn't interested."

"Well," Bethany said, waving her hand, "that doesn't mean much."

"The second time, after we kissed, he said, 'I can't,' and then he ran away. I don't know about you, but that feels like a pretty clear rejection."

"Oh." She bit her lip. "Are you sure?"

"Yes! I'm sure."

The group exchanged a tense glance.

"Maybe, we read Matt wrong?" Rion's tone was unsure.

"No offense, Rion," Bethany said, hand on her hip, "but as much as I love you, you're not the reader of people. That's Sionna."

Sionna blinked. "I—I thought Matt loved Arek," she said simply. "He hid it under layers and layers of sarcasm and annoyance, but it was there."

I sighed, then rubbed my brow. "Maybe he didn't. Or maybe he did and grew out of it. Maybe it wasn't there anymore. I don't know."

Lila banged her fist on the table. "So what? Fine, we don't know Matt's feelings. But we know yours. You love him. And if your little lust pollen stunt—"

"It wasn't lust pollen!"

"If it taught me anything, it is to go after what you want. So why didn't you go after him?"

"I fainted!" I pointed to Sionna. "Ask Sionna! She was there! And by the time I woke up, who knew how far away he could be . . . or how much time it might have taken to reach him." I tugged that loose thread on my blanket until it unraveled. Dropping my voice, I continued, "Besides, I couldn't ask Matt to bond with me. Because he would've done it out of some weird sense of loyalty, and I would've damned him to being stuck with me for the rest of our lives."

"I still think you should go get Matt back." Lila swept her arm out and knocked over her own cup. "Ride out of here and catch up to him."

If only it was that easy. "As our little experiment confirmed, I'm tied to the throne no matter what. I don't even know if I can leave. The magic is so against anyone but me being on the throne that when I tried to abdicate, it almost killed me. Lila picked up the crown just for fun, and it burned her hand. The magic might not even let me walk beyond the walls. Besides, he left because he wanted space. I'm trying really hard to honor that." I swallowed down the lump in my throat. "Even if it means that he's not my soul mate."

Lila grunted in annoyance and crossed her arms. "What did his note say exactly?"

"It said he was sorry, but he couldn't stay, and he would return." She narrowed her eyes at me.

"Well, that isn't very specific."

"Arek," Sionna said softly, "did you ever actually tell him that you loved him? Did he know it without a shadow of a doubt?" I cringed as the memory of the morning conversation I never had with Matt resurfaced. The look on my face was apparently answer enough for all of them.

Lila reached over and slapped my arm. It stung and probably should've hurt more, but I was only partly corporeal.

Rion frowned. "What if he couldn't stay because he couldn't bear seeing you with someone *else*?"

I—I hadn't thought of that. The stubborn little flame of hope brightened again. "I tried to tell him! I was all ready to, the morning after we kissed. But when he woke up, he didn't remember, and Harlow had come to fetch me for breakfast, and there wasn't time to walk through it all. And then Meredith caught him up before I could, and he chose to leave. Look, I know you are all trying to help, but Matt is gone, and we just need to move past that. If I don't... chances are I'm going to die."

As soon as I said it, a wave of dizziness slammed into me. My head spun. I slumped back into the pile of pillows, breathing hard.

"Okay, even if Arek wanted, he is not going anywhere," Bethany said. "He's weak. He needs rest."

Sionna stared at me with sad brown eyes. "Maybe Matt will return."

"Yes," Bethany said, forcing a smile. "He'll come to his senses and sweep back into the castle, and it'll be so romantic."

"Let's just hope he figures it out quick." Lila looked toward the window, frowning. "The first snow will be soon, and we only have until Arek's birthday."

My birthday. The deadline. Three days.

I opened my mouth to retort, but snapped it shut. A tingle worked itself from the top of my head to the soles of my feet. The room wavered, and my stomach flipped. I couldn't explain it, but I felt transparent in my entirety. I tipped to the side.

"Arek!"

"I'm fine."

"You're not."

Four pairs of hands maneuvered me flat onto the mattress. I plopped backward and breathed, staring at the ceiling. That little bit of exertion winded me. My whole body stiffened from my neck to my toes.

"One of us needs to stay with Arek at all times." Bethany placed a hand on my chest, and its warmth swept through me, loosening the clench of my muscles. "I'll take first watch. We still have a few guests in the castle that we need to hustle out of here before the first snow or they'll be witness to whatever happens in the next few days."

"I'm on it," Sionna said. "I'll enlist Harlow to assist."

"Arek, do you have . . . a second choice? Or a third?" Rion asked, ever practical.

Grimacing, I shivered. "Gren," I said through clenched teeth. "If not, then Petal."

"Arek?" Bethany's hands were gentle on my arm. "Are you sure?"

"If it can't be Matt," I said, and my spirit wrenched at the thought, "then at least it should be someone nice to look at."

Forced laughter followed my statement. Spirits, they were trying so hard to remain positive. A tear rolled out from the corner of my eye.

"I have a sparring match scheduled with Gren today. I'll . . . talk to them about things. Size them up."

I raised an eyebrow and turned my head to the side. "You?"

Rion lifted his chin. "I can be subtle when I need to be."

"Don't be too subtle," I said. "We want them to think I'm interested, but not too interested."

Lips pressed into a thin line, Rion nodded. "I can do it."

"Great."

"I can have Meredith talk to Petal. They got along well at the ball."

I gave Sionna a weak smile. "Thanks."

I was exhausted. My eyes slid shut of their own accord, and only the sound of the door opening and closing marked Sionna and Rion's departure. Bethany sat near me on the bed and talked softly to Lila, but I couldn't make out their conversation. I slipped into a doze and dreamed of Matt.

CHAPTER 31

Two days passed in a blur. I spent most of it napping, sliding from consciousness to unconsciousness without much to distinguish the moments in between. The few times I left my room, Bethany slathered makeup on my face and visible parts just in case, and I wore clothes that covered as much of my person as possible.

The group stayed by my side most of the time, switching off between babysitting me and their regular duties. They read books to me from the library when I was in bed and steadied me when I had to walk from my chambers to the throne room.

We received no word from Matt, not that I was expecting any. His note had been clear. But as my time grew short, I was suddenly faced with a horrible choice. Life without Matt or death. But Matt wasn't there and with his departure, he'd made his choice.

My birthday dawned gray and overcast. For once, I was up before the rooster crowed, feeling more awake and alive than I had in days. Rion was asleep in the little room next to mine, and I did my best to slide out of bed without waking him. Cracking my door open, I poked my head out to find a servant waiting there.

"Hey," I whispered.

They were startled. "King Arek?"

"Yeah. It's me. I'd like a bath."

"Happy birthday, sire."

"Thanks. And breakfast for me and Sir Rion."

"Certainly."

"Great, thanks."

I shut the door softly, then resisted the urge to climb into the sheets. I'd only fall back asleep, and I wanted to stay awake for my last day. Instead, I sat on the bench by the table and hefted the princess's journal in my hand. I'd found it on the floor where I'd left it the last night Matt and I were together— it was one of the few things from the library he hadn't taken with him. I'd been reading it in moments I was awake, searching for some piece of advice, but I'd found nothing. And not for the first time since he'd left, I wished Matt was there. Even if he didn't love me, even if he didn't choose to be bound to me, any decision beyond that would be easier with him present.

Within a few minutes, servants shuffled in and poured steaming water into the footed tub near the fire.

"It's snowing, sire," one of the servants said.

"Is it?"

I looked to the window and saw a few flakes drifting on the wind. It snowed on my last birthday, the day before a wizard showed up at my house and sent Matt and me off on a grand adventure.

"Yes, sire. It's good luck for snow on your birthday."

Huh. I'd never heard that. "I willingly accept any good luck the universe wants to throw my way today."

The servant chuckled. Before long, the tub was full, the fire was stoked and hot, and a tray of food and a pitcher of water was on the table.

Sinking into the tub, my skin reddened from the heat, and for the first time in days, I was warmed to my core. Maybe things were looking up. I felt more rested than I had since the masquerade, and I was a little optimistic. I lifted my leg and pointed my toes, and . . . my whole leg was translucent.

Okay. Still fading. Not great.

After my bath, I hauled myself out of the tub, and I dressed in trousers and knee-high boots. I tugged the highest-necked tunic I had over my head and beckoned the same servant into the room to assist me with the laces. He tugged at them until the fabric pressed against my throat, and the collar sat snug beneath my chin. The sleeves slipped down over my wrists, the laces tight on my pulse. After slipping on gloves, I placed my shined and polished crown on my damp hair. I checked the mirror. To anyone else's eyes, I might have been the quintessential picture of a king instead of a frightened boy.

I wished that the princess had a journal entry to help me now. I wondered what she'd think of me reading her private thoughts. I hoped she wouldn't mind, even though they were meant for someone else.

I'd never considered that someone else before. The princess might not be alive, but was her lady? If I survived this, maybe I could fulfill at least someone's last wish.

After the exertion of dressing and eating breakfast, my earlier strength had fled. I had the constitution of a kitten, and I set the journal aside, crossed my arms, and rested my head in the crook of my elbow. I drifted for a while, much longer than I had anticipated.

"Arek?"

I jerked up with a snort. "Oh hey, Rion," I said, rubbing the heels of my hands over my eyes.

"You're up earlier than usual." He ran a hand through his mussed hair. He appeared haggard, circles beneath his eyes, his complexion paler than usual. "You should've woken me."

My gut twisted at the toll that my situation had taken on my friends. "Well, you know, got to make the most of my last day." I gave him my best cheerful voice.

Rion's smile was half-hearted at best. "Glad to see you're in good spirits."

"You know me, I make jokes in tense situations." I cleared my throat. "I ordered us breakfast." I took a piece of toast from the tray and bit off a corner. "It's a little cold now, but it's not bad."

Rion sat next to me on the bench. He stared at the breakfast tray intensely. "Are you going to . . ." He trailed off.

"Maybe?" I said with a shrug. "I have a few hours."

"It would be best if you didn't wait. We don't want to test the magic."

"You sound like Matt."

"There are worse people to sound like."

"True," I said with a nod. Then I pointed to my crown. "But I'm the king. I get to make my own decisions."

"Yes, you do." Rion poked at a sausage with his fork. "How long will you wait?"

"A ceremony at sunset sounds romantic. I'll summon Gren, and if not Gren, then Petal or Enzo or Declan or, spirits, Bethany—if she'll have me."

"And if it's too late?"

"Then I fade away." At his pinched expression, I gripped his shoulder under the guise of giving comfort when I really needed to steady myself. "There are worse things, Rion. We've experienced them. We met a soul who'd been trapped in a tower by an evil dictator who stole the kingdom from her family. We fought a moat monster. We went days without food and fresh water. Fuck, we went weeks without a solid night's sleep. We've been chased across the countryside. Our friends have been hurt in my stead. I hacked off a man's head with a sword that was gifted to me by a magic bog. A bog I was led to by a pixie who tried to steal the life force of my best friend." I sighed heavily. "I did what was laid out for me. I didn't ask to be king. I didn't ask to be tied to a throne. I didn't ask to screw up my relationship with my best friend. But I am. I did. I have. If I have to live a life in a role I didn't want with someone I don't love, then I want to weigh that decision seriously."

"Arek, we understand. We know you will do what is best for you and for the kingdom. We have no doubts about that."

I squeezed Rion's shoulder and let my hand fall. "Good. Thank you. Now, I'm positive that there are people waiting outside this door listening in."

"How'd he know?" Bethany's voice was faint on the other side of the wood.

"Because you're predictable," I yelled.

The door swung inward. Bethany, Lila, Sionna, and Meredith entered.

"Any new developments?" I asked.

"None," Lila said. "No birds. No messengers."

"Right." I rubbed my hands together. "So, what's on the schedule for today?"

"There's cake in the kitchen," Meredith said. "Chocolate. I was told it was your favorite."

"Well then. Let us eat cake."

We ate cake—on the floor of the library, surrounded by what was left of Matt's things, in front of the fire, so the frosting melted. I'd hoped that having food around his precious scrolls might summon Matt to us as if he were a demon, but he didn't come. Not when the sun dipped in the sky, behind the snow clouds, and my time grew short.

I ate the lion's share of the cake, and by the end of my third slice, I was nauseated. The early afternoon slipped away from me while I laughed with my friends, as did the last vestiges of my strength. My whole body tingled. Suddenly it was time for me to make a decision. I knew what I had to do.

"Summon Gren," I said in one of the quiet moments among us.

Sionna reached over and took my hand. "Okay, Arek."

I nodded. "I'd rather talk to them in the throne room." My voice was small, defeated. I couldn't bond with them here, not in the room that had become Matt's and Matt's alone.

Situated between Rion and Sionna, I gained my feet, and with my arms thrown over their necks, I made it to the throne room at a turtle's pace.

"You're a little," Bethany said while I squirmed on the seat, "uh . . . pale." She dabbed a cloth of makeup on my chin and along my jaw. "There. Perfect."

"Hey, before they arrive, if I do fade away, among the three of you, one of you take the crown. Any of you would make a magnificent ruler, and if you want it, take it. But go in it knowing what it'll cost. Don't be like me and crown yourself for giggles."

Sionna cleared her throat. "We've already discussed it among ourselves," she said. "We have a plan. In case."

"Good." I looked out the window. The sun would set within the hour. I'd truly run out of time.

"You summoned me, sire?" Gren asked as they entered through the side door to the throne room. They crossed to stand in front of the throne with a quick, determined stride.

I couldn't deny they were beautiful. Gren had brown hair, lighter than Matt's deeper color, and stood taller and more muscular than him or me. They were a fighter, with broad shoulders, and massive biceps and thighs, and my mouth went a bit dry when they snapped a short bow.

"Yes," I said. "I have something to discuss with you. It's, well, it's . . ." I put my head in my hand and took a breath. "It's weird."

Gren's smile didn't fade, but it went from beaming to curious, and they arched an eyebrow in my direction.

"You are an unconventional king, from what I've gathered in the short time I've been in the castle."

"You're not wrong."

"If I may be so bold, does it have to do with the fading?"

Well, fuck. I scrunched my nose. "You know?"

They shifted on the plush carpet, their boots leaving indents. "There were rumors."

"Great. Freaking great." I threw up my hands. "Well, yes." I stared at the window. "I need a—a . . ." Soul mate was a difficult phrase to say to someone I barely knew. "Co-ruler."

Gren approached the throne. They knelt at my feet, honey eyes tipped toward me, bright and sparkling. They placed their hand atop mine, their fingertips slipping beneath my sleeve to touch the skin of my wrist, and the promise of warmth swept through me. I hadn't realized how much had been leached from me until I felt the touch of their hand covering my chilled skin. "Sire, I'd be honored to be your co-ruler."

I gulped. I should've felt relieved, and I was, but there was a good deal of guilt mixed in as well as a heaping amount of apprehension. "I'm a good king," I blurted. I surprised myself when I said it, and judging by the way Lila's eyebrows went crooked and Sionna put her hand over her heart, my friends were too. "I mean, I'm—I'm . . . You know what? Fuck it. I am a good king." Wow. That wasn't so hard to say the second time. "And as much as I didn't want to be king three months ago, I feel pretty damn good about the job my council and I have done. We're trying our hardest to rule this kingdom well. And to continue being a good king, I have a duty to myself and my kingdom to follow through with the magical laws of this position. Which means I have to bind my soul to some-one else's. I can't promise you I won't screw up, because I basically do all the time, but I can promise that I'm going to do my best."

"That's all anyone can ask of their partner."

I bit my lip. This didn't feel right. It could be that the per-son in front of me was not Matt. It could be that the person in front of me had no idea what they were getting into, and I really didn't have the time to explain. But it also could be that my very being *withered*.

"The kingdom comes first, always. And I can't promise you love." Gren should be worried that this apparently was what "my best" looked like. I saw Bethany face-palm out of the corner of my eye. "And this"—I gestured between us—"is for eternity. It shouldn't be taken lightly."

"I understand," Gren said solemnly, their fingers trailing softly over my skin. I shuddered. "Should I take the day to consider it?"

"No!" the group shouted.

I shot them all a glare. "What my council ... my friends ... are trying to convey is that I've run out of time. I could give you like fifteen minutes to prepare?"

"I don't need it." Gren stood. "When my family received your invitation, we considered that you might be looking for a spouse. I had already planned to stay at the castle either as a knight or a prospect."

Perceptive. Strong. Beautiful. Smart. I could do worse.

I nodded, then forced a smile lest I cried. "Okay. Okay. Yeah." I stood. Gren caught my elbow to keep me from falling. "Let's do this."

My friends gathered close as Gren and I threaded our hands together. Harlow appeared by my side, a long strip of red silk in his hand that he wrapped around our forearms. He tied it off with a taut knot.

"Bethany," I said, looking down where my arm pressed tight to Gren's, "this needs to be done with magic. Are you ready?"

"Yes." Her voice was tense, almost unhappy. She plucked the strings on her harp.

I closed my eyes, swallowed, and pulled myself together. I blew out a breath and raised my gaze to meet Gren's. I could at least give them the courtesy of looking at them while saying the vows.

"I choose to bind—"

The main entryway to the throne room blew open, the doors banging loudly against the stone. Snow swirled in on a bitter wind. A dark figure shot into the room, a large bird, with black feathers, and a beak of terror. Crow flew on the updraft, then circled, and landed on the high back of my throne. Puffed up like a demon, he hissed.

Gren stumbled backward in surprise, pulling me with them until I fell in a tangle on the dais.

"Crow?" Lila said, clucking her tongue. "You're supposed to be keeping watch on the parapet for . . ." She trailed off.

A cloaked figure appeared in the doorway and entered in a flurry, his staff glowing in his hand. His dark hair was damp, falling into his face, flakes of snow rapidly melting into the strands. His cheeks were pinked from the cold and exertion. His chest heaved, but he strode with purpose down the ribbon of carpet. He tossed his hand over his shoulder, and the doors slammed shut.

"Matt!" I jumped to standing. My legs shook. I locked my knees to keep from falling. My heart pounded a fast tattoo, a drumbeat so fierce and loud that it sounded in my ears.

He marched forward, not breaking his stride, until he crossed the entirety of the room, climbed the stairs, and stood right in front of me.

His bottom lip was chapped from exposure. His brown eyes were red rimmed. When he pushed his hood back, his cowlick at the back of his head stood on end.

"Matt," I said softly.

He zeroed in on Gren, and the binding between our arms. "Am I too late?" he whispered.

"No," Sionna said, pulling out a knife. She sliced our bonds, the red silk ribbon falling to the floor in pieces. "You're right on time."

Stunned, I grabbed his cloak, my gloved hand fisted into the fabric. *"Matt."*

"Did you mean it?" he asked. He opened his satchel, plunged his hand inside, and pulled out a scrap of parchment. I looked at him, confused, until it hit me. It was the letter I'd written him the night we kissed. Tears of relief flooded my eyes as I realized I'd unknowingly succeeded; he knew every square inch of truth about how much I loved him. "I found this stuck to the prophecy scroll. Did you mean it, Arek?"

My pulse thudded so hard, I thought it would burst through my skin even though the rest of me felt like a phantom. I nodded. "Every word."

"I love you." He said it so simply, so matter-of-fact, no question in the statement at all. An affirmation. A declaration. "I've loved you since you bloodied your knuckles in my defense. I've only ever loved you."

"I love you," I breathed, my eyes filling. "I love you so much."

His eyebrows drew together. "Then why didn't you tell me? Why . . ." His gaze flicked to our audience, and he leaned in, cheeks flushed. ". . . Why didn't you want to woo me?"

"I thought you didn't want me to. You never showed any interest. I didn't know."

"I followed you in the middle of the night in the dead of

winter from our village on a dangerous quest because a potentially drunk wizard convinced you of a prophecy. How could you not know?"

"I thought you were being a good friend . . . ?" Spirits, I loved his wonderful withering glare. "Fine. I'm oblivious. But why did you leave after we kissed?"

Matt blanched. He looked away, eyes pinching shut. "I didn't remember it until Meredith told me and then . . . it all came back. That I basically threw myself at you in the middle of the ball while you were trying to pursue other people. But Bethany had said something to me about being honest with you, and I drunkenly decided to follow her advice."

"Wait, that's what you meant?"

Matt nodded. "I was so embarrassed. I couldn't face you in the sober light of day, not when I knew you were going to reject me. Not when I would have to watch you with someone else. I couldn't do it." He shrugged. "So, I ran. Not my proudest moment, I admit."

"Matt, I thought you were trying to force yourself to have feelings for me. And if you didn't notice, I kissed you back. Like a lot."

"I thought you were being a good friend," he echoed weakly. "I had made it a few towns over when I finally stopped for the night, and I found your note in my satchel curled up with the prophecy. I turned around as quick as I could, but the snow delayed me. I used so much magic, but . . ." He reached up and slid his fingers along my jaw. "I didn't think I'd make it back in time."

"I'm sorry." A lump caught in my throat. "I'm sorry I made you think that I didn't want you." I pressed my forehead to his, the edge of the crown digging into my brow. It was a small discomfort. "I choose you, Matt. You're the other half of my soul."

Matt's laugh punched out of him, giddy, and joyful, the force of it a gust on my lips. "You couldn't have said this before I left? You had to write a note for me to find? Why do you always have to be so dramatic?"

"Me?" I said, grinning. "I was planning to tell you everything I put in that letter, but you left before I could! You're the one who left an arrival to the last minute. I almost had to bond with someone else."

"It's snowing, sire," Matt said, twisting the honorific into a familiar insult. "I made a two-day ride in one. For you."

The tension bled out of my shoulders. "I waited as long as I could. For you."

Giggling, and that was the only word I could use to describe the sound that came out of me. I pressed my mouth to his and kissed him soundly. He kissed back, as determinedly as he had on the night of the masquerade. My heart soared. My whole being warmed from my core, a feeling I'd sorely missed. I was Matt's and he was mine.

"Not to be the jerk who cuts in," Lila said, voice loud in the otherwise silence, "but Arek, you're practically a ghost."

Matt's eyes snapped open, and he pulled away. "Fuck!"

Oh. That was bad. I tugged my glove off with my teeth, and yeah, my palm was entirely translucent. It was like Lila's words gave the magic permission to act with a vengeance. My legs gave out, and I would have fallen if Gren and Sionna hadn't caught me and maneuvered me to the throne. A headache bloomed fiercely behind my eyes. My whole body tingled, like being stabbed with thousands of tiny shards of glass; I let out a strangled yelp as fire limned my spine. My heart pounded, then seized, locked up in a painful squeeze that was unlike anything I'd ever felt, and oh shit, I was fading. I was *dying*. Right then. Right there. I sucked in a breath, and it stuck in my disappearing lungs. I choked, desperately trying to exhale.

Matt grabbed what was left of my hand and pressed our palms together, threading his fingers through mine. "Does anyone have rope or string or—"

"Here!" Bethany tugged a ribbon from her hair and ran over.

"Wrap it around our joined hands. Quickly. Quickly."

"Here!" Lila said. She pulled the threaded cord from her coin purse. "Add this."

Sionna broke a string of leather from her sword belt. "And this."

Not to be left out, Rion tore the edge from his cloak into a long strip of fabric. Between the four of them, Matt and I were bond together from our forearms, over our wrists, and around our hands.

"Bethany," Matt said. "Are you ready?"

"Yes." She strummed her fingers over the chords. "Let's do this."

I slumped forward. My breaths were reedy inhales and shaky, timid exhales. I pressed my other hand to my chest, but it had disappeared. I gulped, gasped like a fish out of water. Were my lungs gone? Dark spots clouded my vision.

Matt touched my face with his fingertips, tilting it upward. "Arek, I love you. You are the other half of my soul, and I choose to bond with you for this life and the next."

"I love you," I rasped with the little air I had left. Hands on my shoulders pushed me to sitting, and I bent my neck backward, desperately seeking air. My chest heaved. "Other half . . . bond with you . . . this life and next."

As soon as the words left my mouth, a flash of light beamed from between our pressed palms. It lit up the room in a searing shaft, and a sound—like a bang of cymbals, or the crash of waves on a shore—echoed. Magic broke over us, swept through my being, chased out the cold, and replaced it with the warmth and knowledge of the other half of my soul, of Matt. The vise around my chest loosened. Air rushed into my lungs, and I took great heaving gulps of it. The pain fled in a rush of adrenaline, and I sagged in blissful relief as I returned. Vigor and light infused me, and I no longer was half of myself. I was whole. Finally, finally, since the day I'd placed the crown on my head, I was whole.

I still didn't think I could stand, but no matter. I merely yanked Matt into my lap.

"Arek!" he squawked.

He landed crossways; his legs draped over the arm of the throne.

"What are you—"

I kissed him. I swallowed all the words he mumbled against my lips, and I tasted each one. His mouth and body were warm, and I trembled beneath him as my corporeal form returned. He kissed me back, eager and desperate.

"That was close," he said, more a vibration against my mouth than actual words. "I thought I lost you."

"You didn't." I pulled him nearer. "You didn't. I'm here."

Matt broke away and buried his face in the crook of

my neck. His shoulders shook, and he let out a pitiful sob. I clutched him to me.

"What's wrong?" He didn't answer, but his tears soaked my shirt. "Matt?"

"Sorry," he said, voice clogged. "Sorry. I . . . almost didn't make it back. I thought the kiss at the ball was the only kiss I'd ever have with you. I left here thinking I was selfish, so selfish to ruin our friendship with a stupid declaration of love that you never wanted."

I wrapped my arms as tight as I could around him. "You didn't. You didn't ruin anything. If you'd said you loved me, I would've told you the same, because I did. Because I do."

Matt wilted, the tenseness of his body eased, and he slumped so far into me, I couldn't tell where he ended and where I began.

"You let me go," he said, voice low.

"I did."

"When it would've been easier for you to make me stay."

"It would've been, yes. But I wouldn't make you stay somewhere you didn't want to be."

"I do," he said. "I do want to be here."

My relief was palpable. "Good, I'm glad."

He sighed. "King Arek the Kind," he whispered.

I huffed. "For you, I'd be anything."

Matt chuckled wetly, his breath hot on my neck. A shiver worked its way down my spine. The tiny hairs on my arms stood on end.

"However, I think we'd both agree we have to work on our communication."

Matt broke into outright laughs, and he squirmed on my

lap and in my grip, and if he kept it up, there would be an inappropriate boner situation. However, would it really be inappropriate? We were bonded now. It would be a hypothetically appropriate boner. Except we were in public. So maybe still inappropriate, and maybe not so hypothetical anymore.

A throat cleared. I snapped my head up from where I'd tucked it in Matt's hair, and oh yeah. Right. We had an audience. And not a small one. Lila was wedged close to Rion's side, her mouth tipped into a soft smile, and Rion's eyes were wet. Sionna and Meredith clutched hands. Harlow stood by the door, dour and solemn as always, but I could see the relief in his posture. Crow stared at us from above, his neck bent, his beady eyes unblinking and terrifying.

"As happy as we are for you two," Bethany said, grinning, "maybe you'd like to move to somewhere more private."

"Great idea, Lady Bethany, wonderful magical bard of all the land," I said.

She smirked. "Flattery will get you everywhere, sire, but I have a date with a lady named Petal and potentially an individual named Gren as well?" Her voice ticked high into a question, and she winked at Gren.

Gren! I'd totally forgotten about them. I winced. "Oh, um, Gren, I'm sorry?"

They smiled. "No apology required, sire. I'm happy for you." Then they turned to Bethany, a blush staining their cheeks. "And I would be honored to accompany you, Lady Bethany."

Oh, how quickly they moved on.

I helped Matt to stand. Surprisingly, I gained my feet with ease. My strength had returned. Matt, on the other hand, leaned tiredly into my side. With our hands still bound, we descended the dais, and with an awkward wave to our friends, we left the room.

As I guided Matt to my chambers, his head lolled on my shoulder. "I need a nap."

"And we'll have one."

"Good." We made it to the door, and it was awkward work to open it with our hands tied together. "You know," Matt said, not at all helping with opening the door to my chambers, "we're technically bonded now."

I snorted. "If you think we're getting out of having an actual ceremony, I'd like you to break that to Bethany."

Matt paled but laughed. "No. No. I don't think we'll be able to wiggle our way out of that one."

His choice of "wiggle" had me thinking about him in my lap on the throne, and my face flushed. Thankfully, I managed to open the door and pull Matt inside, closing it with my foot. "Thank the spirits for my prowess in writing love letters. Otherwise, I'd be a ghost about now."

Matt raised his eyebrow. "Or bringing someone else to your chambers."

I looked away. "Last resort, Matt. Last resort."

"Hey." He touched my cheek. "I know. I don't blame you."

Throat tight, I leaned into his touch. "Thank you."

"What I was saying, though," he said, wetting his lips, "was that technically we're bonded, and this is our first night together."

Huh. He was not wrong. And if we stuck to tradition, that meant, well, bedroom activities. My pulse raced, and all the renewed blood in my body went south. "You're not too tired?"

Matt's gaze focused on my mouth. He pushed closer until

his body was flush with mine. He wrapped his free hand around the back of my neck. "I've waited years to touch you. Do you think I could wait another second now that I have you?"

Well, then. I grabbed Matt by the front of his shirt, and together we tumbled into my bed.

CHAPTER 32

Matt leaned against the headboard. His dark hair was a mess from my fingers, the back of it sticking up. Shirtless and with a sheet tucked around his waist, he held up a familiar scrap of parchment between his fingers. My letter.

Matt smirked at me. Oh no. *Oh no.*

"Full disclosure. I totally thought you were going to read it, then reject me. I was not in a great headspace."

His smirk grew, his eyes crinkling at the corners. He cleared his throat and unrolled the missive. "'My dearest Matt,'" he began. I lunged from my side of the mattress, but he snatched it away from my outstretched hand. "'I fear I may never be able to say this to you, but I love you, fiercely, with all my heart,' which you then crossed out and replaced with 'being,' which you crossed out again and replaced with 'soul.'"

I groaned. I rolled over and rested my chin on Matt's chest. "Could you please stop? I beg you."

"Oh no. This is a work of art."

"You're an ass."

"Well, they say couples take on each other's traits."

Rolling my eyes with the utmost affection, I poked Matt in the side. "Fine. You read my letter. It's sappy and maudlin and has bad grammar. But you know what's under the wine stain on the prophecy and never told me."

Matt's face colored. He looked away, his eyelashes a sweep across his cheekbones, cheekbones that the girls in the village always talked about as being wasted on him. If only they could see him now, doused in soft morning light, rumpled and beautiful. But they couldn't, because he was mine, and I was never letting him go.

"It's embarrassing."

"And you think an entire ode to your face that I literally wrote down is not?"

Sighing, he tossed the letter on the nightstand. "Fine. It says, 'And the mage will love the chosen one from afar and will stand by his side for the rest of their days.'"

"That's it?"

"What do you mean, that's it? That prophecy basically called me out for pining and then said that I'd be by you and love you forever!" Matt waved his hands. "It said nothing of you loving me in return. I couldn't let you see that. I couldn't let anyone see that."

"Wait." I sat up. "You didn't accidentally spill the wine, did you? It was on purpose!" Matt's ears went red. I sat up. "You filthy liar!" I dug my fingers into Matt's ribs, and he laughed and squirmed away, ticklish.

"Yes, I did it. I spilled the wine on purpose."

"And I bet you could've magicked the stain away."

Matt looked to the ceiling. "Yes. And I thought you realized that the night Meredith spilled the wine all over us in the council room. I cleared that up fine. I thought for sure you'd notice."

"I'm oblivious!"

"Yes. I realize that."

"Are you ever going to tell me what happened with the inn-keeper's son?"

Matt grimaced at that. "Let's leave that one for another time."

Curiosity piqued, I almost pushed the matter further, but, well, I had time. And it struck me then. I had time. I had time with Matt. I had him, and he had me, for the rest of our lives, and into what lay beyond, because we were bound, forever. Hastily, I wiped a stray tear away. "Fine. I guess."

Matt eyed me. "Are you okay?" He slid his hand under my jaw and wiped the moisture away with his thumb. "You're crying."

"I'm overcome with emotion," I said, smiling, soft and fond. "I was thinking about how we have each other forever."

"Forever," he said with a nod. "And always."

My soul agreed. I leaned toward him and roped him in for a firm kiss full of promise, with hope and love and knowledge that there would be more to follow. The prophecy said so.

And peace came over the land and remained for a thousand years.

Epilogue

On the twin thrones of Ere in the realm of Chickpea, I, King Arek the Kind, and my royal consort, Lord Matt the Great, sat and surveyed the throne room. Our official joining celebration was in full swing, and all the guests twirled around the dance floor in bright dresses and dashing suits like confetti on a breeze. Music swelled and echoed. Laughter bloomed. Drinks spilled as toasts rang out. A few months had passed since my birthday. It was spring, almost summer, and the lords and ladies from all over the kingdom had traveled to join us in our celebration.

Bethany had outdone herself with planning. Lila had balanced the budget, though I had to withstand many hours of her complaining about how difficult it was to rein in Bethany's more extravagant ideas. But Bethany was forgiven because she had brokered treaties within Ere itself and with other kingdoms, including the fae. Several of them had come to the castle. Lila kept a shrewd eye on them via Crow, but thus far, they'd done nothing of concern except hound Matt about the magic of his garden.

Knights and guards dotted the perimeter, sober and alert,

and trained by the best first knight in all the land, Sir Rion, and by the best general the realm had ever seen, General Sionna.

Rion and Lila, despite their differences and epic disagreements, were still together, as were Sionna and Meredith. Bethany had a fling with Petal and one with Gren and another with both of them. At the moment, she declared herself single, though a new recruit had recently caught her eye, and she currently danced with her around the floor, dress swishing, hair piled high in an elaborate style, laughing as daintily as ever.

Our friends were happy. We were happy. I was happy. Overcome, I brought Matt's hand to my mouth and kissed his knuckles. The crowd expressed "aww" in unison, which startled me. I'd forgotten it was a celebration in our honor and we were under undue scrutiny, so wrapped up in Matt and everything that was him. We were still firmly in our honeymoon stage, as many of our friends liked to point out, and I reveled in the unabashed freedom to stare at him and memorize the contours of his face and the sounds of his sighs.

Matt laughed, and my heart leapt.

As he read my mind, Matt's smile turned sly. "Tonight, my love," he said, leaning over the arm of his own throne to whisper in my ear, "will be our second first night together."

A flush worked its way up from my neck into my cheeks. I squirmed on my throne, because as much as I'd grown over the course of a year and a half, inconvenient boners were still a thing that happened on occasion.

"Um, excuse me?"

I broke my gaze away from the other half of my soul and found an older woman had approached. She wore a simple gown. She had wrinkles at the corners of her eyes and smile lines around her mouth. Her hair was gray and long and flowing down her back.

"I'm sorry to interrupt. My name is Lady Loren, and I'm not quite sure why I was invited to your celebration, but the invitation said to find you as you had something of mine."

"Oh!" I stood and descended the dais. My heart fluttered as I took her hand in mine and bowed, kissing her knuckles. "It's you."

Her mouth turned down in confusion as she curtsied in return. "I'm sorry, I don't understand. How do you know me?"

I didn't know how to respond. I knew her because of how the princess described her. I knew her because of how she acted in the tack room and on the picnic and during the dancing lessons. I knew her stubbornness and pride, and her love, and her beauty.

Matt joined my side and saved me from my own awkwardness. "We don't," he said. "Well, we do, but only through writing."

She looked between us. "I'm sorry, I still don't understand. Through writing?"

Matt clutched a familiar book in his hands and with great care handed Loren the princess's journal. "We found it in the tower with her."

I watched as understanding dawned. Her hands trembled as she took the journal from Matt. She smoothed her fingers over the binding, and when she opened it, tears rolled down the apples of her cheeks. "It's her journal."

"She mostly wrote about you," I said with a sad smile. "It's your love story."

"She would have wanted you to have it," Matt said, voice

soft and reverent. "If she had been given a choice, she would be with you now."

I looped my arm around Matt's waist, tucked him close to my side. "I know it's a small comfort, but she loved you."

Lady Loren stared at the journal, her expression one of open wonder, her lips parted, her eyes glittering with tears.

"I never forgot her," she whispered. She pressed the book to her chest, and her eyes fluttered shut. "I have always loved her. Even when my obligations forced me to move on, I never loved anyone the way I loved her."

"I know how that feels," Matt said, gaze cutting to me. "I hope reading this will bring you peace."

"Thank you," she breathed, staring at the both of us with gratitude. "Oh, thank you."

"You're welcome." I bowed to her. Matt did as well.

Her smile was tremulous, but she curtsied in return.

"You are welcome here for as long as you want to be," I said. "Enjoy the celebration."

"Your reputation is true, King Arek. I'm glad it was you who took on the burden of the crown. Our kingdom is in wonderful hands."

"It is," Matt said. He leaned into my side. "It is."

We talked a bit longer, but soon she drifted away, holding the book and flipping through the pages.

"That was a good thing you did," Matt said a few moments later. "Inviting her here. Giving her the journal."

"Remember that letter I wrote you?"

He smirked. "How could I forget?"

"I did it because of something the princess had written. 'If I ever get out of here, I'm going to tell her I love her.' She never did get out of that tower. But we did, and it was up to us to pass on her final message."

Matt stared at me with wide eyes. "I love you."

"And I love you."

He kissed my cheek. "Dance with me, sire?" Not an insult, but an endearment, one full of love and warmth.

"I thought you'd never ask, Lord Matt."

I swept him into the cage of my arms and pulled him close, and as the music reached a crescendo, we stepped into the swirling crowd and danced.

ACKNOWLEDGMENTS

This book exists because of a conversation I had with the amazing Julian Winters in 2019 about writing romantic comedies and how I marvel at authors who can write contemporary romcoms since I can't seem to write anything that doesn't involve magic, a spaceship, or unicorns. That conversation led to a joke about writing a romcom in a castle and thus the seeds for *So This Is Ever After* were planted. By the time I drove home from the event we attended, I had characters and a vague plot and a lot of excitement to write this book. So, thank you, Julian, for that spark of an idea and for the encouragement.

The majority of this novel was written during National Novel Writing Month 2019 and the months after. I'm eternally grateful to my best friend, Kristinn, who continues to be my writing buddy and my first reader. She encourages me in my moments of self-doubt and graciously handles my author imposter syndrome with more kindness and patience than I deserve. Also thank you to Jude Sierra, who was one of the first to read the finished product and who provided insight and guidance about all the romance tropes that appear throughout the novel.

Next, I want to thank my agent, Eva Scalzo. Thank you, Eva,

for continuing to champion my books, for being an amazing person to work with, for supporting my vision for my career, and for handling slightly panicked phone calls and understanding my sometimes-weird sense of humor. And thank you to the team at Margaret K. McElderry Books, especially my editor, Kate Prosswimmer, and her assistant, Nicole Fiorica, who worked so hard to bring out all the potential in the storytelling and character arcs and made this book the best it could be. Thank you both for embracing the concept of a book that tells the Ever After part of the story. Thank you to the cover illustrator, Sam Schechter, and the cover designer, Becca Syracuse, for this beautiful, beautiful cover. It really has been a dream to work with you all.

I would like to thank the Science Fiction and Fantasy Club at the College of William and Mary, affectionately called Skiffy. Readers may notice some familiar archetypes in this novel, and I was introduced to those archetypes and roleplaying games in general and all manner of fun sci-fi and fantasy things due to the members of this club. Several members are my life-long friends, including Karyl, Liza, Sean, Seanie, Tom, and Craig. I can't mention Skiffy without acknowledging our dear friend Angela, who left us too soon. She named me FT so long ago, and I know she would've loved this book and is smiling at me from wherever she may be.

I'd like to thank a group of authors who are not only my friends, but amazing colleagues, and who are my cheerleaders, beta readers, support group, confidants, and convention buddies: CB Lee, DL Wainright, Carrie Pack, and Julia Ember.

I'd like to thank Malaprop's bookstore in Asheville, which

is my local amazing indie store and has been so kind to me the past few years. The booksellers are awesome and if you are ever in the Asheville area, please drop by and say hi to Katie.

It wouldn't be my acknowledgment section without thanking my fandom life mate and my fandom twitter pals, who are the greatest when I need a name suggestion or need help deciding on a detail. My internet family—aka pocket friends—always come through, and I can't thank them enough for sticking with me this past decade.

I'd like to thank my family, especially my spouse, Keith, and my three kids, Ezra, Zelda, and Remy, who bring joy and excitement into my life every day. I'd also like to thank my brother, Rob, and my sister-in-law, Chris. If anyone is wondering where my weird jokes and puns originate, blame Rob for gifting me *The Hitchhiker's Guide to the Galaxy* for my thirteenth birthday. Also, Rob is the only person I know who actually reads the acknowledgments. (Hi, Rob!) Also, I want to thank my sisters, Christy and Amanda, who have made the pandemic a little more interesting via memes in our sibling group chat. I would like to thank my nieces and nephews, who tell their school librarians about their aunt's books and talk them up to their teachers and friends.

Lastly, I'd like to thank everyone who reads this book, who either purchased it or borrowed it from a library. Thank you for allowing me to entertain you for a few hours. I'm very appreciative of your time. I hope you enjoyed reading this story as much as I enjoyed writing it. Until next time, I hope you stay safe and happy.

Thank you.

—F.T. LUKENS